Pearly Whites!

Pearly Whites!

By

David Goldstein

To Carol, as always.

Foreword

I would like to thank my editor, John Paine, for his patience, guidance and experience in helping bring this story to fruition.

Chapter 1

The luxury-appointed Airbus H160 was chopping halfway between San Francisco and Oakland when Elizabeth Cleaver received her daily update on the free dental clinic situation. She did not consider herself a fifty-thousand-foot-view kind of person at the Cleaver Foundation. As the inheritor of the multibillion-dollar fund, she was in charge down to the last detail. Liz had grown up in the same commune where her mother had developed the revolutionary green leafy substance, Havana Bandana Cannabis, a perpetual Wall Street darling that drove the foundation's cash reserves.

With her activist background, Liz proudly wore her company logo bandana, Bottega Veneta bell bottoms, and psychedelic tank tops everywhere she went. Loaded in the back of the helicopter were boxes of foundation paraphernalia for free distribution, the bandanas being the most common handout.

Her assistant and girlfriend, Frieda Hansen, dressed in similar garb, was flipping through screens on her mobile phone. Cursing in Swedish, Frieda looked up at Liz and said, "This piece of shit never works when we are in the air!"

Liz nodded sagely. "Yep, something about waves, physics, the tao of electrons. But let's not get wound up in that, sweetie. How bad is the situation in Oakland?"

Dropping the offending phone into her Etro Rainbow shoulder purse, Frieda said, "We have all sorts of poor people needing dental implants. The free clinics are referring patients to these predatory oral surgeons, and the cocksuckers are ripping off the foundation."

Liz was well aware that the foundation was her bank account as well. She took a deep breath and centered herself. Liz practiced daily, even moment to moment, remaining calm. Her beloved late mother, Olivia Cleaver, had arranged meetings two decades back with the Dalai Lama, and that had partially cured her childhood excitability.

"So, what have we learned about this outfit up north? Teethmatics?"

Frieda said, "Teegentics, Liz, Teegentics. Well, they seem to be a real possibility for cheapo implants. If they come to market with this genetic tooth product, we could get this into clinics all around the U.S. I think we could focus initially on parts of the South and Appalachia where rotten teeth seem to come in at conception."

"What about England? Shouldn't we focus there as well?"

Frieda shrugged, and said, "Nah."

They set down at Oakland International, hopped in a waiting limousine that was parked behind a black security SUV, while boxes of company handouts were loaded in the trunk. They then set off for their downtown clinic.

On arrival, the lead security SUV spewed forth an all-female, bandana-clad contingent of former police officers. Each member of the team was dressed in Foundation–approved attire of bell bottoms and bulletproof paisley vests.

They intently surveyed the long line of unfortunate people outside the clinic doors. Once they signaled the driver that all was well, Liz and Frieda climbed out and started working the line, handing out tie-dye bandanas, plastic thermos coffee cups, and dog tags with complementary neck chains, all emblazoned with HBC, to baffled folks awaiting dental care. A few of the men tried to make small talk with Liz and Frieda while ogling them, but the menacing looks of her security contingent shitcanned those attempts.

Liz and Frieda then entered the clinic for their sit-down with the well-paid, dedicated dental technicians that worked a rotating schedule of long hours—except for weekends, holidays, summer vacations, and almost any other excuse to be closed. When Liz had inquired about the closures, Frieda had said, "Well hell, it's free, isn't it?" Liz decided, as usual, that Frieda had made an excellent point.

Once the meeting was completed, they gave the same performance at the three other clinics in the city. Then they roared off to their aerial chariot that would return them to their Pacific coastal estate.

During the drive Frieda had her earbuds in, listening to the news. Liz could see something was getting Frieda worked up, since she was smiling more and more. The woman had great teeth. Finally, she pulled her earbuds out and said, "There is a conference coming up in Denver, and TeeGentics will talk about their product! We should go!"

Liz perked up and said, "We could visit the old sister commune in Nederland, then go spend a weekend at the estate in Aspen afterward. Some of the girls could come with us for a big poolside party. You know how those can go. Remember when we met at the Burning Man?"

With a fond look Frieda scooted close to Liz and took her hand. Burning Man had been pretty wild, filled with the burning of large wooden effigies, body paint and lots of freelance nudity. "You are a blast to party with, Liz!"

Liz nodded, trying to resume her calm. It took a couple minutes to reestablish her chakras. That was her preferred method of controlling her impulses, taught by her beloved late mom after she had squirted half a can of lighter fluid on a grabby male commune member. Not long afterward, the commune shifted to an all-female population. Liz already knew her sexual orientation by that time, so the change led to a lot of escapades that had been great fun.

Once she was feeling in control, she looked at Frieda and said, "Denver, here we come!"

Chauncey Orbaugh III was known to associates and family as "Trace" due to a misspelling of the Spanish number three he had made on a junior high test that he never lived down. Trace had a deliberate morning schedule. Stopping first at Nova Coffee, he ordered an ultra-grande caramel latte with extra sugar. Discarding the lid as he walked out the door, he set course for destination two, waddling across the parking lot to the local Harper's Books to get the latest copy of the *New York Business Journal*.

The short walk was a tepid acknowledgment of his weight problem as well as his exercise for the day. Trace was enormously broad, not particularly tall. Dr. Kelby had recently advised him, "Just keep it up. Before long you will be so round, you can just roll along the sidewalk." That lame joke had led to Trace firing the impudent asshole on the spot. It still annoyed him that the doctor had just laughed, saying, "I'm fired? Why, thank you!"

As he struggled through the double doors of the bookstore, some latte slopped out of his cup and burned his fingers, eliciting a "Jesus Christ!"

The young woman behind the counter jerked her head up at the outburst. Spotting his latte, she called, "Sir, you can't bring that drink in here... sir, please!"

Sucking his wounded digits, he pulled them out of his mouth long enough to flip her off. He sauntered to the magazine rack in front, grabbed the latest edition (he hated online newspapers), and returned to the offended cashier, plopping the paper down in front of her. He took a deliberate gulp of the latte as he studied her reaction.

"That was not nice, sir. My job is to—"

"—not piss off the customers. I own about a third of the stock of this damn company, so I oughta know," he lied, smiling in a cynical way. Trace's holdings in the store were minor, based on online trading.

The young woman's complexion blanched, then turned crimson. She rang up his purchase in silence, avoiding eye contact when she handed him his receipt. That was fine with him. From his perspective, she had all the qualifications of a lifetime register jockey.

Perspective—so important to Trace and how he operated. Here was another fine example of the world going to hell right on his doorstep. He was going to have a word with the CEO, if he could sort out who that was.

Turning to leave, he said, "Better get your resume polished up, chickee."

She stared at him with a mixture of hostility and confusion as he waddled back out of the store, sipping his latte, making best speed to his car.

He tossed the paper in the passenger seat of his convertible, chucked the empty cup on the ground, then began the laborious process of wriggling his bulk into his custom stretched BMW. Many things in Trace's world were customized, not so much because he wanted to have something different from others, though that mattered. It just seemed like exercising was the hard way to lose weight when he had such a demanding schedule and could spend his way out of the problem.

Drawing a sigh of relief at finally being sandwiched into the expanded seat, he floored it out of the parking lot, speeding on to his next stop. It was time to sit down with Werner Brandt and have a come-to-Jesus meeting. Trace did not have any use for the man, even though his firm had lent Brandt millions to fund TeeGentics, Brandt's brainchild.

Yet Brandt had also raised all the technobabble issues after Trace's carefully planted article in a tabloid appeared, outlining the company's fast-track progress. Brandt, clueless as usual about marketing a new product, had nearly derailed Trace's viral marketing campaign with petty concerns about viability and so forth. Trace was not one to let delivering get in the way of selling. Infuriated, he had wanted to give the no-account egghead a guided tour to the exit, but his maternal grandfather, Martin Crosswaithe, who chaired their investment firm, had stepped in. Trace picked his battles very carefully with Martin, so he dropped the matter.

Driving along, he felt his anger bubble up. Hell, some of the idiots taking up boardroom space were talking about using the company for a *tax shelter*. Fuck *that*. He'd weld wings on this smoking pig and make it fly. As he turned onto the TeeGentics campus, he burned rubber, blowing by the startled gate guard.

The object of Trace's scorn could not slump any farther down in his chair. Werner was alternating between rubbing his bloodshot eyes and sipping from a bottle of antacid. While he was exhausted from his all-nighter spent trying to urge his scientists to a new level in their product development, he thought people were understanding more and more: he was not their buddy, but their boss. In a recent example, he had found one of his scientists home-brewing beer underneath one of the lab benches. It had over-fermented and blown up, spewing its contents around the room. The meeting on the incident with the staff had been terse, but nobody seemed to know who the inept brew meister was.

Since then, he had stopped trying to be a scientist and focused on just running the damn place. He was also the face of the company to the media. The change had appealed to his ego, not to mention his wardrobe, and he was starting to have fun in that regard.

Werner stared out the panoramic window of his office, feet propped up on the windowsill, attempting to get a bit of rest, but the awkward position only aggravated his heartburn. Plus, his feet hurt. His new handmade Italian loafers were not breaking in easily.

The window spanned most of the west wall, and this morning it provided a grand view of the extensive parking lot. That suited his grim mood. Barely three months earlier, the *New York Journal* had published what they called an exposé—an inside story leaking his startup company's heady plans to the public. The source for the story had come from a disgruntled former TeeGentics janitor.

As a building maintenance specialist, Earl Jenkins never excelled or even achieved mediocrity while with the company. Despite the lengthy job experience he had cut and pasted off the Internet into his job application, he was neither particularly good nor dedicated to the tasks of building maintenance.

From what Werner later determined, Earl spent most of his time sexually harassing the female employees. Complaints piled up and human resources finally sent an email to Werner informing him that it was time for Earl to hit the road. The man suffered no lack of experience in job-loss scenarios and knew the routine. His final noisy day included a visit from the local cops to eject him from the premises.

Earl declared, "I'm appalled at this draconian, inhumane treatment. I shall endeavor from this juncture forward to ensure that all shall know about the terrible, ghastly things happening within the confines of this hellish facility."

Two days later in the *Journal,* a tale outlining the company's efforts to market lab-grown genetically compatible replacement teeth was splashed across every supermarket stand in North America. Within thirty minutes of the story breaking, Werner had received calls from CNB, the *Pulitzer Post,* and the *Moss Rock Times.*

With TeeGentics's confidential business plans now laid bare to the world, the senior investors and board members, against Werner's strongest objections, decided to proceed boldly with a plan to build a groundswell of consumer interest and demand for a nonexistent dental product.

The worst of the situation was an announcement that the Food and Drug Administration human trials of "Chompers" (the internal, formerly secret code name for the project) were imminent. TeeGentics did not have a viable prototype tooth for the trials. Werner's best scientists had predicted another three years of intense research and lab work to sort out all the complexities, and suddenly here they now were with less than six months till the beginning of the FDA's trial.

His administrative assistant, Sally, appeared. She had a cup of coffee in one hand and a stack of documents in the other. At least that was going right. The woman was so damn efficient, good looking and well dressed.

She said, "Weren't you sitting right here when I went home last night?" She set the cup of steaming black liquid on the desk.

"Another night of probing around in the dark. I now know how clueless people must feel—no hope and no possibility of hope." He attempted a smile and, in fact, felt a bit better seeing her standing there. Sally Dinkleberg always showed up each day with a great smile and an impeccable focus on detail. That kept him on track when he got distracted, which was often.

Sally scrutinized him and said, "Werner, I don't think you can compare your situation with the plight of clueless people."

"You think I'm being melodramatic?"

"I think you're downright pathetic from time to time. How'd you ever manage to raise all this investment capital?"

"Easy. I lied my ass off." He then continued in a more serious vein, "The best people I've got on the team say there is absolutely no way we get this done in six months." He grimaced. "We are screwed."

"Screwed, schmood. Time for a fresh start, Doc. Get someone new onboard to get things energized. You've been collecting applications for the last two months. Hire somebody, damn it."

Werner's stomach tightened at the thought of spending even more of his investment capital and having to explain that expenditure to Trace, the troll he had financed his company with. He shook his head and said, "Hire somebody. You make it sound so easy. It'll take a new person six months just to understand what we're doing, let alone help us make the deadline."

"Hire yourself a go-getter. You need an Oppenheimer."

"Oppenheimer?"

"The nuclear bomb guy from World War II. You need someone like him to get your people cracking. I've even got a candidate. Check out the first guy on this stack. He's trained on our new Acme DNA machine you just bought." She chunked a pile of resumes she had downloaded off the Internet in front of him. Sally was always throwing things on his desk. It was her version of tough love.

Werner shrugged noncommittally. Sipping his coffee, he leaned back in his chair, propping his feet on his desk. It sounded like a great idea. Sally often suggested the smartest ideas after others labored to come up with squat.

Werner said, "How about I hire you? Oh, right, I already did." He then gave her a big smile.

Ignoring him, now on a roll, she added, "I've phone-interviewed the three people on the top of the stack. That first one is a winner, if you ask me. Let me get you some breakfast ordered up from the commissary, and you get started reading. Remember, I put the best candidates on top, so don't go trying to alphabetize anything or do your own sorting."

As she marched out of his office, Werner called after her, "You came in this morning planning all this, didn't you?"

She did not reply and, a moment later, he heard her calling the cafeteria. Taking a big swig of his coffee, he picked the first resume off the pile and began reading. Since Earl Jenkins, he had gotten a lot better at reading resumes. It had made him realize even more that his job was to lead and manage. Sally had made the pitch, and now he could knock it out of the park.

Squealing to a stop in front of the glass and stainless steel lobby of TeeGentics' corporate headquarters, Trace wriggled and writhed his way to his feet, feeling a bit light-headed from the effort. A young man in a lab coat came out and offered to park his car. Trace chucked his keys in the air, not caring if "lab coat" caught them or not, and slew footed it on into the lobby. Another lab coat, this time a young woman, escorted him to Brandt's fourth-floor office.

Puffing and panting from the elevator ride, Trace waved the escort away and gathered his composure. It did not pay to appear weak in front of an adversary. He lifted his fedora and brushed back his thin, greasy black hair. Placing the hat back in what he considered a jaunty position, he waddled on into the reception area. Brandt's secretary coolly greeted him. What was the woman's name? Ah yes—Sally.

He smiled thinly at her as she picked up her phone and said, "Mr. Orbaugh is here for your eleven o'clock." She paused, and then said, "Yes sir, I'll let him know."

Trace, ignoring her, headed for Brandt's inner sanctum. He shoved the door open, nearly hitting Werner in the face.

Werner looked at first surprised, then annoyed, but quickly rearranged his expression to deadpan. He invited Trace in with a wave of his hand. Trace bulled by him, saying, "So, Brandt, what the hell is happening with my money in this black hole of yours?"

Werner stiffened, and with his back still to the man, rolled his eyes at Sally. She gave him a wry grin as he closed his door. "So, how's it hanging, Trace? I haven't seen you since when? Yesterday?"

"Don't get smart with me, Brandt. We've got important business." Trace noticed five empty bottles of Werner's antacid in the trash barrel by his desk, and added "Jesus, you must shit lead pellets from drinking all that crap."

Werner appeared not to hear the comment about his addiction to bismuth and said, "What business?"

"I'm bringing in a new PR firm for product launch next year."

Werner grimaced. "What was wrong with the old firm?"

"You hired them, and they had no damn sense of urgency. Wonder where they got that from? Anyway, time is money. By the way, what have you got to eat? I'm famished."

Werner punched his intercom and requested Sally to have a pastrami and cheese platter, stuffed olives and a bottle of yellow mustard brought up. The speed at which he placed the order made Trace suspect Brandt was trying to defuse his ire by being responsive for a change.

Poker-faced, Trace said, "Good to see you know the routine, Brandt. I thought I'd never get your ass trained." He snarled a smile and continued, "Listen, this is marketing 101. We've got to whip consumers up into a buying frenzy over this fabulous new product of ours. You know, the yes train. Yes, I need new teeth. Yes, old-fashioned dental work is expensive and painful, emphasis on the painful. Yes, TeeGentics has the best new cheap product, and yes, it is pain-free and yes, I will spend all my money on it." He paused for a breath and continued, "This country—hell, the world—needs pretty white teeth and by God, we're gonna sell them a shitpot full!"

"If we pass the FDA trials."

"FDA? I got mee-dix-ah-stiff-one through that bunch, even with the blindness side effect thing. Everybody wants pretty teeth too. The FDA will capitulate, you just watch."

Werner nodded noncommittally, already familiar with the saga of Trace's ED company, Erectus. "What about the problem of teeth mortality during the first week of the growth phase? When they turn black? That's not so pretty or painless if it's in your mouth."

Trace shook his head in disgust. "Piddly-ass details. Fix it, goddamn it! These trials are happening, this product is going to market, and you can be either onboard or standing on the pier when this baby sails. By the way, what exactly are you doing to save our asses?"

The food arrived, to which Trace turned his immediate attention. He began devouring the platter, squirting mustard on every bite. Werner watched in barely disguised amazement and offered, "I've decided to bring onboard a new employee."

Talking around a mouthful, Trace said, "Your funeral. You've already got too much staff."

"We're looking for an Oppenheimer."

Trace raised his thick eyebrows in surprise. "An Oppenheimer? What the hell is that? Jesus, you tech wieners. Never happy with what you got. What the hell is wrong with that Acme DNA slicer/splicer thingamabob we just got from Chi-town?"

"Trace, Oppenheimer ran the atomic bomb project back in World War II."

Trace stopped chewing, swallowed, and then nodded slowly as if Brandt was not a total idiot after all. "So, this Oppenheimer—he'll get things on track?"

"That would be the plan."

"So, who are you talking to?"

Werner glanced at the resume on the top of his stack, and his eyebrows went up as he said, "Uh, Robert Oppenheimer?"

Trace grunted, "The son of a bitch is still alive?"

"No, no, we just happen to have a candidate by that same name. Top MIT graduate, has done some brilliant research from what I see here, and he did well in a phone interview." Werner regretted the last part of his candidate description and decided not to mention that Sally had been the interviewer.

"Research? Jesus, we need some more research, don't we? Hell, Brandt, we need a fuckin' doer, not another cue ball academic."

Werner squirmed, visibly sweating now, and said, "The original Oppenheimer was brilliant and able to solve problems and inspire the people that worked for him."

"Well, we sure as shit could use a little of that around here. You've interviewed this guy?"

"Uh, yeah," Werner lied again.

"I'd like to meet him before you hire. I can tell you in two seconds if he's got what it takes."

"That would be highly irregular—"

"Brandt, what's highly irregular is you've got this damn ship so close to the beach, sirens are waving us onto the jagged rocks. Now get the sombitch in here today. I'll hang around."

Chapter 2

Robert Oppenheimer sat in the TeeGentics lobby with a fine brown leather Italian satchel situated on the floor next to him. He was dressed in an on-sale suit from BarnsMart, and his hair was perfect, reminiscent of a bronze skullcap. His matching tie and handkerchief had arrived just yesterday from eBay, adorned in a red, white, and black logo of his strongest material desire, a Corvette.

Professor Henekey had been right again to suggest submitting his resume to TeeGentics. The professor had been mentoring Robert—or Bob, as he liked to be called—ever since they had met at the Caribbean School of the Americas, when Bob believed that all he ever wanted was a degree in creative writing. Yet Professor Henekey immediately saw his potential and took Bob under his wing. Gently, he guided Bob into the oft-overlooked fields of experimental gene splicing and free-range chemistry. Bob had never imagined you could get a degree in that, but sure enough, that was what it said on the diploma.

He sensed that he had a job offer in hand. A quick call to his old professor, who had encouraged him to apply for this job, confirmed his suspicions. Therefore, he believed he was ready to negotiate from a position of strength on his salary and the other goodies he wanted. It would be interesting to see just how much he could extract from this company.

Sally walked into the lobby to greet him, and he immediately stood up, extending his hand. She said, "Mr. Oppenheimer, so nice to meet you in person after our earlier phone interview." He shook her soft, warm hand and smiled. "It is Dr. Oppenheimer. But, hey, just call me Bob."

Sally's eyes narrowed as she nodded politely. Bob quickly checked off that she was blonde with her hair tied back, slender, tall, had great calf development, and wore low heels. He figured she was trying not to call attention to her height and worked out religiously. He then realized she was more than aware of his survey of her. He grinned disarmingly and said, "Like I say, call me Bob."

She nodded coolly and said, "You'll be meeting with Dr. Brandt and another gentleman, one of our senior board members." She then turned, leading Bob to the elevators.

Bob raised his eyebrows as he tagged along, and his pulse quickened with a shot of adrenaline. *Board member? What the heck was going on?* This had to be great luck—not the black or ugly kind, like what had happened on departure from his last job, when he had accidentally set the main lab on fire when he knocked over a burner while having at it with his favorite female lab assistant. This time it would be different. He could sense it. And only male lab assistants from now on.

Arriving on the fourth floor, Sally stopped down the hall from Werner's office at a large mahogany door displaying an expensive brass plaque that read BOARD ROOM.

On entering, he saw three people—the first was standing near a window, an expensively dressed but disheveled, tired-looking man. Bob waved. He then spotted, seated halfway down a long, gleaming table, an immense fellow wearing a white Panama suit, shirt, tie, and a straw fedora. Finally, to one side, stood an expressionless dude in an Italian waiter outfit with a white towel draped over his forearm.

The disheveled man nodded and said, "Hello, I'm Dr. Brandt."

Bob walked over to Werner and extended his hand, "So nice to meet you, Dr. Brandt. You're the CEO. I am honored to be here with you."

Werner visibly brightened, shook Bob's hand, and gestured for him to meet Trace. He said, "Dr. Oppenheimer, I'm glad that you could make it on such short notice. Let me introduce you to Chauncey Orbaugh."

Bob said, "Mister Orbaugh—my pleasure!"

Trace leered at him and said, "How nice of you to say that. Consider this a special moment."

Bob grinned back, "Chauncey Orbaugh the Third, the financier. Your considerable reputation precedes you."

Trace gave no sign of whether he was impressed or not. He simply said, "Call me Trace."

"Trace it is. Call me Bob."

Bob saw Werner's eyebrows knit and decided the man seemed to be trying to assess the synergy between Trace and himself. Apparently failing in that, Werner said, "Shall we have a seat? We have coffee, tea, soda pop if you like." He indicated for the waiter to step forward.

Trace said, "I'll have some of that expensive single malt scotch you keep around here. How about yourself, Bob? Are you a scotch man?"

Not one to look a gift horse in the mouth, Bob replied "Certainly."

"What about you, Werner?"

"Coffee will be fine. And I'm not sure drinking whisky at an interview is appropriate."

"Whatever. Well then, a Dalmore for Bob and myself." Trace snapped his fingers at the waiter.

Bob smiled as he sat down, studying Werner's reaction to Trace as the server returned with their drinks. The dynamics of the room told him that the fat man was in charge. It did not surprise him. He had learned from a *Timely Life* magazine article that Chauncey Orbaugh's personal and business behavior would scare the bejesus out of most people.

He then noticed that Werner was fiddling with his cuff links to get them properly oriented. Trace made a loud "ahem," at which Werner looked up and saw Trace and Bob watching him.

Giving his jacket a gentle tug, Werner said, "Bob, I understand you had a very good phone interview the other day, and I wanted to take some time to talk a bit more about our activities, learn about your background and how you might find a fit here at TeeGentics."

Bob nodded and waited for more. Trace was eyeing him, sipping his scotch, and eating directly from a jar of jumbo stuffed olives. The man was testing him, he could sense it—he suddenly felt a bit giddy.

Werner continued, "I've reviewed your resume and you frankly have outstanding credentials. Tell me a bit more about these projects you have listed—"

Trace belted out, "Ah, Jesus flipfloppin' on the goddamn cross, Brandt, get to the point."

Turning red, Werner sank petulantly back into his chair and said, "Carry on!"

Trace swiveled around and gazed directly into Bob's eyes. "What the hell do you know about growing teeth, *from* stem cells, *in* test tubes, *for* genetically compatible implants?"

Bob did not hesitate. "I've worked on similar efforts in organ generation. It's going to be a very lucrative technology once it is developed and marketed."

"No shit. Well, Brandt here needs a guy to kick-start our project in the lab and on through the FDA trials to final production. Are you up for the biggest goddamn challenge of your life?"

Bob drew a deep breath. This was moving fast, but he sensed that this was the moment to make demands. He said as calmly as he could, "That depends."

"Depends? Depends on what?" Trace asked, obviously amused.

"On whether we can sort out the financial side of this equation."

Trace leaned back in his chair, popped an olive in his mouth, and took a big swig of scotch. Bob followed suit, swigging from his drink, wishing for an olive himself.

Attempting some reassertion of control, Werner nervously said, "I don't believe that we are at the point of a salary discussion, Bob."

Waving Werner off, Trace grunted, "Hell yes, we are. This is your man, Brandt. Bob here got right to the point. For a price, he'll make your little project sizzle. You'll get your A-bomb on time if you hire this young fellow. Name your terms, whippersnapper, and we'll take care of you."

As Werner squirmed uncomfortably, Bob could tell things had most definitely gotten away from the CEO. In fact, everything had trotted right down the table to Trace. Their project must really be in the shitter for someone like Trace to be personally hiring someone like the person described in Bob's resume.

Trace said, "In case you're feeling powerful and all that, just remember, *Bob*, this is *my* money we're talking about here. I don't appreciate it when somebody squanders it on fucking chips and pop. I expect results, fast, often, and when I say jump."

"Absolutely. My goal would be to give you a bumper crop return on investment and maximize IPO value." He then nodded toward Werner and added, "And of course, bring this product to market on time within corporate guidelines."

Trace smiled magnanimously and nodded his approval. Werner sat back in his chair with a blank, withdrawn look on his face.

Bob smiled inwardly. Professor Henekey had been right again. Putting that he was an MIT graduate and a bunch of complex-sounding projects on his resume had been a stroke of genius.

Trace said, "All I want to know is: when can you start?"

Chapter 3

William Fuller, known to his friends and co-workers as Billy, jogged down the hall to the reception desk at TeeGentics. A half hour earlier, he had learned his new job was to spend the next few weeks getting his new boss, Robert Oppenheimer, familiar with some basics on the Chompers project. Going forward, he would be the man's administrative assistant.

As a youngster, Billy had struggled with relationships in school, being excessively shy, and to top it off, he had begun to have different sexual urges than his counterparts. He realized early on he was gay, and some of the other boys, in typical cruel teenage fashion, called him queer or faggot or a plethora of other insults. This abuse had been the primary reason he started lifting weights and took up martial arts in late high school.

Now six foot tall, he was buff and kept his spiky brown hair dyed blond, though his shyness persisted. Billy had a problem that plagued his otherwise handsome appearance. His teeth were a dingy gray at best. Not that he ignored them. He brushed, flossed, and gargled constantly, and his dentist performed regular whitening treatments, all to no avail. The next steps involved getting quite a few of his teeth veneered, which was expensive and currently outside his modest budget. Because of this, he rarely smiled, and he mumbled a lot. His tendency was to lower his head and barely open his mouth when he spoke.

Emerging into the lobby, Billy arrived at the receptionist's desk. She barely glanced up while telling him Dr. Oppenheimer was waiting in Dr. Brandt's office and that he needed to get up there on the double. Billy mumbled, "Got it," and reversed course for the elevators.

He exited on the fourth floor, the "executive" level. Some of the other employees called the top floor mahogany row, but everything up here had the same look as the other floors—stainless steel and glass. The main difference was a lack of cubicles and instead, large offices with ultra-modern décor, the largest of which was Dr. Brandt's at the end of the corridor.

Billy jogged down the hallway and knocked on the open door to the outer office.

Sally rose, looking toward the doorway, and said, "Can I help you?"

A muscular young man with moussed, spiky blond hair slipped out from behind the doorway. Fascinated, she smiled. She had never noticed Billy moving about the corridors of the "lower floors," as she liked to refer to where those employees of TeeGentics below the fourth floor resided. Taking in the impressive sight, she wondered how in the world she could ever have missed him.

Billy mumbled, "Imherefordoctoroppenheimer."

Sally said, "I'm sorry, I didn't catch that. What are you here for?" She wondered why the man kept his right hand near his mouth. His other hand hung by his side, reflexively grasping, then letting go.

A minor volume increase, but still muffled, "Imherefordoctoroppenheimer."

Sally tried parsing the vague vowel sounds and thought she understood. "Oh, the copier. Sure, follow me. I didn't know there was a problem."

Billy took a deep breath and blurted, "I'm here for Dr. Oppenheimer."

Sally got an eyeful of grayish yellow teeth and her mind reeled. *Meth mouth perhaps?* She then noticed Billy's wounded eyes and felt suddenly sorry for the sad but extremely hot-looking young man. She indicated a chair and said, "Take a seat and I'll let him know you are here. At the moment he is with Dr. Brandt."

Billy went to the chair she indicated and sat down, having duly noted the look of dismay Sally had displayed upon seeing his teeth. He kept his eyes studiously focused on an abstract painting on the wall directly across from him.

Bob sat with a big smile plastered on his face. Werner was droning on and on about the company's mission, the importance of accurate expense reporting, the chain of command, cafeteria hours, keeping track of his new computer notebook, and blah, blah, blah. All Bob could think was, "What a putz."

He felt himself drifting in and out of interest, and when Werner stopped talking, he realized he had zoned out for the last few minutes of the conversation. Werner was looking at him expectantly.

Hesitating for but a moment, Bob grinned and asked, "Who would I talk to if I need further clarification?" It was a gamble but appeared to be the right thing to say.

Werner looked slightly confused as he replied, "Sally can help get you a support contact for setting up your email, though I think if you follow what I just told you, you'll have no problems." He smiled as he added, "MIT graduate and all."

Bob nodded, still grinning as if sharing the little joke with Werner, the grand CEO. He sensed, however, in Werner's attitude and tone, a wee bit of hostility. Well, perhaps more than just a wee bit. Not unexpected, considering the way Trace had flattened Werner's dick on the boardroom floor during the interview. No worries, he would soothe the professor's bruised ego, though Bob was determined to maintain his allegiance to the fat man responsible for this new position.

Werner said, "I've assigned an assistant lab technician to escort you to your office down the hall. He'll be your administrative assistant, per the terms of your employment contract." Bob nodded as he heard more attitude coming from Werner about the hiring package he and Trace had hammered out.

Werner continued, "I'm going to turn you over to him and let you start getting acclimated. There's a two o'clock meeting with the staff, so you can have the next few hours to get ready."

Bob stood and said, "Werner, thanks so much for making me feel at home here at TeeGentics. You're a great boss. We should make a spectacular team." Werner raised an eyebrow and said, "Uh, well, we'll see, won't we? At any rate, let's introduce you to your new assistant." He led Bob out to Sally's office.

A man in a lab coat stood up, holding his right hand near his mouth. Werner looked Billy up and down, then shrugged. "Well, here you go, Bob. Billy Fuller, this is Bob Oppenheimer, your new boss. Bob, Billy. Billy, Bob. Please take him down to his office and show him around this morning. I'll be seeing both of you in the afternoon meeting."

Billy nodded shyly and Bob stuck out his hand. "Nice to meet you, Billy. How's it hanging?" He figured he might as well start off friendly, until he could get this guy replaced with a suitable female. He had already forgotten the promise he made to himself earlier to avoid entanglements.

The two shook, with Billy staring down at the floor, mumbling, "Fine." Cocking his head, Bob smiled, not understanding the muffled reply, and not caring anyway. He replied, "All right, then. Well, lead the way." Billy exited out into the corridor. Bob, with a dreamy smile, waved at Sally and Werner as he followed.

When they arrived, Billy stopped in the outer office, which contained his desk, while Bob proceeded through the inner door to his new digs, making a survey. It was a window office, facing the west, just as he had negotiated. There was, however, a tall, thick Monterey pine blocking his view of the scenery. It seemed peculiarly placed, especially as he peered out the window to the left and right. It was the only tree on the campus near the building. Puzzled, he looked down.

Bob immediately realized the tree was freshly transplanted on the balcony below that had been converted. A groundskeeper was standing next to it with a water hose, soaking down the tree perimeter. The man saw Bob gazing down and waved at him. Bob waved back, noting to himself that Werner must have been a lot more pissed off than he had guessed. How much must it have cost to get that tree put in place? Well, he figured he could deal with Werner's hostility and later with the tree, especially when he started delivering results. Besides, there was always Trace, who seemed to enjoy making Werner's life miserable. Bob knew he should be cautious, though. One used a weapon like Trace with great care.

Lovingly touching his new desk, he smiled and said, "Billy, I'm just gonna go ahead and spend a bit of time in here getting settled in. Come find me when you're ready for lunch, and we'll head down together." Bob heard an "Okay," then a chair squeaking. He decided that was probably *his* new assistant checking out his new desk. It gave Bob a warm feeling and he let out a contented sigh.

On his desk was a phone with a bunch of buttons in different colors. He picked up the receiver, heard a dial tone and set it back down. A new laptop with three flat-screen monitors bracketed one end of his desk. He stretched forward and extended his arms, grasping the edges of his new burled walnut treasure, again part of his negotiation with Trace, and another contented, dreamy look settled over his face. Negotiating was fun, though he had no idea what he would do next to deliver on his side of the deal. He shrugged at the thought, not wanting to spoil the moment.

Chapter 4

Thankfully, the original meeting Werner had scheduled wound up delayed several days. Subsequently, Bob spent time getting settled in. So today was the day to meet the commoners, starting with a meal together.

Lunch was uneventful enough. Bob decided that the scientists sitting around him, talking of formulae, chromosomes, gene sequences and amino acids, had other things besides an exquisite meal on their minds. In the future he would either be ordering in from his office or going out for meals. Going through the line, he asked for au gratin potatoes to go with the cube steak lying gray and tired on his plastic plate—the elderly server added canned cream corn instead. One nibble of the meat blob convinced him that the cream corn was infinitely better prepared.

Pushing his tray aside, he decided that hunger would drive him this afternoon. Besides, all this biomatter with pretensions of being a meal fired his imagination for a big T-bone, bloody and rare, lyonnaise potatoes, some tender asparagus tips, all complemented with a fine pinot noir at an exclusive restaurant. Heck, he could afford it now that he was employed again.

Bob's thoughts drifted to his new living quarters. His signing bonus was more than adequate for an exclusive luxury home lease. Built atop a cliff, he had a great view of the Pacific coastline from his backyard, though this time he had made sure it was not obscured by a massive tree.

To go with the new digs, he had needed furnishings, having left much of his earthly effects behind in his recent hasty departure from his previous employer. He had settled on modern Scandinavian styling—and Helga Krantz.

Red hair, blue eyes, a good tan and wonderful smile had been Helga's sales pitch at Gustav's Creations. He bought whatever she recommended on the condition of immediate delivery—and dinner that evening. After a week of such elaborate dinners and fine liqueurs, he awoke in his new stainless steel, king-size bed with blond wood headboard. Getting up, he padded into the kitchen.

Cooking breakfast in the nude was Helga. He grinned, thinking that sex at the kitchen counter would enhance the breakfast experience. This became a rather drawn-out affair, with Bob concluding that her interest, like his, was as much in sex as in food preparation, which was just fine by him. She was inclined during these moments of culinary passion to moan in German, banging the nearest skillet or pot on the cutting board. She would smile and get an impish look when he asked later what she had been saying, declining all requests for translation.

She became a regular part of his new routine, and she quickly agreed to move in.

Then the car—he had been dreaming of this for quite a while—a red Corvette. He could have bought a Porsche or a Jag, but he had decided long ago that when it came to automobiles, it was good old red, white, and blue for him. The Vette he bought was all leather interior with lots of bells, whistles, and "doohickeys"—his salesman's favorite descriptive. It also came with factory-installed rattles that had him returning to the dealer frequently at first.

He then took it to a performance shop for a dual turbocharger upgrade, stage two exhaust system, stage three stereo and a stage four rear spoiler loaded with custom red LED lights that would blind anyone behind him when he hit the brakes or flipped on a turn signal. Warranty now voided but heck, the car was ridiculously fast—he had already received two tickets because he could not keep his foot out of the fly-by-wire gas pedal. The salesman had assured him during his purchase that this was just like the stuff they used in the F-35 fighter jet.

Bob's mind wandered back to the present. He began watching the people around him. As the other staff finished their lunch, they stood, one by one, and carried their trays dutifully to a window that had a sign hung at eye level. Inscribed in tiny print was the "lunch tray drop-off protocol." Per these instructions, the staff scraped their plates, sorted their flatware, and emptied their cups, then proceeded out of the lunchroom back to their various cubes and labs. It made him shudder.

Fuck that, he decided, he was management. He strode out for his afternoon meeting, leaving his uneaten tray full of food on the table. He felt that he had to get his bluff in up-front and show all these eggheads who was boss. Maybe he would smoke one of the big ass Cuban cigars he had bought from the nervous little man at the tobacco shop near the office. That would show his disdain for all that was holy around this building of stuffed shirts.

He was exhilarated. This was so much better than that black hole of a depression he had fallen into after he barely escaped being run out of town on a rail from his last job. Best not to think about that, he decided. Professor Henekey had enrolled Bob in serious therapy time with a hypnotist so Bob could sail past all the negative memories. He did remember for sure that one day he just woke up thinking it was a grand morning and that he was feeling great. He had emerged from his funk, ready for a new job.

As it turned out—it was this job.

Wandering in fondling a fat cigar, Bob spotted Sally, who was occupied with ensuring that this first staff meeting went off without a hitch, and she was bustling about. She had set up a podium, talked with the kitchen manager, arranged for delivery of coffee and pastries, and then directed Earl's replacement, Chip, to set out chairs in orderly rows.

"So, you got the shit detail?" Bob asked, trying to get her to warm up to him. "Working for Brandt seems below you."

Her expression was a mixture of puzzlement and coolness as she said, "Sorry for your confusion, I had advised Dr. Brandt that I would look to the arrangements and flow of this meeting. He will be down for introductions and will then turn everything over to … you." Sally then excused herself to direct a small contingent of lab-coated busboys from the kitchen in setting up the refreshments.

Research teams began to drift into the room, clumping into little groups based on their functions and pecking order. The various department managers sat in the front row, team leads in the second, and so on. Bob took his seat, which had been positioned by the podium facing the audience, and looked around for a sign to see, if like the lunchroom, there was some set of instructions to show these people what to do.

Werner dragged in, nervousness and fatigue expressed in his movements. He walked up to the podium and said, "Everyone, please take a seat and let's get started. I know how all of you are chomping to be out of this meeting and back to your work."

The group let out a collective groan at the pun, and a few jokes circulated around the room. Werner waited for these to pass before he continued. Bob thought that right here was half of the company's problem. There was no discipline and Werner just demonstrated that he was a weak, ineffectual bozo of a leader, certainly not someone who could demand respect.

Werner continued, "I know you've been hearing the rumors about the new manager we've brought on board after an extensive review of qualified applicants. His name bubbled right to the top. And here he is, Robert Oppenheimer. He prefers to be called Bob.

We are expecting big things out of Bob, and not just because of his name." Werner paused, and Bob realized the man was expecting a laugh. The scientists look around at each other, at Bob, then back to Werner.

Werner shrugged and went on, "Bob, say hello to your team."

Everyone looked at Bob as he gave a big smile and waved at them. There was a brief round of subdued, broken applause.

Werner continued, "Bob comes to us with some excellent credentials and a positive attitude about getting this project delivered on time. I can tell you that the senior management of this company is … in wonder at having him onboard. Bob will be taking over the day-to-day focus on research and working out the kinks in the Chompers product. With that in mind, I ask each and every one of you to welcome him aboard and give him your support. He's got a big responsibility, just as we all do."

Harry Bingham, Werner's oldest friend and lead scientist of TeeGentics, raised his hand from the front row.

Werner said, "Not now, Harry."

Apparently not so easy to dismiss, Harry left his hand in the air.

"Where was I, ah, yes," Werner tried to resume his intro spiel. Harry began waving the hand back and forth. Everyone was now watching. Werner slumped and said, "What?"

"On time? Deliver this project on time? Are we talking about that ridiculous schedule the investors came up with? And who is Dr. Oppenheimer? God?"

Werner stared intently at the podium; it appeared he was trying to determine its construction. Bob found the little drama amusing.

Werner finally replied, "Harry, give it a rest. We all know the issues."

"Werner, this is crazy. I don't care if Bob here has the fucking CIA stealing the technology we need."

Bob jumped in with, "Harry, you wouldn't mind if I said something here, would you?" The group's gaze shifted from Werner and Harry to Bob and Harry.

Harry leaned back in his chair and gestured for Bob to continue. "Help yourself. We're one big happy family here."

"Thanks, Harry. Werner, do you mind?" Another group gaze shift to Werner, who debated the wisdom of relinquishing control, then waved a dismissive hand in Bob's general direction and stepped away.

Bob strode to the podium, grasped the microphone and pulled it out of its holder, wishing he could flip a cable like he was a 1960's Las Vegas entertainer, but the thing was wireless. He cursed to himself as he stepped out from behind the podium. "It is my meeting after all, isn't it, Harry? Seems you're kinda raining on my parade. Not a very auspicious start."

Harry shrugged and pasted on a grin. "Welcome to TeeGentics, Bob."

Bob nodded, smiling as he fixed his gaze on Harry. Harry eyed him back, undaunted. Bob, finally realizing that a stare-down was not going to work, shifted his attention back to the rest of the scientists, saying, "TeeGentics has bitten off a very ambitious project with genetically grown teeth." A collective moan went up and he realized he had unintentionally made a pun.

He smiled and continued, "So, now, I'm here to make us all winners, to bring in the herd, so to speak, and to make this happen, we've got to change our modus operandi. We've got to get out front on the latest techniques, we've got to introduce invention in our thinking, we've got to—"

"—Get real goddamn lucky. That is, if we are gonna continue with this *product to market in six months* crap." Harry smiled at Bob as a laugh went up around the room.

Bob lost his cool with the last comment, and he suddenly wished Trace was there to shut down this Harry guy. The man was like a heckler at a Las Vegas show. He said, "Harry, Harry, Harry—okay, you're done here, ah, I believe, yes, you are."

"You gonna fire me, boss man?" Harry asked, still grinning.

Bob hesitated, then smiled, and said, "No, sorry, Harry. I mean, let's think about our next steps. I suppose if you were up here, I might be giving you a hard time, though I understand you have been through some tough times with this project."

Harry, raised an eyebrow, smile softening, and looking less confident now, "Sorry, Bob, I was not trying to make your life difficult."

"I understand. You people have been under a lot of pressure. I hope, in my own way, to move things along. We should talk on the side."

Harry nodded now, cooperative, "Just say when."

Bob nodded back, planning on never talking to Harry again. "Absolutely. Well, that seems to have just about covered everything. Werner?"

Werner, looking a bit confused himself, said, "Okay, folks, back to work. Thanks for your time."

People stood; several hushed conversations broke out. The rest dribbled out the door in silence, a few glancing Bob's way with the same curious look he had gotten in the cafeteria earlier.

It occurred to Bob this project might be harder than he had initially anticipated. Of course, until now, he had given scant thought to that problem. He suddenly needed a stiff drink. He decided he would pack it in early and start back in on all this minutia in the morning when he felt better. He returned to his office, grabbed his satchel, and breezed by Billy without a word. He was on his way to an extended stop at Flannery's bar, his favorite new hangout only a few blocks from his condo.

As he climbed in his car, he spotted Harry, his nemesis from the earlier group meeting walking out of Teegentics. He waved and Harry waved back. Bob's mood lifted, thinking to himself, *what a putz.* When he later saw Trace, he mentioned the confrontation that had occurred in the meeting. A couple days later, he learned that Harry was no longer with the company and that the new lead scientist was a Black woman named Fiona Kendle who would directly report to Bob. When he ran into Werner in the hallway outside their office, the man was stiff and less friendly than ever.

Chapter 5

Sitting directly across the boardroom table from Bob was Trace, munching on a massive pastrami and provolone on marbled rye, punctuating his consumption with a slurp of beer and occasional crunch of dill pickle. Holding the sandwich in his right hand and a mustard bottle in his left, Trace methodically applied the yellow condiment between each bite. To Bob, the yellow squiggles were starting to look like a Rorschach pattern he had once been asked to interpret in therapy sessions his mother had sent him to in his youth. In junior high he was caught standing on a dumpster while spying through a window into the girls' locker room.

It was not Trace's love of plain old mustard, however, that had Bob feeling agitated. He could accept that Trace did not like Dijon. It was the whole reason for the meeting itself that had him off-kilter. Nothing could have been further from Bob's mind than actually performing the science part of his job. Yet here he was, thinking, *I am being grilled by fatso about doing just that.*

Trace paused during his assault on his sandwich to say, "Listen, Oppie, I didn't hire your expensive ass to have you whip these eggheads into meringue. I could have hired much cheaper than you to take on that piddly task. No, what I expect are results in the way of a fucking viable tooth, or this job will be very short-lived. I don't have to tell you what sort of difficulties we are under to get this product into trials and out on the market. Our schedule and your employment contract are quite inflexible in that regard."

Bob considered his reply, because the more he had learned about Trace since the interview, the more he feared the man. He knew he had bullshitted his way into this position, and he was truly embracing all the salary and perks of his handiwork. However, he had neglected to anticipate Trace standing with a big foot an inch from his balls all the time.

Trace was expectantly staring at him, and he realized he could not hesitate any longer. So, he said, "I know just what you mean. I'm all over this personally now. I'm here at the crack of dawn, in the lab every damn night, learning the technology, suggesting innovation, and kicking the asses of these nitwits that Brandt assigned me—and yes, I suppose we can hire somebody else for that last part if you want. Anyway, uh, we'll have, ah, tangible results inside a month. I guarantee it." He watched Trace's expression for signs of how the man was digesting this line.

Trace nodded thoughtfully, opened his mouth to say something, hesitated, and then took another bite of the sandwich. While chewing, he squeezed the mustard bottle. It made a farting sound and came up empty. He put the sandwich down, unscrewed the cap on the bottle and peered inside with one eye. Trace said, "Oppie, get me one of those butter knives over there behind ya. There's still some of this crap hiding in here somewhere, and it is time to root it out."

Wondering if the crap message was directed at him as well as the mustard bottle, Bob stood up abruptly, looking for the knife. While he rattled through the drawers, Trace said, "Listen, you've been here three weeks now. I think that's plenty of time for a man with your credentials to come up to speed. Give me some goddamn sign of life here."

Bob tried to look busy, but he had pretty well surveyed both drawers and the butter knife was lying in the first one, on top, in plain sight. Trace said, "I believe, by now, you should be staring at that knife." Bob steeled himself and forced a grin. He grabbed the knife, turned around and handed it to Trace. "Sure. Here is what I'm on to." At this point, Bob was purely spinning his reply. "What we need is a DNA fertilizer, you know, a supercharger ... to ... keep the implant teeth ... from dying. I've got leads on three different lines of attack on this problem, and I can have all this wrapped up in a month..." His explanation trailed off.

Trace nodded again, still rattling around in the mustard bottle with the knife and finally came up with a big slug of the yellow stuff. He grunted and slowly spread it on his sandwich, set the knife down, and leaned back in his chair. "Listen, Oppie, I'm not a patient man when it comes to my money being wasted. We all have our problems. Mine, right now, is getting more mustard. Yours, hell, yours is keeping my ass happy, and as we have already discussed, that means a good tooth, right fucking now, not later. I'll take you at your word on the fertilizer, but don't fuck with me." He resumed eating the sandwich.

After a moment, as Trace focused on gestation, it dawned on Bob that the conversation was over. Briefly, he waited in confusion about whether he should stay or go but he then stood, thinking he wanted to run, not walk out the door. He managed to move his legs with the right amount of authority.

As he wandered back to his office, Bob was filled with dread. This project was one tough nut to crack, far tougher than he had ever anticipated, and since his background in genetics was actually nonexistent, his anticipation of the difficulty had been nil. When he sat back down at his desk, his mind was racing.

Suddenly, a look of determination shone in his eyes. He turned to his computer screen and brought up the best online research source he knew—Wikipedia. He felt his powers surge. He would start from the very beginning and read everything he could find on teeth, genetics, and, well, whatever.

Billy knocked tentatively at Bob's door around eleven that evening. There was no answer, though he heard what sounded like light snoring.

Billy had gotten into the habit of staying at work barely ten minutes longer than his boss just in case Bob forgot something and wandered back. This had worked out well until today. Bob was hardly a workaholic. Billy had been getting off around three in the afternoon and enjoying his reduced work schedule.

Even so, Billy was considering requesting a transfer. Previously, senior scientists had directed him to various mundane tasks. They rarely paid attention to whether he got things done or not, and that had allowed him to goof off. However, Bob generated too much pressure, with Trace constantly calling or sometimes just barging into the office, demanding status reports that were never available. The typical scenario was that Billy had to first be insulted, and in that regard, Trace could be highly creative. He then had to find Bob for a handoff. A handoff could be challenging. Bob could be anywhere at any particular time of the workday, including at home with his German girlfriend.

On the plus side was the professor, Sam, the person that Billy often initiated the calls to each day for Bob. Sam was apparently this very smart person that Bob knew from back in his college days. After the first call Billy made, the professor would recognize his voice and talk with him for a few minutes. Billy wound up over a series of calls telling Sam about his partner, Jerome, his bodybuilding, martial arts skills and culinary interests. Sam always seemed interested in what Billy had to say. It made him feel special.

In any case, today Bob was staying uncharacteristically late, and Billy was starving. It was hard to sustain all his muscle mass with the tired, overcooked gray meat stuff that TeeGentics served in the cafeteria. Billy was not even sure it was meat. He really wanted to go home, so he braved another knock on the door, this time a bit louder. He heard a snort, then the sound of some papers being shuffled. He said, "Bob, are you busy? Could we talk?"

Billy heard Bob's chair squeak loudly, followed by a sigh. Then Bob's detached voice said, "Jesus, what the hell time is it?"

Billy decided to enter Bob's office. Poking his head in, he saw Bob sitting behind his desk, rubbing his eyes and yawning. Bob looked startled when he saw Billy looking at him.

"Jesus Christ, don't you ever fucking knock? Can't you see I'm busy?" Bob said, reengaged now in shuffling some papers to look busy.

Billy looked down at his shoes and mumbled, "I did knock."

"Speak up, damn it. What the hell is wrong with you, mumbling all the time?"

Billy stood mute, scared.

Bob said, "You're a peculiar one, Billy. What the hell do you do, besides work?"

Billy tried to answer, but Bob cut him off, "Me, I like to watch the sun go down in the evenings. I sure as hell don't want to lift weights. Why do you lift those weights so much, anyway?"

Again, Billy tried answering and again Bob cut him off, "Never mind, I don't want to know. What the fuck time is it, anyway?"

Billy said, "After eleven, boss. Everybody is gone."

Bob stood abruptly and said, "Well shit, let's call it a day. This is too damn much like work." Bob began stuffing the random papers he had been shuffling into his satchel. Billy left to lock his computer for the night. Bob breezed past Billy's desk and said, "Hey, lock mine too before you go."

Feeling annoyed at the last-second assignment, Billy clenched his fists, but then walked back into Bob's office. He was about to lock the computer when his curiosity got the better of him and he looked at what his boss had been reading. Bob had at least two dozen web browser windows open, most of them related to topics on genetics or teeth. He began clicking through them.

Some of the stuff was straightforward information that he had seen or heard when looking over the shoulders of the scientists he had worked for earlier. Some of it was a bit weird. Bob was reading about different animal teeth, on cloning sheep and puppies and finally, a recipe for homemade tomato basil soup.

Billy wondered if Bob actually understood what was going on at the company. For himself, he had spent enough time around the scientists to realize at a basic level what the new product being developed was supposed to do. Perhaps Bob was on some track to introduce something revolutionary, though Billy was puzzled where the soup fit into the genetic stew.

He decided it was above his paygrade as he flipped out the lights to head home.

Chapter 6

Sitting at their reserved private dining table on the window-wrapped top-floor room at the Denver TeeGentics conference, Liz and Frieda awaited the arrival of Werner Brandt to talk to them about his company.

Liz had tried during the morning question and answer session to nail down the CEO of the company on something, anything. However, Dr. Brandt had studiously avoided her raised hand, instead taking questions from various points around the room, which sounded as scripted as his replies. She had noticed, however, the other participants in the audience, primarily male, seemed impressed with the presence of the two women in mod squad attire who had added leather jackets to their normal outfits. Denver was a bit chilly compared to San Francisco this time of year.

Liz realized the whole thing had been conjured up as a PR event for Teegentics, and her suspicions were confirmed when she noticed Dr. Brandt looking down and reading from his notes after each question. Clever, even for a man. Seeking an end run, she used her high-level Wall Street financial contacts to put her in touch with Teegentics headquarters, where she had talked to a rather rude man named Chauncey Orbaugh. Rude at first anyway. Once the man had become aware of who Liz was, her foundation and their monetary backing and need for low-cost dental care for their low-wage patients, he changed his tune.

"Call me Trace."

Liz nodded, working on her self-control. She was having a hard time suppressing thoughts of sautéing the man. "Trace. Listen, don't want to use up your obviously invaluable time, but our foundation really is interested in becoming one of the leaders in the charge to get this technology out to our public."

Trace said, "Sounds terrific. Let me get Brandt to get with you when the dog and pony show is over."

When Werner came in, dressed in a top-end Armani suit, he smiled at the two women and said, "Dr. Werner Brandt, CEO."

Wrinkling their eyebrows at how effusive he was, both women introduced themselves. Frieda exchanged a look with Liz that said, "Good Cop, Bad Cop." It was a practiced routine they used on uppity males.

Frieda started in, "So, Dr. Brandt. Have a seat." She indicated the chair across the table. She continued, "Lunch is coming. We summoned our chef and he arrived this morning. The fare of the conference is, well, shit."

Werner nodded, "I know, but we were footing the whole bill for this event, and as you know, being fiscally responsible is part of being a CEO."

Frieda raised her eyebrows. "But we paid to attend your conference. We paid to fly from California. Okay, we took the foundation's jet. Then, to get around the crappy food, we flew in a chef."

Werner looked a bit nervous, so Liz stepped in with a soothing tone. "Can I call you Werner? And please, call me Liz." Werner shifted his attention to her and nodded, looking relieved. Liz continued, "Werner, we are really interested in your product. It sounds so promising for the people we are trying to help. If your technology is for real, we want to be the leading proponents and suppliers of your products to our patients. Believe me, it could make a huge difference for Teegentics, especially right out of the gate when your stock hits the market."

Werner nodded. Before he had come up to talk to them, Trace had given him a ten-minute, profanity-laced briefing about the "fucking huge size of this opportunity!"

Werner had a practiced reply: "We could have you tour our campus, show you what we are doing. The labs, the scientists. Of course, we would avoid the cafeteria. We have some great restaurants in Santa De Lola." He smiled at her.

Frieda jumped back in, "So, another dog and pony show, as your employer Chauncy Orbaugh referred to this conference?"

Werner reflexively ran his finger around the inside of his collar. Liz thought the man seemed awfully jumpy for a CEO. She said, "Listen, this is not an inquisition. I just have to be careful. The foundation I lead really expects due diligence on deals like this, we just have to be thorough. So, when would be a good date for that trip?"

"Son of a bitch!" Trace swore as Werner swooned over some recently arrived Brioni suits he had splayed out on the boardroom table. Trace was looking at an email that Werner had forwarded to him about the Cleaver Foundation's requirements for a visit to Teegentics that had led to this hastily arranged meeting.

When Werner had brought his new suits with him, Trace said, "What the fuck, Brandt?"

Werner had nodded. "Yep, they are pretty nice. I like the pattern in the fabric. Each is unique. I have this one for meetings with the scientists, this one for board meetings, and this one for … something. You know."

Trace scrunched his nose like a foul smell had come his way. "I prefer the customs I get from those inexpensive tailors over in the trailer park here in Santa De Lola. Quality at low prices."

"Sounds like a real deal, Trace."

Trace was not sure if Brandt was serious or derisive with that last comment, but he said, "I will be looking to see if you can keep track of what shit you wear where. Now, this foundation business."

With a wry grin Werner said, "Oh, yes, our latest greatest idea, Trace. You sure you want to deal with them?"

"They got billions to spend."

"You did read the email?"

Trace sighed, "Yes, I read the fucking email. Still, I reiterate, there are billions on the line here that could make a real difference to our situation."

Werner still looked amused as he said, "So, a landing pad for a helicopter? I guess I flat-ass just forgot to get that installed when we built the place."

Trace sighed again and said, "We can concrete in those ugly bushes in the lobby island, slap a circle on it, be done."

Offended, Werner retorted, "As CEO, I selected the shrubbery myself, Trace!"

"Figures." Trace looked thoughtful, "Hey, I got an even cheaper way to do it. Not to worry. I need a bit of time, though. Write them back and set up a meeting for a couple of weeks out. Besides, maybe we will have a fucking product by then to show off."

Werner raised an eyebrow and said, "Ever the optimist, eh, Trace?"

"Fuckin' A."

Chapter 7

Trace gazed pensively out the window, watching England coming up to meet the landing gear of his grandfather's Gulfstream. A light thu-thump indicated the flying was over and the pilot eased the nose of the aircraft down to the runway as they rapidly decelerated. The plane then taxied along for several minutes to a private hangar and an idling Rolls Royce.

The copilot exited the cockpit, opened the special double-wide door while a ground crew positioned a portable stairway, and unloaded the luggage in the belly of the aircraft. Trace busied himself gathering his things, which he had strewn about the cabin during the flight. Cramming it all into an oversize leather satchel, he sighed, wishing he could have avoided this trip.

Without a word to the crew, Trace began laboriously climbing down the stairway, his stomach rubbing and bumping the railing at each step. Finally on the ground and breathing heavily, legs feeling unsteady, he wobbled over to the Rolls, wondering if London air had somehow gotten thinner.

A waiting driver opened the door for him as he settled in. Trace helped himself to some scotch from an elegant decanter placed conveniently nearby in the small bar. He closed his eyes and took a deep gulp, then refilled his glass.

Trace's luggage was loaded in the trunk, and they whisked away silently, headed for the Mayfair district of central London.

Trace sipped the whisky now, barely acknowledging his surroundings, thinking about how his English mother had tortured him with spending nearly half his youth growing up in this shithole miserable city. He had never liked it here, preferring the warmer, sunny climate of his now deceased father's home in San Francisco. London was too proper, too British, too cloudy, and too rainy. His maternal grandfather had further fueled his dislike for living here. Martin Crosswaithe had harangued Trace for years to lose "a few stone" and when he failed to do that, the old fool went on and on about proper British bearing and how Trace had none of it but should, at the very least, try to emulate some semblance of such behavior. Trace so hated his grandfather he would have dumped the family ties decades back except for one reason—the enormous money and influence that Martin wielded. The old man realized that was Trace's primary driver in life and used it constantly to manipulate him.

Turning on to Piccadilly, he noted they were nearing their destination, so he swigged down the whiskey, refilled his glass, and downed another quick shot. Thus fortified, he looked out his window as they entered a side street just off Hyde Park. They stopped in front of tall, elaborately constructed wrought-iron gates finished in glossy black with gilded tips that slowly swung open. Entering the property, the driver negotiated a packed gravel drive to the front of the massive residence, passing ancient oaks and elms that dotted the exquisitely manicured grounds. Trace sighed as he then spotted Nigel, his grandfather's ancient butler, who stood waiting on the stone entry steps.

Trace extracted himself from the Rolls as the driver held the door. He looked around the familiar grounds as Nigel supervised the staff in porting his luggage into the home. Finishing his inspection, Trace climbed the stairs to the front door. Standing somewhat bowed, the butler waited patiently for him to make his way.

Nigel began with, "Master Chauncey, I'm so delighted to see you again." He was probably the only person in the world that called Trace by his given name. Trace ignored the old butler, and as he passed, Nigel added, "I see your attitude has not improved a great deal with age, your eminence."

Trace considered turning around and tossing an insult Nigel's way, but instead continued on. He had learned the hard way that arguing with the old butler was a total waste of time. In fact, it often left him feeling like he had been pummeled. Continuing on, Trace was about to turn the corner of the great hall when Nigel called to his receding back, "That's very good, sir, very good indeed. Your temper has certainly improved over the years from when you were a petulant, though rather overweight little child." Trace closed his eyes and kept walking.

Taking the elevator to his old third-floor bedroom, he noted his clothing had already been unpacked and hung in a large armoire. He entered the adjoining bath to shower, emerging half an hour later, feeling a bit more alive after his long flight. One of the staff had laid out his tuxedo for the evening on the bed and applied a fresh polish to his dress shoes. A decanter of whisky and a glass sat on a nearby table. Ignoring the tumbler, Trace lifted the decanter, taking a direct, deep drink. He then poured himself a double, downed that and poured another, which he sipped on while getting dressed. His dread for the evening's events was growing, and even the whisky was having a hard time diluting his emotions.

Martin Crosswaithe sat quietly at the head of an ancient oak table in a second-story study, listening to the junior members of his organization as they ran down a list of current activities in the group's investments. Nobody present was under the age of sixty-seven, so junior was a relative term.

As the chairman of this group of financiers, Martin left the mundane details of administration to them. They were, after all, younger and their intellects better suited to mind-numbing details. Martin considered himself a big picture person, and for the past twenty years he had focused on one overarching strategic initiative above all else—income growth. It drove his investment strategies with projects such as TeeGentics. When Trace had brought this biogen start-up to his attention with its plan of regenerating teeth, it dovetailed perfectly with his plans.

Feeling his age, he addressed the French contingent, Pierre Larose. "Pierre, what is the status of your company, Regen?"

Pierre looked up from his number three spot and said, "The status. Well, as a company that is only two months old, it is making proper headway in stem cell renewal. However, we are in a market today where some of the best in this area of genetic research are working for other top firms. More than a few work for your own TeeGentics."

Martin impatiently barked, "Pay what you must. We need the best, the brightest and you know our sense of ... urgency. I want no more excuses about finding talent." He thought, "I am surrounded by incompetent idiots!"

Expressionless, Pierre merely nodded. Martin calmed, remembering Pierre's other role of chief enforcer. The man could be relentless and deadly when needed.

Following a knock on the massive double oak doors at the far end of the study, Nigel stepped through and said, "Sir, dinner is served."

"Has my grandson arrived?

Nigel nodded. "He disembarked two hours ago. I believe he is in his room, at this moment seriously depleting our supply of scotch."

Martin did not disguise his annoyance. "Just make sure he is at the dinner table on time, would you, Nigel?"

"I imagine that won't be a problem, sir, what with Master Chauncey's fondness for all things edible." He turned on his heel and left.

Martin stood, as did Pierre and the other six men that made up the little group. They filed out in the opposite order they had arrived and moved to designated seats along the table in the grand dining room.

Twenty minutes later, Trace staggered in, a nearly empty whisky decanter dangling from his hand. The dining room was at the far end of the three-story-high great hall, an imposing chamber constructed of stone and ancient wood from European forests that had been annihilated for such purposes nearly two centuries earlier.

The walk from his third-floor bedroom down the stairs had left him breathless. As he entered, he noted that the entire group of sycophants that the old man surrounded himself with were present and accounted for. He hated them all and had made a point over the years of learning all their weaknesses and vices. One never knew when a bit of knowledge could save one's ass, especially with this group. For a fact, he had not survived this long with this lot on just his good looks and luck.

Nigel noted his entrance and quickly directed a young footman to guide Trace to his seat. A neophyte in his new role, Carl, approached and smiled and with no prior experience, he made the mistake of acquiring eye contact with Trace.

Trace, his words slurred, said, "What, no curtsy? Are we ever slipping around here, yes-sir-ree-billy-bo-bob." He paused, trying to focus on Carl. Failing that, he said, "So, the old bastard butler sent you to take care of me, did he?" Trace tried on his most practiced drunken glare, first at Nigel, then at Carl, then back to Nigel. Nigel merely smiled back. Carl, for his part, looked surprised and a bit confused. Trying on his best footman demeanor and tactful language, he said, "Master Orbaugh, excuse me, profoundly.

I meant not to offend. If you would but follow me, I will see to your seating."

Trace leered and said, "You'll see to my seating? Lead me by my balls, perhaps? Yah gonna grab my ass and tickle it with great aplomb?" Then he hiccupped, staring blearily at the helpless man in front of him. Carl looked at Nigel and Nigel flashed a hand signal back, his left forefinger down his right forearm.

Nigel was a fan of American baseball and loved the signals the coaches used to communicate with the players. He had studied them, devising his own signals, handed out extensive printouts explaining what they meant, and had frequent training sessions to ensure compliance of the staff.

Carl recognized the one that Nigel had code-named "Bunt." Sadly, Carl had struggled with keeping clear in his mind the difference between a baseball "bunt" and a football "punt." Was he to attack, retreat, flank or stand still? With a drunken Trace slurring odd insults at him, and with the rest of the senior investors following the drama, he made up his own translation. Glaring back, lowering his right shoulder, he assumed a defensive stance.

Nigel began furiously relaying in new signals, but Carl was now focused on his own play.

Trace interpreted Carl's stance to be part of some elaborate scheme by Nigel, and possibly his grandfather, to humiliate him in front of the group—it would not be the first time that had happened. Therefore, his sumo wrestler training, from a two-week summer camp in Japan when he was ten, took over. Taking a last gulp of the scotch, he thumped the empty decanter on the dining table, lowered his right shoulder, and parodied the same stance as Carl.

Martin, remarkably spry for his age, levered to his feet. From the far end of the long dining table, his voice rang out: "Just what in the hell do you think you are doing, Trace? Is it conceivable that you could even possibly begin to explain this behavior?"

Carl's attention shifted from Trace to his grandfather. Trace saw Carl's distraction as an opening. He leaped into action with a high-pitched "Hi ya!"

Hearing Trace's battle call, an alarmed Carl lunged forward, blindly as it turned out. All he succeeded in doing was losing his balance. Trace was already chemically off balance. When the two struck each other, it was a glancing contact which sent both men ricocheting to their respective left.

Carl landed on the flagstone floor face first, breaking a tooth, and began yelping in pain.

Trace's fall was much more elaborate. He careened into the ancient dining table, his torso aligned nearly dead center to his place setting—the one that Carl had so desperately wanted to guide him to.

It was a considerable chunk of oak, ample in every way, representing Martin Crosswaithe's financially substantial family history. As he struck the table slightly below mid-gut, it forced his considerable girth to conform to its polished surfaces. His feet came off the ground, and he slid across the center, clearing a swath through the silverware, fine China, some large candelabras, an outstanding 1982 Chateau Margaux and upon arrival to the far side, seated and with eyes now wide open in panic was the most elderly and unsuspecting partner of Martin's firm, fresh that morning from the Netherlands, one Rutger Frans Bauer. Both men and all the dinner paraphernalia hit the floor in a loud crash.

Rutger's head broke Trace's fall, and Trace's fall broke Rutger's jaw. Trace's momentum carried him on for a distance away from the injured, stunned old man, rolling to a stop face down. For a moment, dead silence—but only for a moment.

Nigel reached Carl, furiously jerking the addled footman to his feet. Martin reached Rutger and knelt down next to his oldest friend. Trace reached drunkenly around for a small revolver protruding from his back pocket.

Pierre, seeing Trace's move, strode quickly over, brushed Trace's wavering hand aside, and snatched the revolver, slipping the weapon into his cummerbund. Returning to his chair, he lifted his glass filled with the 1982 Margaux he had salvaged from the wreckage. He aerated the wine with a big swirl and took a swig. No one noticed this during all the confusion except Trace, who was hollering, demanding his gun back.

Almost everyone was talking or shouting now, except Nigel, who was making wild gesticulations to the remaining staff to remove Carl from the room. Trace, still face down on his belly, chin on the floor, greasy, stringy hair in his eyes, was gasping unintelligibly for someone to help him up.

Carl was still yelping and, between yelps, threatening to sue. Martin was now cursing that his foolish daughter had exhibited the unbelievably poor taste to get married to an American and to then give birth to this moron of a grandson now beached on the floor in front of him.

Without even an appetizer served, dinner was over. First assessed was Rutger. Martin's private physician was summoned and, after a cursory examination, arranged for the old man to be taken to the hospital. Next was Trace. Nigel's remaining squad of footmen wrestled him up onto a stool for examination, at which time he threw up, scattering everyone around him except the doctor, who nearly threw up himself from having his shoes covered in the goo. The sawbones soldiered on and determined that except for a badly sprained wrist and some severe bruising on his belly, Trace was unscathed.

Carl, as protocol dictated, received treatment last and with the least amount of effort—i.e., he was summarily ejected from the premises. Summoning some bobbies that worked part-time on Martin's payroll, Nigel provided them with instructions to escort the former footman away from the grand old mansion.

In his huge wood-paneled study, Martin sat behind an ornately carved desk, outwardly calm, observing his grandson. Inside, he was seething. He had decided long ago that Trace was mostly a neanderthal, and the dinner table debacle had most definitely helped to reinforce that belief.

Nigel stood nearby, waiting, watching. Martin had long ago vowed never to meet with Trace alone. The man was suitable for certain work, sometimes very useful, but dangerous and a bully. He had seen the mental instability when Trace was but a boy and had worked to shape that behavior to his advantage. Still, he considered his grandson a loaded gun. And with a loaded gun, you never took chances.

It had been a miserable week for everyone around the estate since the dinner incident. Trace had been nearly impossible to deal with. Martin had taken the expedient of having Nigel remove all liquor and place it under lock and key *and* guard—one could never take too many precautions with his grandson.

Besides that, a young barrister had called, claiming to represent the former footman, Carl. The attorney wanted a speedy settlement. Nigel had taken the call, and on hearing the demand, asked if the young man had any idea whatsoever whom he thought he was dealing with. Then he said good day, quietly placing the old-fashioned handpiece back on the phone. He then dispatched a couple of his more experienced "footmen" to visit Carl to "discuss" the matter.

The old financier, Rutger, was getting expert care, but due to his age, he was definitely struggling with his injuries. This particular point really angered Martin—to think his old friend was in the hospital because of his own wayward flesh and blood.

This morning, Trace was hungover, sweating, and uncomfortable. Sitting down, he complained that his whole gut ached. Martin was rather enjoying the discomfort of his grandson and would not have minded watching him suffer for a while longer.

However, he needed to talk about some business issues, the reason for this damnable summoning to begin with.

"Trace, we seem to be at an impasse. This company, TeeGentics, is floundering badly, and without the product and the FDA trials, the trials that you so ingeniously arranged to have begun before the product was remotely ready, we have nothing less than a disaster on our hands. It is nearly impossible to resuscitate the marketing energy and consumer goodwill of a lost product announcement. You learned this long ago, yet you chose to push this—this boneheaded position."

In pain, eyes shut, with arms across his chest, Trace rocked back and forth. He opened one eye to look at his grandfather and then Nigel.

He said, "Gramps, give me a break. You know as well as I do that time is really the issue here. We don't have a lot of it."

Martin leaned back in his chair, "So, your financial concern for me is what drove this decision to reveal a product we don't have to a clamoring public? You did all this just for me?"

Trace dropped his head. "Of course, Gramps—only for you. Why else?"

Martin snorted, looked at Nigel, who was smiling derisively, and said, "Yes, why else would you ever act on your own? Well, I must say, it was a gutsy move, Trace, a gutsy *stupid* move." He paused to let that sink in and then continued, "I suppose I could let this go if it were just me. However, the rest of our partners are not nearly so forgiving. In fact, there are already a few calls for your head."

Trace opened his other eye, now eyeing his grandfather's expression.

Martin said, "I can see from your look, you are wondering if I am the one driving your problem. Rest assured, the other partners are not amused with failure, and they need no encouragement in this matter. In fact, only your association with the family has kept you safe. I am all that is between you and—shall we say—the end of the line." Martin stood, planting his clenched fists on his desktop, and leaned toward Trace. "Your only choice is to fix this, to fix it now, and to not allow any additional slip-ups. Do you understand? I will not protect you for long in this matter. This has become very personal for me. After that ridiculous fiasco at the dinner table, you and I are nearly done."

Trace nodded and a small sardonic smile broke through his pained expression. "I'm sure you will do what you can, Gramps, to protect me. You always do."

Martin said, "You know, I think this has been a worthwhile trip for you, after all." He nodded to Nigel and then added, "Now I must go, Trace, I am needed elsewhere. Have a nice flight back to the U.S. Say hello to your mother for me." That comment was a final dig, as Trace and his mother had not spoken in years, mostly due to the wedges Martin had driven into their relationship. He said nothing. Martin strode imperially from the study, Nigel falling in behind him.

Trace returned to his room, finding his bags packed and a note saying in fifteen minutes the limo would transport him to the Gulfstream for the trip home. Fine, he would go home. At least he could drink and eat something on the plane, and he could regain some focus. He proceeded down to the grand entry. No one was there to see him off and that was fine too—no false goodbyes, no good lucks, or any other stiff-upper-lip efforts at civility.

A few minutes later, the Rolls pulled up. On cue, Nigel's staff brought his luggage around and loaded it while he eased himself out the front door, down the large stone stairs and into the limo, painfully grunting as he climbed into the back seat. He did not immediately reach for the whisky decanter, as he had on his arrival. Deep in thought, he felt a weight lift from his psyche with the idea of leaving this place. Once on the way to Heathrow, he leaned back, let out a big sigh and poured himself a stiff drink.

He was musing about how exactly to have Nigel murdered when his phone rang. It was Bob. After the fourth ring he answered. "Bob, I hope this is good news. I haven't got time for any other." Trace did not want to hear another laundry list of sorry excuses and techno-babbling out of the mouth of the man that might have been a major hiring mistake. As he listened, he sank down in his seat, shaking his head. Bob was possibly the worst liar he had ever met when it came to cooking up excuses for failure. Hell, at least Brandt really did not know how to lie. He was just incompetent.

Trace said, "Well, hold onto your pecker. I'll be back in California in about ten hours, and you can personally blow smoke up my ass with all this lab effort shit you are doing." He hung up without saying goodbye and sipped long and deep from his drink.

Chapter 8

Bob had gone to sleep at midnight, coming straight in from work and quickly climbing into bed. Awakened two hours later by a ringing phone, he moaned as he put his hands over his ears. Helga had a shapely leg draped over him, which he had to wiggle out from under to reach his own personal source of torment.

It was Trace. "I called the lab, and they said you had gone home. What the fuck? Does this mean you've got this thing sorted out?"

Bob rubbed his eyes, trying to gather his thoughts while Trace blared at him. Helga sat up, yawning, stretching her naked body. He had a sudden urge to pay urgent attention to her, which he suppressed. Since his return from London, Trace had begun calling him at any time, day, or night, insisting on status and updates. It was extremely disconcerting, as Bob was at a standstill. More accurately, he had not achieved the slightest momentum. He had tried in his own limited way, sneaking into the lab after hours, when none of the other scientists could see him. He had been mixing and matching DNA like a lunatic, running the concoctions through the Acme DNA splicer that he had been learning more about on the phone with Sam. In the end, though, he mostly wound up with foul smells.

He took a deep breath and said, "Ah, yeah, Trace, wow, uh, yeah, things are moving right along—some good progress." Helga smiled at him as he talked, stretching back, making kissy faces, and playing with one of her nipples. He tore his eyes away from her, knowing he needed to focus on Trace.

"Progress, my ass. Get moving, now. Get down to that lab. Get your ace assistant, Billy, down there with you and get me a viable product. Or your ass is gonna get fired."

Bob started to say something calming when he realized the conversation was over. Trace had hung up on him.

He sat on the edge of his bed, head in his hands, just trying to stay awake. Looking over at Helga, who had fallen back to sleep, he knew what he had to do.

Getting up, he slipped on a robe and wandered to the bathroom. He was relieving himself when the phone rang again. He decided to ignore it, letting it go to voicemail. He went to Helga, rolled her over on her stomach and straddled her. A moment later, it began ringing again—he let it go again as she was now awake, arching her back and pushing against him. Maybe ten seconds later, it began ringing again. He grabbed the phone and shouted, "All right, Trace, I'm up, okay, I'm *up!*" He had gone limp, and Helga began to slip back into slumber.

The other end was silent, and then Bob heard a shuffling sound. Finally, Billy's meek voice: "Uh, I'm really sorry, Bob, to be bothering you this time of night. Mr. Orbaugh called me and said for me to meet you at the lab and to call you and coordinate our efforts."

"He did, did he?"

"Uh ... yeah, well, sort of. He was actually a lot ruder than that."

"Fine, fine. Give me a minute," Bob sat thinking, and when no thought occurred, he said, "All right then, Billy, let's get to it.

I'm taking a damn shower first, however. See you at the goddamn lab."

He slammed down the phone. It felt good to slam down the phone on Billy, even if the man was not the source of his pain. He shrugged, heading for the bathroom once again.

He stopped halfway across the bedroom, feeling a surge of desperation. *This is so fucked up*, he thought. Everything that he tried in the lab died, and his constant emails and calls to his Caribbean mentor had only gotten him more confused. Sam had spent hours trying to explain the operation of the Acme DNA thingie to Bob, and Bob had tried his best to program it, but it seemed like the machine did not like him.

He went to his satchel and dug out a little black leather-bound book. He thumbed through it to the letter H. Bob hesitated, thinking about how he had the latitude in his contract to bring "any and all" appropriate resources to bear on the project. What he needed was his mentor, Professor Samuel Henekey, the man that had helped direct him to this very position—though it would be Bob's ass if this backfired. He shrugged—it would be his ass no matter what.

He dialed the number, and on the second ring Professor Henekey picked up. Without preamble, Bob launched straight into the problem as he understood it, which was to say, not much. He closed his rather sketchy explanation of the issues with, "Sam, the only thing I am worried about is that Trace will say no to this idea of bringing you on board, but I really need you here now."

Sam was receptive to the idea. "Well, we knew this was always a possibility, so why don't you fly me up to headquarters for an interview? I think if I were to meet Trace, we would hit it off just fine."

Bob seized upon this idea. "Do you think so, Sam? God, I hope so because this man is like a piranha. You can't even imagine."

Sam chuckled and said, "I think so, Bob. I think it will all be fine."

"Great, so when can you get here? I hate to rush you like this, but times, they are a bit fucked up."

"Book the flight for me to arrive this evening if possible. I think at this point, the sooner I get there the sooner we can get the project moving forward and back on schedule."

It sounded great to Bob. "I'll get Billy to see to the reservations when I get into the lab, and he will send you an email confirmation." They closed with some pleasantries.

A big grin spread across his face. He would be back with Sam if they could sell Trace, and Sam was good at that sort of thing. It made him feel good just to think about it. Fifteen minutes later, he headed out the door with a plan, one that he hoped would get this project done and Trace off his ass. He could not wipe the smile off his face all the way to the office.

Bob corralled Billy as soon as he got in and told him what he needed. Billy said, "Dr. Sam is coming here? Wonderful!"

Bob looked at him suspiciously and said, "Why is that wonderful for you?"

Billy shrugged. "I just like talking with him when you have me make calls. He's genuinely nice." Bob wrinkled his brow at the reasoning, but then Billy's comment made sense. Everybody liked Sam.

Later that morning, he got an email from his mentor outlining some details on their plan for working on the teeth. Sam included a bullet list of things to say in the interim, since Trace was giving him such a hard time.

Like clockwork, at noon, Trace called him into a one-on-one meeting in the boardroom. Bob showed up feeling more confident than he had felt since his initial interview, and Trace noticed his mood in the first few minutes.

It started, as always, with Trace saying, "So, where the fuck are we, Bob? Since we last talked, I have spent around two more fucking million dollars on keeping this place afloat while the sharks smell blood in the water. Wanna go for a swim?"

Bob grinned. "I have a prepared briefing for you."

"That's a first. Where are your usual scribbled notes outlining lab failures?"

Bob maintained his grin, not wanting to get derailed. He was going to run over the five key bullet points on what they were going to be doing no matter what Trace said. "First off, I have determined that we have been fighting a problem with the Acme DNA splicer since I got here."

"What sort of a problem? Jesus, the thing cost a small fortune. Get the company in here and get it fixed."

Bob nodded. "What needs to be done is already in the works. We need to do two key things, first, a code update and secondly, a recalibration of the phase lock oscillator circuitry after we install the update."

Trace was impressed. "I have no fucking idea what all that means, but it sounds good."

Bob also had no idea what it meant, but the comment did exactly what Sam had said it would do—it got Trace off his back. He continued with more of the details in his notes and before long, they were damn near singing Kumbaya.

Bob left around four to go home, took a shower, then got ready to meet Sam at the airport at seven. Though he had been awake at this point for twenty-six hours, he still felt jazzed. Sam wanted to go to dinner on his arrival, so Bob made reservations at a place called Kimoto's, some fancy joint that served a ten-course meal with ten different boozes—guaranteeing one big-ass check at the end.

On the dot of seven, Sam's plane landed. Any plane getting anywhere on time was a miracle these days, and to think that Sam had made all his connecting flights and gotten through customs without a hitch was like a monkey coming up with the square root of pi. Bob liked to call it Sam luck.

Bob made his way to the baggage area and waited. Ten minutes later, he saw his old professor, a regal-looking middle-aged Black man, at least a head taller than the rest of the crowd around him. As he waved with a huge smile, Bob marveled at how white and perfect his mentor's teeth were.

Sam approached with his hand extended. As Bob reached out, he pulled it back and said, "*Qapla!*"

"What?"

Sam held up a book and said, "That's the Klingon word for success! Been reading on the plane."

Bob looked at the title, "The Klingon Dictionary." He grinned. Sam was always doing cool stuff. "What about the handshake?"

"Klingons head butt. We can do that if you want."

Bob's grin faded a bit. "Um, maybe some other time." Sam guffawed. All of Bob's worries evaporated with the feel-good Sam was pushing his way. Sam then stepped away to grab his bags from the carousel. The next thing Bob knew, they were gathering up luggage and hauling it like mules to Helga's Mercedes. Bob had begged it off the woman for the evening. Though he had bought it for her just a month ago, she kept both sets of keys hidden from him. She finally had agreed to loan it to him after he gave in and let her have the Vette for the next week. The woman drove a hard bargain.

As they climbed in the Mercedes, Sam said in his deep baritone, "I am ready to eat. Have you got something special in mind?" Bob nodded. A half hour later they were at their table for dinner. Bob noticed Sam was ignoring his silverware, using only his hands to eat. He said, "Uh, are you going au naturel?"

Sam grinned, "Klingons don't use flatware. You grasp your food, engage with it!"

Bob nodded, not understanding at all what Sam was talking about, but the booze had kicked in and he felt good.

Bob's earlier jazzed-up mood had passed, but he did not feel sleepy, even as they worked their way through the various liqueurs that were served with each entrée. Normally, drinking like this after so little sleep would have put him out like a light. He attributed it to how he never felt tired around Sam, another one of the small miracles he often experienced around the man. He was feeling a bit drunk, however, and at one point the waiter brought out some fancy champagne and two dinky plates with a weird-looking morsel on them. He could have sworn the waiter said the food was nitrogen-fried quail meat with some reduction.

Bob asked, "What about this course? Klingon acceptable?"

"Normally it would be served raw, freshly killed."

He and Sam started giggling and making jokes, because as food went, there was nothing exceptional about the dinner except the price, the funky methods of preparation and the booze.

At the end of the meal, Sam said, "Nothing like this where I've been living lately. Thanks for the dinner." He and Bob toasted and then he added, "Any good bars nearby? I could use a nice Macallan."

Bob signaled the waiter for the check, then staggered a bit when under way to the Mercedes. They went directly to his Irish bar, Flannery's, and ordered a bottle of whiskey with two glasses. Sam drank in moderation, while Bob got sloshed. They then wandered out to the Mercedes for the short trip to Bob's place.

As he was backing up out of his spot, a car honked, and Bob hit the brakes just in time to avoid an accident.

Bob got out and felt his great evening buzz go right out the window—it was a cop car. He almost started weeping and said, "Oh Jesus, oh, Jesus."

Sam got out on his side. "Officers. Can we help?"

Two annoyed cops climbed out and had them lean on the back of the Mercedes with their hands on the trunk. Bob, scared but still very drunk, slurred, "Guys, ya don't wanna do this. I mean, no damage done, right?"

The first cop, a big redheaded fellow, told him to shut up and unceremoniously handcuffed him. He ordered him to lie face down on the road next to his rear bumper.

The second officer approached Sam and told him to turn around. Sam just smiled and said, "Officer, give me a sobriety test if you want, but I can get us home. You would honor us if you did."

The officer hesitated and his scowl flickered. He had Sam do the sobriety walk, the breath test, and nothing seemed amiss.

The radio in the squad car started going off—a backup request for any nearby officers that could respond to an in-progress burglary. The two cops looked at each other and shrugged. They hauled Bob to his feet, uncuffed him, and told Sam, "You be sure and drive."

Bob gave a weak smile and slurred, "Thanks guys."

Frowning, the cops departed for their backup call.

"Let's call it a night. Rather than stay at your place, put me on expenses with TeeGentics at the Ritz Carlton. You can sleep it off there."

Bob nodded blearily and said, "Of course, great idea."

At the hotel, they checked in. Bob was out as soon as he hit the couch.

The next morning, Helga was angry about her missing new car and called Bob, demanding to know where the hell he had been all night. She then climbed in the Vette and, cursing in German, burned rubber for half a block on her way to work.

Later, Bob found Sam doing a set of slow-moving exercises that looked like tai chi, but he was not enough of an expert to know. Sam headed off to the shower while Bob sipped some French press coffee that had been brought up.

Sam emerged outfitted with a sash over the front of his suit. He sat across from Bob, poured himself some coffee and said, "Soon, we meet with the Trace. Let's take this approach to get him into a cooperative mood."

He then outlined a simple introduction for Bob to provide and said he would handle the rest. It appealed to Bob, as he sensed success would come with his old mentor now present. Besides, he wanted to keep the cash flow coming into his own bank account.

Chapter 9

Rising early, Liz decided to go for a run to clear her mind. It had always been that way for her. As a teenager, she had been declared champion by her mom's staff in the all-state commune distance runner competition, though only a few other grade-school age kids had entered with her.

She changed into her jogging outfit and slipped on a pedometer. She set an arbitrary distance in her mind of two miles along one of her normal routes that took her over several hiking trails on the estate, what had formerly been the commune. It had been about six months since she had done this, but figured she was good to go.

A quarter mile in, she was finding herself sucking air, so she backed down the pace to complete her distance. After another quarter mile, she stopped, caught her breath, and trudged back to the mansion for a shower. It would take a bit to get back up to her old distance.

Emerging from the bathroom while toweling off her hair, she slipped into a paisley cotton robe and sat down with her laptop to do some online research on TeeGentics. Since Frieda had turned her on to the company, she had noticed that every day more and more press came out about how great TeeGentics was and how absolutely wonderful their new product was going to be.

It was exciting or maybe all bullshit. The company would come up in an incredibly positive way in various Internet search engines. She clicked through seven or eight pages of links, trying to find one negative thing about the company.

She said to Frieda, "This company sounds like a gift from the gods."

Frieda shrugged. "Well, at any rate, it looks like they are plenty cheap. Don't forget, we got some creative accounting to eat up the millions we spent converting the commune into these palatial grounds we live in now."

Liz raised an eyebrow. "This is our sanctuary, allowing us to live our mission. Palatial maybe, but necessary."

"Whatever."

They both giggled. Liz continued her research for another hour. After finding nothing more of interest, she went into their bedroom and found Frieda doing crunches. The woman religiously worked out, did yoga, pull-ups, push-ups, handstands, you name it.

Liz said, "Hey, let's meet up downstairs out on patio one for some coffee and rolls." Early on, before the numbering scheme, they often had to call each other on their phones to get themselves to the right common location.

Frieda nodded, "I'll get the order into Chef Alfonzo." She then headed to the shower with her phone to her ear, giving rapid-fire orders to the chef.

Liz sighed with contentment as she headed to the elevator and the first floor.

Patio One was one of her favorites: it had a view of the San Francisco Bay Bridge in the far distance. She found Frieda already there, directing the male wait staff in arranging the coffee and rolls.

It turned out that these men could do some things okay. Frieda had recently ordered all of them never make eye contact with Liz, because it brought out her "dragon."

Once seated, Frieda said, "So, this upcoming trip. Looks like the schmoes up at TeeGentics are actually building a helipad to make us happy."

They both laughed. Liz said, "Yep, even that rude man called Trace capitulated pretty easily, which may mean they are desperate. When are we going?"

"Another week. You think this is worth our time?"

Liz considered. "Well, we need a clinic in Santa De Lola, and there is some coastal real estate I'd like to look at in the area. Let's combine the three activities."

Frieda gave a thumbs-up and sipped her coffee.

Liz sighed in contentment, then strolled over to take in the vista. She stared at the San Francisco bridge, then looked over at the large pond directly below the patio. A great idea came to her in a flash. They should build a replica of the bridge across the pond that would lead to a whole new patio area for parties. She would get Frieda on the task today.

Chapter 10

Trace was surfing one of his favorite websites on a TeeGentics company laptop that was set up for him in the boardroom for his briefings. The site in question specialized in the best deli meats—corned beef, pastrami, German bologna, all of the highest quality. The stuff was shipped out of New York City via a courier. If he ordered in the morning before noon Eastern, it was guaranteed to arrive at any location in the continental U.S. within seven hours or the costs were refunded. The price per pound was ridiculous, but the meat was sublime. He was about to place an order when Bob banged on the double doors.

Trace sighed. "The door is open, Bob. Come on in, be quiet and give me a minute."

Bob entered with Sam directly behind him. Saying nothing, Trace raised his eyebrows, wondering *what now?* He refocused—he had four minutes to get his order in, and he was at the point of entering his credit card information.

Bob watched with curiosity and said, "What site is that?"

Trace said, "You can't afford it, even with what I pay you, so don't ask." He pulled his wallet out of his inside suit pocket and started digging through it for his credit card—he had a ton of notes and other trivia in the wallet as well. He finally pried it loose and quickly entered the number. The computer beeped and the order

68

application told him his card was invalid. Trace said, "The fuck? Invalid, my ass." He entered it again—same beep, same message.

Bob said, "Perhaps I can help."

Trace glared at him. "Listen, Oppie, you stick to teeth, I'll do the fancy finance stuff." He entered the number again, and this time it took the order, but came back and said it was past noon Eastern and that his order would be delivered tomorrow. "Tomorrow? You have got to be shittin' me."

He considered calling this New York bunch and chewing them out, but Bob looked at Trace as if he was about to pee on himself with excitement. He sighed and said, "Shit. What's up and who's your bro here?"

"Trace, some exciting news. I have here Professor Samuel Henekey." As he said, it, he gyrated his hand around in a semicircle like a master of ceremonies at the circus.

Trace shifted his gaze to Sam, who was smiling at him. Trace cracked a grimace and said, "Professor, is it? Professor of what?"

Sam spoke before Bob had a chance. "Genetics, mathematics, computer science. I like Monopoly too, suits my desire to dominate."

Trace sighed and replied, "Nuther egghead, though I like the dominate part. No offense, Sam," his tone belying his last words. He shifted his gaze back to Bob. "What's this all about? My left nut tells me this is gonna cost me money."

"Sam is here at my request . . . my summons, ugh, to, um, help us get things, you know, finished up!"

Trace's baleful gaze made Bob swallow hard. He said, "So, is Sam working for free, or are you splitting your pay with him?"

Bob gulped and said, "Well, now, Trace, in my contract it says I can bring people and resources to bear to get this project done. I need to bring Sam on for that exact purpose."

Trace smirked. "Wow, quoting your employment contract. Impressive. Now, convince me, Bob, why I should hire someone you recommend."

Sam leaned toward Trace, who automatically leaned back in the opposite direction with an uncomfortable expression. "Trace, it's nice to meet you."

Trace's guarded look remained. "Why, Sam, yes, I am glad to meet you."

"You know what, Trace? Bob's idea to bring me on board, if you allow it, is a good decision. Honor will be served, and cash reserves will be accumulated."

Trace frowned and said, "Bob? Making a good decision?"

Sam nodded. "Yes, Bob. Think positive here. I got the secret sauce."

Trace's cynical smile returned. "I see. So, you think you can get this ball rolling finally?"

As Sam looked at Bob, Trace felt compelled to follow Sam's gaze. His lead scientist was looking zoned out, a placid grin on his face. That seemed normal enough. He looked back to Sam.

He couldn't put a pudgy finger on it, but lately, Trace felt like he as well as Werner and company were all moving in slow motion. He supposed it was the stress of running this three-ring calamity called TeeGentics. Maybe Sam could fix all the broke shit, one never knew. Plus, if they got the Cleaver Foundation in their court, this could be one huge payday. He decided, *go for it.*

Sam helped cement that decision when he said, "Yes, I can. Get an offer letter written up. Salary and stock option requirements are right on this piece of paper. I will get things going today with Bob in the lab. Be back to sign it at the close of business. *Qapla!*" Sam slid the folded paper in front of Trace.

Trace got wide-eyed when he looked at what was written on the slip. Then a small frown emerged. He said, "*Qapla.* Klingon. I like it. Well, you better be worth it, Professor. I am putting you on a sixty-day trial basis."

Everybody breathed a sigh of relief. Trace said, "By the way, the Cleaver Foundation folks are on the way over this morning. Would like you all out front in the lobby drive with the rest of the team. Gonna give them a grand welcome, the tour, and Sam, this is a great opportunity to help get them on board with our product."

Sam said, "The hippie trust fund awardee Liz Cleaver? That broad is worth a bundle."

Bob had Billy lead Sam down to his new office. When they arrived, Sam motioned to Billy to take a seat and relax while he pulled some items out of a small backpack he had brought with him.

Billy was enjoying the break. Sam was not like Bob, aka, Mr. Hyper. He watched as Sam set a small figurine on his desk facing him.

Sam caught Billy's interest in the object. "You like martial arts, right?"

Billy nodded.

Sam said, "Well, I've gotten into the Klingon style of combat."

"I used to love those episodes on Star Trek! And that Worf you have there with the bat'leth is cool!"

"Got it online. Tons of stuff out there. I even have a variety of Klingon-based Monopoly games."

Billy stood and acted as if he was swinging a bat'leth. Sam laughed, "We need to work out together."

A knock at the open door, and Billy, mildly embarrassed, saw Fiona Kendle standing at the door. She was watching him and Sam with a small smile.

"Hello Dr. Henekey. I'm Dr. Kendle, call me Fiona." She extended her hand.

Sam smiled. "Well, hello. Call me Sam."

Billy watched the two looking each other over and sensed they were instantly attracted. He decided to give them a moment alone and said, "Uh, Sam, I should get going."

Sam, without shifting his attention, replied, "Sure, Billy. Thanks for getting me situated."

Billy made a quick exit.

Fiona withdrew her hand, and took a step back from Sam. He indicated for her to take the chair just vacated by Billy.

Once seated, she noted the Worf figurine. "Commander Worf! I love Star Trek!"

Sam looked pleased as he said, "I collect a bit of memorabilia."

Fiona said, "I used to go to conventions with my dad when I was a kid. Great fun." She paused, then added, "So, I understand you are going to be working with us in regard to the DNA splicer. I heard that you think that there are issues? I've been wondering about that thing for a while."

Sam nodded, "I know there are. We have the same unit at the university I came from, albeit a slightly earlier version. I have written some routines that sorted out some code bugs in the splicer. We can use them here."

Fiona smiled, "Wow! Then it looks like we will be spending time together. I do a lot of the genetic work and have the science team under me."

Sam leaned forward and said, "I look forward to working with you."

They continued smiling at each other, Fiona finally breaking it off with, "Well, time to get ready for our visitors."

Chapter 11

Werner, Sally, Trace, Bob and Sam along with Fiona Kendle and her science staff stood in front of the lobby entrance as they awaited the approach of the Cleaver Foundation helicopter and its passengers. Werner was looking intently at the new helipad and suddenly started walking toward it. "Trace, what the fuck did you install here?"

Trace, looking offended, hollered at Werner's receding back, "A fucking pad. What the hell. It'll work. Now get back here, the helicopter is coming in."

Liz was looking out her window as they made their descent to the campus. Their new pilot, Corrina, spotted the helipad, and all of them could see the CEO, Werner Brandt, approaching. It was like they were royalty, what with the CEO and all the other staff waiting out front to meet them. It gave Liz a tingle and she smiled at Frieda, who suddenly had a concerned look on her face. Liz lost the smile and wondered what was going on as their pilot said, "Oh shit!"

Trace was now alarmed and hollering at Werner because the blue swimming pool tarp with a hand-painted red circle in the middle (custom fitted to the shape of the lobby garden island), was coming loose. The large helicopter's downwash had popped a series of rather flimsy wooden stakes out of the ground.

Winded, Trace hollered again, "Brandt, get your ass back here!" but the noise level of the helicopter drowned him out.

For his part, Werner finally understood what was going on with the pad, and his internal green light switched to flashing red. He reversed course and fled back toward the assembled group at the best CEO speed he could muster, throwing his arms up around his head to block minor debris that was catching up with him.

When the helicopter was only five feet from touchdown, the tarp ripped completely loose, floating about and then rippling along the ground, swiftly gaining momentum. Along with that was a rapidly developing dust storm from the semi-compacted, exposed soil. The tarp and the dust storm appeared to be chasing the fleeing Werner.

As the helicopter touched down, the tarp, along with lots of dirt and detached shrubbery, blew into the assembled staff. Werner, being the closest, went down with the tarp on top of him, while the others were swallowed in a dustbowl-like assault not seen since the 1930s in Oklahoma. Bits of debris struck the glass windows of the lobby, cracking a few, though none shattered.

As the blades of the helicopter wound down to silence, everybody rushed over to find Werner. Trace was not leading the charge. He was on his phone with his contractor venting, "You motherfuckers better get your sorry asses out here pronto. What a fucking disaster!"

Sam arrived first, then Sally. The two of them attempted to lift the tarp, but it was too heavy, so they enlisted Bob and a few more scientists. Still no success. Finally, Sam pulled out a large Bat'leth–shaped Swiss army knife, felt around, and found where Werner was located, then sliced a large enough opening to let in some air.

The impromptu team then pulled back this bit of canvas as Sam continued to slice a larger opening. Finally, Werner was able to crawl out right where Sam was squatting. With a certain amount of humiliation, he emerged between Sam's legs, his new Brioni suit looking shredded. Sam helped Werner to his feet and smiled.

Werner, dazed, said, "Who are you?"

Sam said, "The new man on campus, boss. Nice to meet you, Werner. Trace and Bob have been telling me a heck of a lot about you. You know, your reputation precedes you."

Still dazed, Werner just nodded as he shook Sam's outstretched hand.

Liz and Frieda along with their new pilot had climbed out and were staring at the sight of the Teegentics folks extricating Werner out from the tarp and what looked like his rebirth between a large Black man's legs.

Frieda shook her head. "Helipad, my ass. We still doing this?"

Liz said, "Maybe we should reschedule." Then she saw Sally dusting Werner off, wondering why any woman would help a man in such a fashion. Curiosity overcame her desire to leave, and she said, "Let's stick around for a bit. The price might have just gotten cheaper."

Werner spotted his guests and, after a quick huddle with Bob and Trace, sent Bob to greet them while Werner limped back to his office to try and salvage his appearance. Trace muttered something about murdering the landscapers and wandered off out of sight.

Bob hollered at Werner, "Get that leg looked at," referring to the badly skinned knee Werner was hobbling off on. Sally gave him a dirty look as she helped her boss to the lobby doors.

Bob then sauntered over to Liz and Frieda, who were watching their pilot as she checked their helicopter for damage. "Welcome, ladies. Boy, was that something or what? I mean, not often do we see that sort of stuff going on here at TeeGentics." He then flashed a big smile at them.

Liz squinted her eyes in annoyance and said, "I would certainly hope this is not a common occurrence. Is Werner Brandt okay?"

"Oh sure, yep, he's tough, you know, CEO man. Can take a lickin', keep on limpin'."

Liz gave Bob a quizzical look, then a wry glance over to Frieda, who was rolling her eyes.

Frieda said, "So, you are what? Or who? Or do I care?"

Bob, realizing he had not introduced himself, dove in. "Oh, sorry, hey. Bob Oppenheimer here. Lead on the project, as in project lead. Yep. Leading away with our staff. Management, you know. So, are you ladies ready for the big tour? I mean, after all, you're here, might as well!"

Liz smiled and said, "Oh, you betcha ass."

Frieda giggled and Bob wondered if Liz was making fun of him. Then he thought how fucked up the arrival had been, dust storm and all, and decided he should smooth it over. He said, "Follow me, ladies. By the way, love the outfits. Very retro. Especially the tank tops."

Frieda appeared about to say something nasty when Liz flashed a hand signal to her. Oblivious, Bob led them to the lobby entrance, dodging the new driveway tumbleweeds and the tarp. At the reception desk, he was advised they were all to meet in the boardroom.

Werner was now relatively dusted off, though he could not get a couple of new cowlicks in his hair under control. Sally was off looking for some industrial grade hair spray or as she had joked, "Shellac if nothing else could be found". The company nurse had attended to his scraped knee, and he had gotten into the "Boardroom" Brioni. That the suit did not match his tie or shoes was trying, but as Sally had said, "It looks better than that street beggar outfit," which is what his old suit now constituted. *Yep,* he thought, *a ten thousand dollar street beggar outfit.*

Sally came back and with skillful use of a blow dryer, hair spray and a brush, got the offending licks back in their place.

Werner stood, grimacing in pain at his banged-up knee but flooded with determination to win over the Cleaver Foundation, he headed for the boardroom.

As he entered, he found Liz and Frieda sitting with Bob, Sam, and Fiona. The women were busy talking. Bob and Sam, not so much.

Werner barely made it into the room as the three women stood. Liz looked at Werner and said, "Your lead scientist, Fiona, is going to take us on the tour. Would it be possible for your … assistant, Sally, to attend with us?"

Werner said, "Ah, sure. I mean, should we talk first, or what?" One of his cowlicks popped loose. Both Liz and Frieda's eyes opened a bit wider. Liz said, "No, that won't be necessary. We are running behind. For now, let's do the tour. You get some rest. Then we'll be in touch." The women headed out the door for the lab.

Werner shook his head, trying to clear some dizziness, which popped another cowlick loose. He sat down, feeling exactly like he'd been run over by a giant tarp. With a puzzled expression he looked over at Bob and Sam.

"So, Sam, how did you wind up here? I heard nothing about you coming on board."

Sam smiled reassuringly and said, "Well, boss, I was flown in to help Bob here, my old student, get the lab sorted out. I have a lot of experience with the equipment you are using."

Being called "boss" gave Werner a small boost. Still, he replied, "So do we. Not all that good, I think."

Sam shrugged and said, "Yep, well, I code a lot and I think I can fix the bugs in the Acme DNA splicer. We have a similar model at the lab at my old university."

Werner was impressed. He said, "So, how long to get that sorted out?"

"Not long. A week, maybe two?"

Werner said, "Wow! Okay, well, Sam. I guess welcome aboard. Keep us posted."

"You got it, boss. And we should get to work, whadaya think, Bob?"

Bob nodded his head for a bit longer than necessary. Sam gave a sideways look of amusement to Werner, who in a tired voice said, "Tally ho, mofos."

Despite the rocky beginning of the visit, Liz was impressed as Fiona showed them the lab, lots of equations, plus some teeth samples that had not died yet. Fiona said nothing to raise alarm. Sam then dropped by and talked with them for a few minutes.

Liz noticed Fiona gazing raptly at Sam. Well, she thought, *he is good-looking, for a man.* Then she thought, *That Fiona is one cool woman, that cinnamon complexion—I need to stop now and pay attention. To the briefing.*

Liz, Frieda and Fiona were getting along well, but the other one, Sally, kept to herself and took notes on a clipboard, briefly explaining to Liz that since Werner was not on the tour, she would need to brief him afterward.

Liz shrugged, figuring today was already weird enough. Trying to sort out Sally could wait for another time.

The tour completed, Fiona led Liz and Frieda back to their ride. Corinna, the pilot, was waiting and said, "We should have no problem lifting off now."

Walking out to the waiting helicopter, Liz saw a new tarp had been cut into sections and securely tied and staked down around the craft to protect its fuselage from getting peppered with loose debris during liftoff. Along with that, several half-ton trucks were parked around the edges of the tarp to ensure nothing could come loose again.

Corinna said, "I inspected this after that landscape crew put this in place. It should hold just fine."

Liz nodded, and both Frieda and Corinna boarded. She then turned to Fiona, pulled out a bandana from her purse and said, "Here you go. A memento."

Fiona laughed and said, "I will be sure to keep an eye on this one. Put it under glass."

Liz laughed with her and said, "What a cluster, huh?"

Fiona, giggling, said, "That freakin' tarp! That was Trace's idea! He's standing back by his BMW watching."

Liz spotted the man, putting a face to the name. They kept laughing until they both had to stop from lack of air. Liz shook hands with Fiona and extended an invitation, "How about you and Sam come to my place for dinner with Frieda and me soon? We want to know more about the tech, and you two make a nice couple."

Fiona blushed, and Liz said, "Oh, I could see how you were looking at him." She pulled out another bandana and said "For Sam."

Fiona, biting the edge of her lower lip, smiled and said, "Sounds like a great idea on the dinner, and maybe … about Sam too."

Liz grinned, thinking the place still had potential. She just had to get Fiona more into the mix, given all the testosterone-polluted science.

Climbing into her seat, Liz situated herself while Corinna ran down her checklist. The departure was uneventful, and as they headed on to their next stop to look at some local real estate, she saw the short fat man waddle over from his car, waving his hat at the mess around him and giving what looked like a very animated lecture to the landscape workers.

Over the next few weeks, Trace would meet with Bob and Sam in the boardroom for regular pastrami-fueled updates. He breathed a sigh of relief that things were beginning to move along now that Sam was on board, which vindicated his initial impulsive decision to hire Bob that was probably iffy at best. Yet here he was with what appeared to be a functional team getting stuff done. He decided going forward to stick with his impulses as it once again had worked for him.

The problem, as he now saw it, was not if they would get there, but when. Would it be in time for the IPO? From a marketing and stock price perspective, it had to be. Because of that, Trace continued to visit the lab on a regular basis, the first time at Sam's behest, later, because he was seeing some actual awesome shit down there on *Two*—the second floor, which housed not only the primary lab, but their data center and Fiona's team. Masses of complex computing equipment, racked up on a raised floor, surrounded the lab—a gem of isolation in the middle of tech central.

Some of the first stuff he saw was the cell and DNA structures that Sam was developing on their computer modeling software per Fiona's guidance. The images showed double-helix molecules with an associated half-ladder thangie aligned for bonding to the existing DNA—that was damn cool, whatever it was. On later visits they actually had cells growing in an amber liquid. Sam called it the nutritional medium, and that was pretty jazzy too. It was a lot different than the Werner *death by slide presentation* sessions back when the company first started. It was clear even to Trace's untrained eye that something profoundly different was going on.

The most amazing thing, though, was an intermediate step between the computer models and the material floating in the amber liquid. He watched Sam enter the computer model of the DNA into the Acme DNA Splicer. The machine had the most unusual hum—multi-harmonic was what Sam had called it—along with a faint blue glow emanating from all around it when it was running, though there were no sort of windows or view ports on the device. He had told Sam that was funky.

It really scared the shit out of him when Bob, under Sam's direction, opened the front of the machine to extract the early samples for analysis. The blue glow spilled out, filling the room. Moments before, Sam had asked Trace to step out during this part, but he had refused, and Sam had just shrugged. Bob and Sam had on some special goggles that allowed them to see what they were doing. As it turned out, the intense light effectively rendered Trace blind for ten minutes afterward. He was extremely agitated until Sam told him not to worry and, like an egg timer winding down, Trace's vision restored—except for some floaters that dissipated the next day.

He then did something he never did. Trace actually apologized for getting in the way and then asked if he could have his own pair of goggles. Sam told him he would take the request under advisement, which again got a chuckle from Trace rather than a termination notice.

Ultimately, however, Trace was still afraid for both this venture and his hide. Martin was calling regularly wanting to know "precisely how are you going to salvage this mess you have made?" It was a damn good question. He decided to get his own slide presentation put together for Martin of the new shit in the lab with pictures and endless bullet points. When that was done, he would have Billy schedule a virtual conference call.

Chapter 12

Werner sat in Bob's office for the first time ever, wondering why he was meeting him instead of Sam. In their earlier brief morning conversation, Bob had refused to elaborate when he requested a meeting, except to say it was "really important." Really important? How could anything Bob was up to be "really important"?

Werner finally agreed only because he could sense Bob's excitement over the phone. While he was waiting, Trace came waddling in and sat down next to Werner.

Two weeks earlier, the two had got caught up in a major yelling contest in the lobby, and only the arrival of a local news team responding to a new set of rumors that Trace had started broke it up. Werner had to reset himself, then take the reporters to his office, and chat them up. He barely made it through the interview; afterward, he threw up in the lobby bathroom. Trace had been out of sight and mind since then, no longer bothering him. While that had made him feel good at first, more recently he wondered what the hell the man was up to.

Billy entered the room, and in a low voice said, "I'm sorry, Dr. Brandt, Mr. Orbaugh. Bob just called and said he will be another five minutes."

Trace frowned and said, "Quit mumbling. What the hell did you just say?" Billy raised his voice just a bit and repeated himself.

Trace nodded and then went back to staring at the far wall. He seemed unusually calm about the delay, which again made Werner wonder.

They entered another round of silent waiting. Ten minutes later, Bob arrived. Hurrying in, he tossed his lab coat over the back of his chair, sat down behind his desk and then gave them a big smile. "Eureka."

Trace sat up and said, "This better be eureka. I mean, I could use some fucking exceptional eureka after that status report last Friday."

Bob then looked excitedly at Werner, apparently needing more adulation than what Trace was doling out.

Werner sighed, "So, Bob, sounds good so far. What's happened and what did you tell Trace you didn't tell me?"

Bob ignored the part of Werner's question about Trace and said, "You know the problem you brought me on for, the dying, blackening teeth?"

Trace said, "No, hell, we fucking forgot—refresh our memories here."

Bob gulped at the sarcasm but plunged ahead with his explanation. "Well, we've whupped it. We can go to trial with the FDA."

Trace was ecstatic. "Well, finally! Jesus, we are all going to shit in tall cotton if this is true. Give us the lowdown, Oppie."

Bob grinned nervously. "Two weeks ago, we hit on something we thought was going to work. Trace, you knew about these new versions of the product—by the way, they look better than anything we've ever made before. Talk about gorgeous. They are holding up fine."

Werner felt a pang of jealousy, realizing from Bob's last comment just how much he had missed in the last couple of months while playing CEO, not talking to the scientists or visiting the lab. He stood up and said, "Take me to the lab. Now, Bob. I want to see this."

Bob grinned and, looking at Trace, said, "Wanna come along?"

Trace nodded. "Let's quit gallivanting around here! Show us the product." He pulled Bob aside as Werner strode ahead of them and said, "Don't let on again, like you just did, about how much I have been involved here lately, okay? Brandt doesn't need to know squat except what I tell him."

Bob winked conspiratorially. Trace rolled his eyes and sighed.

They emerged from the elevator on the second floor and stopped outside the lab in a small airlock to don clean-room suits, clean-room hats, and little clean-room booties. Bob looked them over, smiled brightly, keyed in his door code, and the group entered.

Near the center of the gleaming steel and glass room stood a table constructed of the same materials. On its surface were forty clear acrylic boxes, each filled with an amber liquid. The containers were being fed nutrients by a variety of hoses, all color-coded for their specific compounds. Routed cable bundles fed into each box as well, attached to complex sensors monitoring the exact mix of nutrients, temperatures, growth progress and myriad other conditions. Bob said, "This is the latest generation that we started two weeks ago. As you can see, they are all healthy as they can be."

Trace peered into one of the boxes at a suspended white pristine tooth. He said, "Damn, these look better than any sample I've ever seen down here. What went right?"

A melodic, deep voice from the end of the table said, "We changed the nutrient formula. It was quite simple, really."

Trace grinned, hearing the voice. Werner turned and smiled as well. Sam and Fiona were standing together, smiling at them. They nodded as one to Werner.

Werner raised an eyebrow. "Sam. What a relief to have had you come on board. Fiona, I am even better seeing you in here."

Trace looked surprised. Werner smiled grimly at him and said, "Sam and I met the day of your tarp fiasco when he cut me out from under the damn thing."

"With a Klingon blade, I might add," Sam exclaimed.

Fiona smiled and jested, "Sometimes, only a blade will do."

Bob jumped in, seeing an opportunity to show his project management credentials, and said, "Hey, I needed Sam to reset the project. It was ever so clear to me that we were off course. He was available and I brought him onboard. You know, my contract and all. It allows … this sort of stuff." The last couple words trailed off as Werner tilted his head slightly.

Sam shifted his attention to Trace, extending his hand again. "Hello, boss."

Trace said, "Been there, done that," but extended his hand anyway. Sam grasped Trace's elbow just below the elbow, throwing Trace off balance with a huge shake.

Turning his attention back to Bob and Werner, Sam declared, "Werner, let's look at your grand idea!"

Leading the way, Fiona dove into a detailed explanation. "We also fixed some minor issues in the Acme DNA splicer that Sam resolved, then a recalibration and now the new nutrient. This is truly a joint achievement we forged." The two smiled at each other, then took a Klingon–style tai chi pose for holding a bat'leth.

Werner raised an eyebrow at the scene his two scientists had created and scratched his head. "Recalibration? Shoot, we've been at this for a while now, and it was going to take more than an adjustment or two to make *this* work. You must know the code in this box really well."

As he spoke, he again surveyed the contents of the boxes. This was finally it. He was seeing his original dream in front of him.

All he could think about was the value of his stock. He was going to be one rich ass man!

Bob smiled and said, "Dudes. Our product—these very teeth—can be ready for implanting next week. We have a volunteer right out of my own office."

Werner thought about that, then said, "Implant? Already? What do you think, Fiona? I'm personally still not sure about implants just yet."

Trace said, "Brandt, you are incredible. Here we have teeth, ready for implant, and you want to hamstring us with a thousand pages of light reading, justification, x rays, z rays, and who dah fuck knows what else. Jesus."

Fiona said, "I think we can have minimal exposure with just one tooth. Sam?"

Sam nodded in agreement. "Fiona here is the genetic expert, and everything she has shown me looks fine."

Trace said, "Well, there you go, Werner."

Werner decided what the hell and said, "Well, I guess we could try it out on a few volunteers. NDAs and all that, release of liability. I can get the lawyers to type it up."

Trace said, "Cover our asses! I for one am ready to ship these babies! Bob, Sam, Fiona, consider yourselves to have each just earned a big bonus, more stock options." Bob started bubbling thanks as Trace ignored him and turned back to the rows of the floating genetic teeth.

Shaking his head, Trace lifted his fedora, slipped a chubby hand through his thinning hair, and upon returning his hat at a jaunty angle said, "Wow. Just—fucking—*wow*!"

Chapter 13

B illy ran his tongue sensuously around his new front teeth, grinning self-consciously.

The first week after the removal of his natural teeth and the insertion of the new ones had been painful. After that, the new teeth rapidly settled into their new home. At any mirror he was near, he marveled at the shiny white wonders now located front and center in his mouth.

The teeth made him think about his partner, and he winced inside a bit. Jerome had been distant and not at all happy that Billy had made this decision to volunteer for the company trials without consulting him. Nevertheless, after the procedure, when he first looked in the mirror, Billy decided Jerome would just have to get over it. After years of bad-looking teeth and the associated humiliation, Billy had been willing to pay any price to fix them— and this had been *free*.

A lesser concern of Billy's was that Werner had been unhappy as well, though not with him. What a one-sided row that had been! The tirade from Werner had started with, "Jesus, his top four front teeth? All at once? No one should get more than one of these things at a time! Why don't you just call up one of those damn tabloids and tell them we are determined to kill somebody so we can be on the front page every goddamn day?"

With a nervous titter Bob said, "Now, Werner, calm down. Billy signed the release of liability you got us, so we're covered. He couldn't sue us if he grew tits on top of his head."

Werner said, "What if something goes wrong and these teeth have problems that force us to remove them? He'll look like a goddamn Arkansas hillbilly!"

Bob quipped, "Don't you mean Mississippi?"

Werner grimaced and said, "Yeah, right. Sam, what do you think?"

Hands clasped behind his back. "I trust Bob, he has good judgment in these matters. His decision and his honor are both on the line. And I have given the strictest attention to Billy since the transplants. I think he will be fine."

Bob grinned and said, "See?" like that explained it all. Werner nodded. He was learning to trust Sam, if not Bob.

Bob added, "Werner, have you even looked at Billy's new teeth? My god, the man wants to replace all the others right now. I can see why; I've never seen someone with more godawful natural teeth."

Werner nodded and added, "Yes, I have looked. That's another thing—you guys are treating his inflammation way too aggressively. His teeth look like they've been in there for six months, not two weeks."

Sam said, "Werner, we've done nothing but a few saltwater rinses. He just has a remarkable constitution, and the teeth are performing as designed."

Bob added, "Yeah, it is impressive how well he has already healed up. You know, five more people, all with missing teeth, were transplanted at the same time and we're seeing the same results. Two of them had been missing the tooth we replaced for over a decade."

Werner looked pointedly at Bob and said, "So, what does that tell you?"

Bob got a blank expression as he apparently struggled to determine what it meant. Werner sighed and, as if talking to a child, said, "We need to understand this good fortune, because the FDA is going to question how in the hell we did it. We need to start getting our ducks in a row as soon as possible."

Bob looked quickly over to Sam, then back to Werner and said, "Sure, sure. We're working on it, uh, nearly day and night. There is just so darn much going on right now like, ah, you know, expanding our capacity for prototype, ah, getting the teeth plugged into volunteers for our own trials, preparing the big press release Trace wants to get out—"

Werner interjected, "And getting ready for the FDA. We can't botch that part. We must have their approval to release this to the market. They will look up our asses with a microscope, survey our science, our data, our trials and on and on and on," Before he could say more, his phone rang. Werner glanced at the number. "I've got to take this."

Phone to his ear, he stepped away from Bob and Sam. It was Sally.

Werner listened, then said only "Okay ... okay. Give me five minutes." Phone back in pocket, he said, "Listen, we all have a conference call coming up with the board and the investors. Put a two-page summary on this healing-acceleration phenomenon on my desk by close of business on Friday. I need some weekend reading."

Billy thought about all that he had overheard from Werner in the discussion. So far he had felt fine after the implants except for one thing.

"Sam, I just wanted to express how happy I am about these teeth. One thing, though, I am tired all the time."

Sam smiled. "You've gone through a lot of teething trauma. No worries, this too shall pass."

Billy nodded, then wandered back to his desk. He yawned, and in a moment was asleep with his head atop his crossed arms.

Fiona and Sam came through and Fiona exclaimed, "Patak! Paid to sleep, are we?" Sam started laughing and startled awake, Billy looked embarrassed. Fiona pressed on, "Is that drool?"

Sam stepped close to Billy and slapped him on the back. "I believe it is, Fiona!" Everybody started laughing, however Billy's was rather strained.

Frieda came skipping into the kitchen, where Liz was having her morning coffee with Chef Alfonso and Langley. Planting her feet like she was making a superhero landing, she gave Liz a kiss on the cheek, then sat down next to her as Chef signaled for one of the kitchen staff to bring her a drink.

Liz, smiling, said, "I can see you are enthused this morning. What's up?"

Frieda had a conspiratorial look in her eye. "For your ears only."

Chef took the hint and poked Langley in the side. The two headed back to the freezer area to let the women talk.

Liz said, "So what's up that one of the few men I like has to leave the room?"

"I have a way for us to use TeeGentics to hide the cost on the commune overbuild we did. Not an overnight thing, but we can run the transactions offshore, and come back showing we spent three times as much."

Liz said, "Well, it's a start. But we spent thirty million plus on this joint if you want to call that an overbuild."

Frieda nodded, then added, "Hey, creative accounting needs names for line items like this place. And I think we can make even more money buying stock when they go public. Basically, more offshore stuff. Buy it, sell it, trade it, push cash around in shell companies, comes back clean. We can also hold some stock, our gyrations will push the price up, then same thing again. Rinse, repeat."

Liz said, "Now you're talking. Above my head, of course, but it sounds good. I got a little announcement too. We have a call to be on with TeeGentics. What do you think about investing directly? Would that help? These guys need to build a plant to make these things. Shit is getting flakey on their credit."

Frieda nodded slowly, then said, "I think that could dovetail with the rest of the stuff I am talking about."

Liz grinned and said, "Girl, running a foundation is all sorts of fun!" She sipped her coffee and buzzed on the counter-mounted intercom for Chef and Langley to return.

That evening, Liz was standing at the helipad as the foundation's helicopter set down. She stepped up and as the passenger door slid open, Fiona and Sam emerged. A robotic stairway rolled up to the door and locked itself in position, and they took the three steps down to the ground.

Fiona was bright eyed, Sam smiling. Both were dressed in jean shorts and wearing T shirts that said *Klingon Drinking Team* below an image of a mug of blood wine.

Fiona said, "I have never taken a helicopter ride in my life! That was a blast!"

Liz chuckled. "Well, I hope that is not the high point of your evening." Fiona blushed just like she had at TeeGentics. It was like hanging out with a teenager, and Liz found her to be a pleasant personality, with the blush telling her things must be proceeding as she hoped with the couple. She then looked at Sam and said, "Welcome, Professor. Can I call you Sam?"

He said, "Certainly, and is Liz okay with you?"

"No formality at this place. I am really glad you two accepted the dinner offer. First, your HBC dog tags, just a little memento." She hung them around each of their necks, like they had just arrived in Hawaii. "If you'll follow me, we can see what Chef Alfonso has put together for us."

Sam gave a sideways look of derision to Fiona as Liz turned to lead them away. Fiona shook her head in amusement.

They walked from the pad via a flagstone pathway to the mansion. Frieda greeted them there and the small talk commenced as they headed for Patio Eight, where dinner was being set up.

Liz said, "Listen, this may run late. If you two don't mind, why not just stay over? We have lots of room."

Sam said, "Uh, well, we didn't pack anything."

Liz turned, seeing Sam was holding Fiona's hand. She grinned and said, "We got everything here you need. Come on now, please?"

Sam and Fiona looked at each other, and Fiona said, "What the heck. Sure."

During some appetizers and chardonnay, Frieda said, "So how are things going at work?"

Fiona said, "Really well. We have teeth in trials now with some volunteers. Sam got a few things sorted out in some code we use along with some genetic mods I made. I think we have a winner now."

Liz said, "Sam, you're quiet."

Sam looked at the three women and said, "Well, yep, we have done some implants now. Just not sure how much we should talk about it."

Liz nodded and said, "Well, for what it's worth, this is a big deal to the foundation and frankly, we are looking at even more investment. We are under NDA with TeeGentics, so I think there is no issue talking to us."

Sam appeared to consider. "I suppose you are right." He looked back at Fiona, and Liz thought maybe they should just send the two up to their room.

They had some more discussion, dinner, deserts, more booze and by the time they were done, Fiona was sitting in Sam's lap in a lounge chair while Frieda told stories about growing up in Sweden.

Around midnight, Liz escorted the two to their suite. "If you all need anything, just ring Langley." She handed a suite key card to Sam and said, "Behave yourself! Just kidding!"

They all laughed, and Sam and Fiona were finally alone together as the door clicked close.

Liz went down to find Frieda in their room, watching a big screen of the surveillance cameras in Fiona and Sam's suite. They had multiple angles to see everything. Liz gave her a kiss on the cheek, rubbed a boob on her arm and said, "You perv. Did I miss anything?"

Chapter 14

A nervous Werner tried to gather his focus for the telephone conference call that was about to commence.

Sally, electric in her efficiency, unyielding in her dedication, welcomed board members as well as several people from Martin's group of investors and advised them that Werner would be joining them in just a moment.

Sally then took roll call and said, "Looks like they are all here, boss, except for Mr. Orbaugh."

Werner said, "Anybody know where Trace is? Oh, Trace! Oh, okay, so moving on!"

He paused for effect, then continued, "Welcome everyone else, and thank you for attending on such short notice. On the agenda are a series of minor funding and accounting activities. We can get to those if anyone is interested, but one of the big news items is about the FDA. They have assigned their team of half-assed scientists, and that is exciting. So now we are preparing for our trials—"

The call was temporarily blanketed with noise as Trace tweaked the position of his microphone and then said, "Well, hell, here we are."

Werner said, "You're late, Trace. I was just explaining to the rest of the board about the FDA trials."

Trace snorted and said, "Sure, fine, great. Well, I have an announcement about that as well. Let me take the wheel here for a minute, Brandt. First off, I am happy to announce the Cleaver Foundation is partnering up with us."

Another guest joined the call. It was Liz and company. She piped up, "Hey, everyone. *Kalimeris.* That's Greek for *good morning* for all you ... philistines out there."

Werner, wondering who on the call was a philistine, said, "Hey, Liz! Welcome! And, thanks Trace, yes, this is major. I was going to get to that announcement until you disrupted things by being late to the call and making a lot of noise. Anyway, we would like everyone to know, with this foundation, we will have immediate sales, even before the IPO and having to complete our filings with the SEC. This is massive."

Trace added, "Plus, we have our own project management team to liaison with these bureaucratic FDA dufus boat anchor idiots."

Irked, Werner said, "Trace, if you don't mind, I had already made the FDA announcement. Then you jumped to the Cleaver Foundation, which I was going to get to, and now we are back to the FDA. Even I am getting confused."

Trace laughed and said, "Hey, nothing wrong with emphasizing good news, no matter the order! And Bob Oppenheimer is going to be in charge of talking to these FDA morons."

Werner could hear Bob and Sam chuckling in the background. He decided to roll with the team so he could look on top of things as a CEO should, and said, "Well, carry on, as we previously discussed."

Trace said, "Previously? Discussed? Right! Okay, to explain the details, I'm turning this over to Bob Oppenheimer for a few."

Bob's voice came on, saying, "Hello, board members, and a hearty good morning to all." There was a long pause. When the others on the call realized the meeting might not move forward until they responded, a round of mumbled "mornings" and "hellos" went around.

Bob continued, "So, has everyone got coffee? Who needs coffee? We could—"

Trace said, "Oppie, it's a fucking conference call, you don't serve coffee."

Bob chuckled nervously and said, "Sure, boss, sure. I was just making a silly joke, ice breaker sort of thing, I, uh, well, never mind." He cleared his throat and continued reading from the notes Trace had provided. He continued, "Okay, then. Our FDA liaison is Dr. Hisashi Kimura. He has a team of folks assigned to him to help us get our product through to market. He brings—"

Trace interrupted, "What this stuffed shirt really brings is a path to wealth. We just need to manage his ass." A subdued round of laughter went around the call.

Bob said, "Right, Trace, right—fame, fortune, wealth, money, stock options... anyway, one of our newest and brightest will be assisting me, and I just found out today, he speaks fluent Klingon. How about a round of applause for Professor Samuel Henekey!"

Trace cut in, "Hey, no applause. Sam doesn't need it and this call has already gone on way too long, it's lunchtime. Okay, Sam, take it away, you got two minutes."

Sam chuckled, "*Yay chavlu' 'e' bajnISlu!* That's Klingon for 'Victory must be earned.' And thank you, Trace. I am honored to have this responsibility with TeeGentics. I'm also looking forward to more of the same fine support the company has provided so far. Here we are at just the right moment in human history, on the cusp of massive change, driven by the knowledge we are gaining about ourselves. And we are talking *neral* of money now. *Neral!* Uh, that's Klingon for shitloads for you philistines."

Trace said, "Uh, right on, bro. Hell of a segue way back to me! So, in conclusion, I think we got this whipped. Back to you, Werner."

Werner, shaking his head, said, "Okay. Well, one last thing. The Cleaver Foundation folks will be back here in the next few days to talk about our arrangements, and we will of course get the right people engaged in those discussions. That should be a wrap."

Liz, sounding miffed, added, "Yes, let's not spend too much time on who the fuck is baling your asses out."

Werner, suddenly apologetic as he could be, "Liz, of course, we appreciate you. Yep, even love is not too big a word. Not at all. Nope."

Liz snorted in derision and ended the call with, "Fuck me, what have I done?"

There was another beep as Trace's connection terminated, immediately followed by a series of "goodbyes" and "have a nice day" as the others on the call dropped. Werner eased to his feet, still limping from his knee injury, feeling like he had no idea what just happened.

Shrugging off any fear or doubt, he went back online to shop for a diamond-encrusted Rolex watch.

ob and Sam sat in the boardroom with FDA officials Dr. Hisashi Kimura and his assistant, Eddie Childress. On a tray placed between the four men was a pot of coffee and a pile of pastries big enough to feed a platoon.

Bob wriggled nervously in his chair, eyeing the FDA people, waiting for the first salvo of questions he could not possibly answer. Sam sat stiffly, shoulders erect, eyeing a blueberry muffin, and said, "*Dochvetlh vIneH!*"

Bob, puzzled, said, "What?"

"It translates roughly to: I want that damn muffin."

Directly across the table from Bob sat Dr. Kimura, who went by the name Sash. He had long ago given up trying to understand the vagaries of undisciplined Western minds. It was alien to his way of thinking and, in his opinion, any logical way of viewing the world.

When he first got off the plane from Japan as a student, he had been a reserved observer of the people he met in California. Sash had read a lot about the code of bushido growing up in Japan and wanted to integrate its best principles in his behavior.

Americans, however, never knew their place. They trampled on the traditions of others without a clue or a care. During his college days at Berkeley, after a few heated arguments and one suspension for almost getting in a fight, a dean threatened to expel him. Sash decided then and there he was in America for an education, not culture conversion.

He therefore earned doctorates in both biology and chemistry. On a spring break back in Japan during his final year of college, he looked at his parents' tiny apartment home, the crowded streets of Tokyo, and decided to apply for American citizenship. With Sash's education his application flew through. At the same time, Sash's younger brother, Hiroyuki, asked to come live with him, to which Sash happily accommodated. A year later, Hiro surprised him and applied for citizenship, which he achieved during two enlistments in the U.S Army. Sash was proud of Hiro—it fit his ideas of service to one's people and country.

This was why sitting with the staff of TeeGentics left him with a bad taste in his mouth for what he considered one of several downsides of his adopted country.

Bob, for his part, had been watching Sash with a puzzled expression. Sash said, "Dr. Oppenheimer, why are you staring at me?" He had a deep, almost guttural tone that commanded attention.

His directness startled Bob, who said, "Sorry, Dr. Kimura. Was I really staring?" He smiled, trying to turn on the charm.

Eddie Childress said, "I think Dr. Kimura knows when someone is staring at him."

Sam smiled brightly at the two men and said, "I'm sorry, but I must have one of these fine pastries. These will not get eaten by merely admiring them." He reached over, snagged the blueberry, and poured himself a cup of coffee.

Sash reached over for a cruller while Eddie poured coffee for their side of the table.

Bob grabbed hold of a cinnamon roll and took a big bite. Eddie started working on a bear claw with practiced efficiency.

Sash said, "Professor Henekey. You may call me Sash. I insist on it."

Sam sipped his coffee and said, "Call me Sam."

Sash grinned. "Sash and Sam. We should go to the Catskills."

Bob smiled and said, "Sash, you can call me Bob."

Sash, suddenly serious, said, "Dr. Oppenheimer, you may only address me as Dr. Kimura." Bob's mouth hung open in surprise, his now exposed cinnamon roll needing a bit more chewing. Sash gave out a big belt of a laugh, saying, "Just kidding, Bob. What's with your sense of humor?"

Everyone started laughing, though Bob was forcing it. He looked at Sam, who was deep in a belly laugh, over to Sash, then to Eddie. *What the fuck?* he thought.

Sash stopped abruptly and said, "Enough." Everyone stopped and then giggled. Sash, looking around, grinned and added, "So, here are the guideline documents. I know you have probably reviewed them. Let's talk about some protocols we commonly use to move the process forward and hope you get your product to market."

Bob perked up. "So, Sash, how long till we can sell this stuff? I mean, we are getting ready to build our plant now."

Sash frowned and said in a slow, deliberate voice, "Plant? Bob, there is no guarantee that your product will *ever* get released, let alone produced. We have some serious work ahead of us. If all goes well, we are looking at maybe one year, perhaps two. Worst case, that is."

Bob's feel-good level transformed to a tightening of his sphincter. He sputtered, "Tuh, tuh, two years? Our investors will never go for that."

Silence fell across the room, as if Bob had farted out loud. Sash clicked his pen several times. "Bob, just so you understand, no one at the FDA gives a rat's ass about your investors. We are, ultimately, concerned about public safety as relates to your product."

Bob said, "But, Sash, they're just teeth. You know, enamel, stuff, and, hey, hey, where are you guys going?"

The two FDA men began collecting their effects. Sash's intense gaze made Bob flinch. He said, "Don't worry, Bob. We will see you in the afternoon session. We are going to review some of this … material."

When they were gone, Bob turned to Sam, and said, "Did he just say fucking two years? Trace is going to kill me. This is beyond screwed up." Feeling dejected, he added, "That's twenty-four months, right? My god, I'll lose my job, the Vette, the condo, Helga…" He trailed off, thinking of further losses.

Fiona strolled in and sat next to Sam. He grinned and slid the box of pastries over to her. She started studying the pile and pulled out a huge oatmeal raisin cookie. She leaned back in her chair, munching away, saying, "You got that for me, didn't you?"

Sam and Fiona gave their now customary nod of being warrior equals. She sighed contentedly.

Sam finished his blueberry muffin and reached for a big apple fritter. He snorted at Bob, "You worry too much, my young friend. Trace can handle our Dr. Sash. This will go just fine. No, that is not the problem. The problem is that all these fine pastries will go to waste."

Bob snapped back to the present at Sam's cheery assessment, realizing he was most likely quite correct. He proceeded to root through the pile for a cheese Danish.

Sash and Eddie returned for the afternoon session, bringing the rest of their team of scientists with them. Bob and Sam went over the setup of the company from a technical perspective, then led a tour of the lab to see a few teeth, which suitably impressed the FDA folk, including Sash. It was a heady feeling to see the teeth—this was innovative biotechnology—and everyone agreed it was hard to believe human knowledge had progressed so far.

The FDA team also wanted to see one of the transplant volunteers. Bob had wanted to parade Billy in, but Sam cautioned against it. Billy was exhibiting more of the fatigue problem and had now lost even more weight. The single-tooth volunteers, while having mentioned feeling a bit tired from time to time, hadn't showed any other issues, and all had received complete physicals that said they were otherwise fine.

Like Billy, the volunteers all exhibited perfect adaptation to their new teeth. The FDA team, for a single afternoon and cursory inspection, were suitably impressed.

At the end of afternoon session with the FDA, Trace summoned Sam and Bob to the boardroom. Bob led off with a briefing for Trace, hoping to low-key the time intervals. He said, "Good news all around, Trace. The FDA team saw our handiwork up close and personal. The lab and now the transplant volunteers—it never fails to impress."

Trace said, "Uh-huh. What about the lead man, Kimura?"

Bob's stomach churned a bit, wondering if he ought to mention Sash's two-year comments. Trace picked right up on his hesitation.

"Sitting there and not answering my questions is just like you hollered in my ear, 'Fucked, we're fucking fucked!' What did the man say? Never mind." He swiveled from Bob to Sam. "Since Oppie here is struggling with basic syllables, why not help the ole bomb man out?"

Sam leaned back in his chair with a thoughtful look. "Dr. Kimura is a real ideologue, i.e., a problem. He is not the type to be pushed around or even persuaded in other more subtle ways that you have such extensive experience with."

Trace nodded. "Bribe proof. It figures. I checked up on this guy when I heard he was the one we'd get. You just confirmed it, he's an asshole. Okay, fine, good to know. Sam, of anyone around here, I believe you first. You're my results man."

Lately, Bob had noticed that only Sam easily deflected Trace's vitriolic outbursts or got actual compliments. It was weird to watch sometimes the way he would just back off or become agreeable, then turn right around and bite deeply into Bob like he was a block of cheddar.

Trace asked, "So what about the timeline? I need to know what was said in the meeting."

Bob got weak in the knees. This was the part he dreaded, but he spit it out, not wanting another lambasting, "Ah, well, Sash indicated like maybe two years, more or less."

That ignited the expected outburst from Trace. "Two years? Hell, why not two decades? We have to get this certification completed in less than four months now. We got an IPO scheduled and there is a shitload of money beyond your wildest dreams riding on time frames."

Bob, full of uncertainty, said, "I'm not sure I know how to bump things along faster with the FDA."

Trace waved dismissively, "I know that! Fuck it. I'll fix it. A few bribes in the right places and this guy'll be boltin' bumpers on Fords in Detroit. We'll have our IPO execute on schedule."

The meeting wrapped up and Trace waddled out the door, saying he was late for his afternoon massage.

Sam signaled Bob to stay. When they were sure the fat man was gone, Sam said, "The real issue, what *is* going on with Billy? He is not rejecting the teeth, but it is putting an enormous drain on him. More than he admits. The other trial members are showing similar but lesser symptoms. The four teeth are demanding more of his constitution than anticipated."

With Sam's comment, Bob freaked out and said, "Trace finds out about this, he'll go ballistic. What with the IPO talk and all, and if Kimura sees Billy, I'd say we're in the weeds on that front as well. You were right to keep a lid on him."

Sam smiled and said, "Trust the Trace on Kimura. We have our own issues to attend to, so let's bring Billy in. Fiona and I have been working on something that should take care of this whole problem."

Bob called his office, summoning Billy to the boardroom, wondering what Sam had in mind. Billy arrived a few minutes later. Sam indicated for him to sit down in the chair next to him.

Sam said, "Hello there, young man. How are you doing today?"

Billy shrugged and, in an example of his newfound appreciation of his lovely teeth, did not cover his mouth as he spoke. "Good, Sam. The teeth, they look, well, terrific. I want to do the bottom four, like you said I could. Today if possible."

Bob glanced curiously at Sam on hearing Billy's comment. It was the first time he had heard of any more transplants for Billy.

Sam just smiled and said, "Certainly, Billy, but first we need to fix this fatigue problem. I've been working on something I'd like you to try."

"Absolutely, Sam. Anything you want me to do."

Sam said, "Now, that's my boy. Bob, would you bring over a bottle of scotch? We'll all have a couple of drinks and then Billy can have his medicine."

Bob went over to the liquor cabinet and pulled down a bottle of Macallan from the top shelf, curious as to what the heck Sam had come up with now.

He placed a glass in front of Billy, who asked if he could have some cola in his drink. Sam shrugged and said, "Sure, Billy. The soda should affect nothing we do here." After a nod from Sam, Bob scrounged around in the liquor cabinet until he located a liter bottle with a thick coat of dust on it. Pop was certainly not in big demand in this boardroom.

He blew the dust off and handed it to his mentor. Sam expertly mixed a solid three ounces of scotch with an ounce of coke over ice.

Billy grinned, nodded, and sipped his drink. Bob and Sam drank theirs neat. They chatted about northern California weather, presidential politics, and the price of superior booze. Billy rapidly felt the effects of the scotch and jabbered on about how demanding his partner Jerome was.

Sam smiled while keeping an eye on the level in Billy's glass. He then fixed a second drink, more scotch, less coke, and as Billy took a sip, he pulled a zip-locked baggy out of his pocket and laid it on the table. Billy and Bob look intently at the dark reddish-brown powdered contents of the baggy.

Sam said, "Now, Billy, let me mix this in your third drink. I think you will feel a whole lot better afterward. Just one caution—this won't last but a day or two. I only want to see if it works. If it does, I have a more permanent fix, just for you."

Billy, who never drank during the day, and never more than the occasional beer or wine with a steak, was not used to the effects of scotch. Completing his second glass, chewing the ice, feeling the alcohol wash through his body, he imagined himself melting into his chair.

For Billy's next drink, Sam unzipped the baggy and then removed a ring of kitchen measuring spoons from his lab coat pocket. Eyes wide, Billy and Bob leaned forward to watch. Dipping out the dark powder with the smallest of the spoons, then carefully leveling it with the edge of his pinky, he dumped the powder into Billy's empty glass, adding three measured jiggers of scotch, no coke, no ice. He laughed, saying, "Stirred, not shaken!"

Billy giggled nervously and reached for the glass, but Sam commanded, "Wait." The three returned to watching the glass of amber liquid. Its contents began to darken, taking on the reddish-brown color of the powder.

Slowly, a deep red glow began in the middle of the glass, spreading out from its center. Bob gasped. Billy chortled, quickly looking at the two men and back to the glass. The liquid bubbled just twice, making the sound, "Blip...blop."

Satisfied, Sam commanded, "Drink up, Billy, drink up. Do it now!"

Billy grabbed the glass, first tentatively sipping the concoction. He had never had scotch neat, did not know its woody, bracing taste, and with the additive that Sam had provided, he did not really know if this was the true taste of the liquid anyway. He just knew that it tasted good, and he leaned back his head, slurping it down, wiping his finger across his mouth. A solitary drop escaped, and he said, "Oops!"

He sat the tumbler down, carefully licking the drop. He then saw Sam watching him intently. Bob had pushed away from them in his chair, rolling back a few feet until he bumped the boardroom wall, sipping his drink, watching his secretary and his mentor.

Billy felt an extension of the earlier warm sensation spreading through him, reaching down to his toes and what felt like all the way out into his scalp and beyond to the tips of his spiky blond hair. It gave him goose bumps. He became warmer and warmer, and then began to sweat. He grinned tightly at Sam. Sam smiled back, maintaining his vigilance.

Billy started to speak, but it came out as a squeaky, squirrel-like sound. He gave Sam an odd look, tried to stand, but ended up grasping the end of the table to keep from falling out of his chair. His vision swam. Sam and Bob seemed to be a million miles away suddenly.

Sam did not move to help him, and Billy wondered suddenly just what the hell was in the powder. Then an adrenal-spiked surge jolted him—he felt like a fire was flashing down to his nerve endings. His muscles burned and his back arched involuntarily, then darkness.

Billy opened his eyes. Sam and Bob were each pouring themselves another round of scotch. It was dark outside the boardroom windows.

His head had slumped forward onto his hands while dozing, and he had drooled onto the tabletop, but finally, he was awake, and he abruptly sat up. He felt like he was floating on air.

Sam said, "Billy, welcome back, partner. Have a nice lil' nap?"

Sam and Bob were smiling at him, and he could see they were both snockered. He said, "I feel fine. Matter of fact, I feel fabulous." Billy stood and, feeling the physique he had sculpted so methodically in the gym for years, flexed his biceps. The one he had hurt two days earlier during curls had no pain in it at all. The injury had not been severe, in fact, was common with body builders who often suffered strains as part of their regimen. He knew in another week it would be all right, but weirdly, it now felt healed. He bent forward and his back, which typically ached from an old martial arts injury, did not let out a peep. He looked at Sam incredulously and added, "Matter of fact, I don't think I've ever felt this good before. Wow! Sam, you ought to sell that stuff over the counter in a health food store. It would make you a rich man!"

Sam grinned, saying, "Billy, you look good, man. Come have a drink with us."

Billy giggled and said, "Three fingers, Sam. This is my new official health drink."

Sam laughed as he poured. "Looks like we are fixed, man. It will take me a few days to shore you up for good. Be aware, probably late tomorrow or the next morning this will wear off, so the fatigue will return. Just do me a favor—keep some good notes on how you feel, and we will take care of you."

Billy wanted to go home and tell Jerome all about this, but he could not leave just yet. First, a few drinks with his friends and then he would hit the road.

About eleven in the evening and another bottle later, Bob said, "Jesus, we need to wrap it up for the day. I'm blasted." He staggered to his feet and began looking for ashtrays to empty, though no one at TeeGentics was allowed to smoke on the premises. It was an old habit, one he had gotten when he worked in a bar and grill in his youth. Only after a few moments of wandering about the room did he realize the room was free of ashtrays.

Sam had an amused expression as he watched Bob tilt from side to side around the room. He said, "Yes, and I have a bit of work at the house to get done."

Bob and Billy looked at each other. Billy said, "What sort of work? Laundry?"

Sam laughed. Fiona would be waiting and all he could think about was removing her clothing. He said, "Yep, laundry. All over the floor."

Billy waved at them as he wandered out the door. He rambled down the hall, the last few shots of booze spreading out through him like it had earlier that day. Scotch, he had determined, was good. When he got to his old Pinto, he decided to stop by the liquor store and see if he could get another bottle or two for home consumption.

He pulled into Harold's Discount liquor parking lot, and as he was closing his door, a loud, rumbling black Chevy pickup pulled in alongside. He went on in and began perusing the shelves of liquor, looking for Macallan since that had been on the label on the bottles they had been drinking from earlier. Baffled that he could not find any, he strolled up front to inquire.

The black pickup bunch were slumping around the store, two of them talking loudly about the strip joint they had just left. The driver, a mountainous, hairy man with dyed red hair, a bandana and sleeveless red T-shirt, told his companions to shut the fuck up and get the beer. Billy found the hairy man's voice grating, which was unusual—typically, Billy would get nervous around that sort of verbal aggression.

He approached the counter. An ancient, shriveled, balding clerk by the cash register looked him up and down and said, "What can I do for yah, buddy?"

Billy smiled and said, "I'm looking for Macallan. It's a brand of scotch."

The old man shrugged, saying, "Well, all we got is what yah see. That Glen Livet, now that's a good one a lot of people buy."

Billy narrowed his eyes and said, "So, could you order the Macallan for me? I like it."

The old man shrugged again, a slight edge to his voice, saying, "Maybe. Let me look in my book."

The three men with the beer came up behind Billy. The hairy one was fidgeting impatiently. The old man was flipping through his book, saying, "Macallan, Macallan, hmm. Okay, here we go. Hey, this shit is expensive!" The edge disappeared from the clerk's voice as he looked up with a grin. Billy leaned forward to take a look, and the old man half closed the book, adding, "I can't show you my costs, buddy, I'd get fired." Billy shrugged, not really giving a hoot what the cost was.

The big hairy man said, "Well, are yah gonna order that crap or do we have to stand here all night while you decide?"

Billy looked over his shoulder and said, "I'll be done in a minute, big boy." He turned his attention back to the old man.

"'I'll be done in a minute, big boy'? God, does that ever sound queer. What are yah, blondie, queer?" His cronies giggled, and even the old man smirked.

Billy turned around and said, "You talk big, for a moron. Anyone ever tell you that before?" *Was that him saying that?* he wondered, and then decided that it felt good to not be pushed around.

Hairy man lost his smile and said, "Moron? Hey boys, the fairy just called me a moron. Well, let me show you what a moron can do, faggot."

The skinny, sallow companion said, "Get him, Clem. I don't like that Hollywood hairdo he's got, anyway."

Billy laughed, and in an exaggerated female impersonation, snapping his fingers, he mocked, "Clem? Clem? Jesus, what was yo momma thinking when she named you? Was she watchin' the *Beverly Hillbillies* while getting' fucked in the ass by some hayseed dick? Are you the result? If so, I do believe you have showed me what a moron can do."

Clem took the case of beer off his shoulder and handed it to the skinny, sallow companion, who buckled under the load until he could set it down on the counter. He said, "All right, queer, let's go outside."

The old clerk chimed in with, "Good idea! I'm about to call the cops."

Billy replied, "Sure, hon," and turned, swishing in drag queen fashion to the door, staggering just a bit, as Clem followed.

Two steps into the parking lot, Clem attacked from behind.

Billy, even drunk, had time to plan his first move. Reaching behind him, pivoting as he did, his right hand grabbed Clem by his testicles. Clem shrieked in pain. Billy hollered, "Macallan!"

Letting go of Clem's nuts, he locked the man in a fierce headlock, then punched Clem in the nose. Clem sagged. Feeling a bit woozy, Billy let go of the man and staggered off. Clem fell to the ground in a one-round knockout, no longer wondering about gayness.

Billy pivoted about on one leg to face the other two, never having felt so strong in his life. He screamed, "Macallan!

Clem's two friends, absorbing with their eyes but not accepting what their brains were telling them, pressed a rather disorganized attack. Their usual assignment was mop-up. Tonight, however, they were the reserves thrown into a pitched battle.

Sallow man belatedly grabbed for a pistol he kept in his belt behind his back. Billy grabbed the other attacker, slinging the hapless fellow into him. They both went down, and the gun came loose. Billy grabbed it and flung it into an empty field across the street.

Billy smiled and said, "Tell Clem, it was nothing personal." He then belched and walked back into the store to order the Macallan. He looked at the shriveled old man behind the counter and said, "Make that a case."

The old man, jittery, quavered, "Great, I can get you a fifteen percent discount on a full case. Yes sir. Now I'll need a deposit to get ... that ... ordered?" The old man's voice trailed off and Billy sensed the old man's fear.

How cool, he thought. As he smiled, the old man was mesmerized at the sight of the four white upper front teeth in Billy's mouth. Billy opened his wallet, pulled out a credit card and said, "Receipt, please?"

Transaction complete, Billy left the store, staggered a bit, then steadied himself. He strode past the three men without giving them a glance, climbed in his Pinto and drove off, weaving side to side.

Chapter 16

The latest trip to London was completely unexpected and primed with a sense of urgency. Trace provided access to a chartered private jet and instructions for Bob and Sam to get their asses in the air.

They stayed at Martin Crosswaithe's and ferried back and forth to the hospital via one of the five Rolls-Royces stowed in the converted old stables located behind the mansion.

The day before, Trace had woken Bob at two in the morning. Bob griped for just a moment about needing sack time and about all the long hours. Trace cut him off, informing him of the trip and its purpose. Apparently, an elderly friend of Trace's grandfather, Rutger Frans Bauer, was not recovering from a broken jaw he had suffered in an accident and was barely hanging on.

"Listen, the old fart needs a couple teeth to make him pretty and some of that Sam go juice you all used on Billy. The doc says there isn't anything they can actually do at this point. Let's get a move on."

Bob replied, "What if the FDA finds out from some doc in London that we installed a couple of these in a foreign country? We'd be risking the entire project."

Trace snorted, saying, "The old sawbones attending Rutger won't say squat. You worry too much about shit you know nothing about. Just do like I say, jump on the jet with Sam and some teeth and get your asses over there. I also need you back here pronto, so don't fuck around touring Piccadilly."

Bob said, "I don't know about this, Trace. As project manager, it makes me nervous."

Trace shot back, "Quit your whining and get moving."

Trying to change the subject, Bob asked, "So this was a bad accident for the old gent?"

Trace was hardly able to stop laughing, finally managing, "Oh yeah, it was a real doozy!" The call ended with Bob staring blankly at his phone.

He yawned, trying to wake up. When he felt a bit more alive, he called Sam. He sounded like he had not been sleeping and was excited at the prospect of possibly seeing Destination Star Trek, as the convention was being held this year in London. Apparently, as Sam was happy to educate Bob on the topic, he had been to England a few times before. Bob shrugged, hung up and began packing.

Helga had taken to camping out on the couch due to all the nighttime interruptions of her sleep. On his way out the door, he gave her a light slap on her rear. She moaned and then pulled her blanket over her head when he tried to give her a farewell kiss. Somewhat mystified by her reaction, he shrugged but kept moving.

Sam and Bob had to quickly rig up a way to keep the teeth alive during the flight, but that had turned out to be a minor issue for Bob, as Sam did all the work. The real issue in Bob's mind was that they were sticking two teeth in a fossil of an old man weakened by injury.

Bob said, "Sam, you think the old codger will be able to hold up?"

Sam gave a *who knows* shrug and said, "He's old, could die any moment." He paused, and then added, "I want to try a toned-down version of the injection I've prepared for Billy when we get back. I think it would be safe enough and should last the old man for the rest of his life."

Bob felt ambivalent about expressing any additional reservations. Then he decided that if Sam thought it would work, who was he to question his favorite source of wisdom?

He was still sorting through the night Billy drank the glowing whisky. That was the weirdest thing he could ever remember, drunk or sober, followed by the reported fight incident at the liquor store, which Billy had proudly mentioned the following morning. "Sam, what exactly was in that stuff you gave Billy?"

Sam laughed and said, "Billy was just taking care of himself, as any warrior would. There be no problem, mahn, with my revitalizer." Since Sam chose to conclude the thought with his "island speak," as Bob called it, to make light of the incident, Bob thought, *What me worry?*

Sam then reached into his carry-on luggage and pulled out one of his Klingon Monopoly games. "Let's play. Properties are now planets, money is actually military forces, and Chance and Community chest are Combat and Honor."

Bob nodded and jumped in. He was dead on the board after four dice rolls. Sam set it up for a new game, same result. Once more, again, same result.

"You're not very good at this, Bob."

Bob nodded in agreement.

At a private medical facility in London, a doctor introduced them to Rutger, who looked puny, or at least that was what Bob's grandma used to always say about nearly dead plants she would constantly overwater and fertilize. Rutger was suffering pain and trauma from his broken jaw. He scribbled on a notepad a lot about the person that had caused his trauma, and it quickly became clear that the culprit was Trace.

That fact did not surprise Bob at all. Rutger wanted to talk about the incident, but when he tried to croak out the story with his bad jaw, he would get emotional. Then his blood pressure would spike, and the doctors would have to rush in to get the old fellow calmed down, which simply delayed their progress.

Before their arrival the old man's physician had removed the two sheared-off teeth they had been sent to replace, so they were set to begin. Rutger managed to joke, "I understand you are here to save me!" Sam laughed and soon he and Rutger were chums. Sam told funny stories and Rutger, holding the side of his face, grimaced while laughing.

The teeth insertions went well enough. The next morning Rutger was up, looking in his large bathroom mirror, admiring them. He was hanging on white-knuckled to the vanity while two Dutch nurses on Rutger's payroll were nearly apoplectic at the fact the old man refused to follow their orders and return to his bed. Sam and Bob looked at each other; it was obvious that the teeth, without the "revitalizer," were having a significant impact on Rutger.

Sam said, "Rutger, we have a second stage to your treatment. It is painful at first, but within a very short time you will feel ... much better, and the teeth will tighten right up in the sockets."

Rutger grinned. "So that's all there is to it? A bit of pain? I'm old. You can't get this old without pain."

With Rutger's doctor insisting on performing the procedure under Sam's guidance, they extracted bone marrow from Rutger. Sam went off to do his special mix, and the modified marrow was then injected back into Rutger's bone. It hurt like hell, and to their surprise, Rutger cursed in Klingon throughout the procedure. Bob understood none of it. Sam just laughed and patted Rutger on the shoulder, saying, "*Heghlu'meH QaQ jajvam*" and the old man nodded in agreement. "It may be a good day to die, but I prefer not. You got your accent down, I must say." Sam smiled and said, "We should talk!"

Which raised two questions in Bob's mind. First was, "How does Rutger know Klingon?" Sam advised Trekkies had been around for decades. Bob later asked, "Well, then, how the heck does modifying bone marrow work?"

Sam expounded on the subject. "It's straightforward, really. Our special blend is first merged with the cells from Rutger's marrow, making them more efficient. After being injected back in the bone, the marrow will over time generate all the new...hybrid cells to make him feel fine from now on."

The return trip was uneventful; they went straight to the campus from the airport. Billy was waiting for them, looking rundown. True to Sam's prediction, the scotch-borne medication he had given him had worn off.

"Sam, I feel awful. To top it off, I had a filling fall out, of all things."

Sam's eyes widened and he immediately led Billy to the dental chair they had in the lab, asking Billy to open wide so he could look. Bob tagged along and he could see why Sam was getting so excited. Sam looked up, grinned, and said, "We better get on the phone to London."

Bob said, "Can't this wait till tomorrow? I'm jetlagged. Bushed. Out of gas."

Sam said, "Take a look at Billy's tooth, the one that lost the filling."

Bob yawned, swapping places with Sam. He gandered at the tooth in question once it was pointed out; it looked fine to him. He stood and said to Billy, "Why'd you have a filling in a tooth with no cavities?"

Billy looked perplexed and said, "It had a cavity. I remember when the dentist filled it."

Bob looked puzzled and said, "Open your mouth again." He grabbed a dental mirror while donning a little headband affixed with a halogen light. He flipped it on and looked closer. The tooth was perfect, pearly white. He sat up abruptly, dropping the mirror in Billy's mouth, who gagged and coughed, yanking out the instrument, saying, "Are ya trying to kill me?"

Dazed by what he had seen, Bob turned to Sam. "It looks just like one of the transplants. I mean just like a transplant. What the heck?"

Billy's jaw literally dropped.

Sam said, "Uh, this is bad for business. However, you want to make that call to London, or shall I?"

Billy said, "What for?"

Bob's brow furrowed, and for a change enlightenment dawned on him. "We need to make sure Rutger has all his fillings removed immediately?"

Sam nodded, then said, "Yah, might keep him from choking to death. And we need to make an adjustment in that bone marrow shit. We want to sell our teeth, not have them fixing old problems in customers' mouths for free."

Bob said, "Good point, good point."

Sam then advised Billy that it was time for his own bone-marrow transplant to address the fatigue issue. He was going to knock him out, because it was painful. Relieved, Billy nodded agreeably and said, "I need it, my ass has been dragging full time lately."

Bob went off and snoozed in the corner during the procedure and was later awakened by Billy, who said, "I'm going home to get some sleep. Sam told me to tell you to clean up the area before you go." He then limped off, his left leg still hurting from the bone marrow treatment.

Bob blinked his eyes a few times, yawned, then fell back to sleep.

Chapter 17

Times Square provided a welcome change of pace for Werner, somewhat easing the insult of this errand boy interview with CNB that Trace had forced on him at the last minute. Plus, he had a shopping expedition planned for additional clothes and accessories at Brioni's. They were even going to come by and pick him up. He smiled, thinking, *Money good for Mongo!*

He believed that he now had TeeGentics running like a top. The product was on track, and the Cleaver Foundation was keeping them afloat in the interim. Whenever he got put on the spot by a reporter, he was much more difficult to derail. Trace rarely talked to Werner, but they did discuss this trip, and both agreed, he was the man for the job.

There had been one peculiar situation before he left. Billy had gotten smart with him in the hallway the other day when Werner tried to elicit some information.

Billy said, "I can't talk about what Bob and Sam do, and I have no knowledge about a trip on a jet."

Werner said, "Trip on a jet? What are you talking about? Don't forget who you are working for, Billy."

Billy looked chagrined and said, "Sorry, boss. Oh, I have to get some bagels for Bob." He hurried off, leaving Werner wondering who ate bagels at three in the afternoon. He shrugged it off as stupid Bob stuff.

Now in Times Square, Werner contemplated his trip to New York for his upcoming interview with Bear Leibowitz. It would have been fine, but at the last minute, as Werner boarded the chartered Gulfstream, Bob braked to a hard stop in his silly-looking Corvette. He yanked out an overnight bag and handed it to the ground crew to load aboard.

Werner had said, "And just where do you think you are going?"

Bob smiled. "Hey, CEO man! I'm under orders from Trace to hitch a ride."

Werner said, "Trace? Are you on my CNB interview?" Sharing the limelight with Bob was a depressing thought.

Bob broke into a gosh-golly-gee-whiz grin, looked down while stubbing his toe in the tarmac, and said, "Oh, heck no, Werner. Other business. Not sure it's even worth the trip."

Werner nodded, thinking that talking to underlings was a waste of time. He climbed aboard, gently hung his suit coat in a closet right behind the cockpit, got out his laptop and started surfing stock prices and finance news. He and Bob hardly spoke during the flight except when Werner made a couple of obligatory queries as to how things were going, was there anything they needed, etc.

Bob grinned. "If I'd have known about all the extra duties, I'd have asked for more money back when you and Trace hired me."

Werner turned to his window, ignoring Bob for the rest of the trip.

Separate limos were waiting for them when they landed in LaGuardia, and they split up with a "Hey, good luck" and "Later, bud" sort of strained banter.

On the way, he wrote some notes for the talking points he needed to cover in his interview. He was going to accentuate the positive. Good teeth, affordable costs, dedicated teams of scientists, job creation, to name just a few. Satisfied, he nodded to himself. Werner got to the hotel, picked up his room key and hurried off in case Bob came in behind him or was hanging around in the lobby area.

The next morning, he went down for breakfast. With no sign of Bob, he considered himself off to a good start. He ordered a fruit bowl, a thick slice of grilled ham, two eggs over easy, hash browns, wheat toast, jam, orange juice and coffee. Like the previous night's big meal, he was on expenses and intended to make Trace pay. After the meal, he went through his notes, rehearsing his lines. He would start out with "Bear, TeeGentics is *the* thought leader in genetically developed teeth implants!" He then made his way out front for a cab and the short trip over to CNB. There was still no sign of Bob.

When he arrived, the receptionist smiled, signed him in and called for an escort. A young Black man named Antwon arrived, leading him to his room where the associate indicated he take a seat. A makeup person came by to get him ready to be under the lights. An assistant director dropped by to talk a bit about Bear's preferred way of interviewing, and if there was anything in particular that Werner was concerned about.

Werner listed five items, and by item two, the assistant director stopped writing on his yellow legal pad. He frowned at Werner, pulled out his phone, making an act of looking at it, then saying, "Gotta go, be back soon," and abruptly departed.

Werner waited, flipping through about a half dozen old magazines, then watching a TV monitor in the green room. He again walked through his bullet points, and his lead-in statement while nodding to himself.

Antwon buzzed by, saying "five minutes." Werner stood, straightened his tie, and checked the hang of his suit. He began pacing. Nervousness fluttered up through him, emanating from the pit of his stomach. He started to perspire. Antwon returned to pick him up and, upon seeing the beads of sweat on his charge's forehead, he irately waved at Werner to follow him, dragging out a walkie-talkie to call makeup. The makeup woman came running on the set as Werner sat down. Another assistant attached a microphone to the lapel on his suit as the woman carefully dabbed the moisture off his face, shrugging, "That'll have to do."

The set was suddenly vacated of staff. Bear sat down across the table from him in the new *Position Room*. In the old *Position Room*, everyone had been required to stand all the time. In the new one, people could also sit—it was advertised by CNB as accommodating personal preferences after a flap with an older guest that fallen off a walker during an episode. Werner had decided to sit.

A production assistant counted down from five, and Bear turned to the camera, smiling, and said, "Welcome back to the *Position Room*. Today, we are talking with Dr. Werner Brandt about his company TeeGentics and the exciting field of affordable, genetically engineered teeth. First, however, a brief update on some of the latest progress from the fruits of the Human Genome Project and how it is reaping so many rewards in medical science while at the same time raising many bioethical concerns."

A story began playing on the video monitor, describing activities in genetic science over the last two decades. Bear leaned back in his chair, smiled at Werner, giving the only clue that they were not on the air at that moment. A young assistant brought some papers for Bear to approve. He glanced at them and told her, "Not now, goddamn it." Huffing, she left. Bear scratched his side, yawned, joking with the camera operator about the assistant that just left. Werner was thinking he did not care much for Bear at that point.

Five minutes later, a buzzer sounded briefly, a red light came on behind the cameras and a counter on the wall started counting down from ten. Bear sat up, focused on the camera and when the counter got to zero, he said, "Welcome back to *the Position Room*. We are back with Dr. Werner Brandt, founder, and CEO of the exciting new company, TeeGentics."

Werner summoned up some confidence. "Hello Bear, glad to be here to talk about my company. We are, as you know, *the* thought leaders—"

"We want to hear everything you have to say, Dr. Brandt, but now we have a fascinating interview that our own Dr. Adarsh Agate, conducted earlier today with Elizabeth Cleaver of the legendary Cleaver Foundation. She agreed to this interview and traveled to our headquarters in Chicago. She has a compelling new perspective on the story." He then turned as if to somebody in the room, but Werner didn't see anything except a little piece of paper on the wall that said, "Stare here, Bear." The anchor continued, "Adarsh, can you tell us what Ms. Cleaver and you talked about?"

Adarsh's face suddenly projected on a big multi-tiled projection screen behind them. He said, "Bear, we certainly live in exciting times with recent medical advances in applied genetic research. I met earlier today with Liz Cleaver of the Cleaver Foundation, and here is what she had to say."

Adarsh was sitting with Liz, adorned in her normal activist attire. Adarsh was wearing a tie-dye bandana that she had awarded him earlier.

Werner, watching all this in a daze, wondered when Bear would speak to him. He tried to reorganize his lines and get his thoughts straight as he realized that as a multibillionaire, Liz sure could get around. She seemed very used to this sort of high-flying promotion of herself and the foundation. She was good-looking too and he briefly wondered if she dated men as well as women.

Adarsh continued, "Liz, can you tell us what the Cleaver Foundations position is on genetically grown teeth?"

Raising her eyebrows, she said, "Well, Adarsh, the foundation, with its extensive network of free dental clinics in underserved communities in cities like Chicago, needs this sort of technology. We will be far more effective helping the dentally challenged."

Adarsh nodded and said, "We've conducted an extensive investigation of our own, Liz, and we have Meyer Kowalski with us here today. He's an experienced private eye who has some interesting information."

Befuddled, her eyes fluttered. "Who? Private Koldaski?"

The scene cut to Meyer Kowalski in a studio in Denver. He looked uncomfortably nervous as he fiddled with a bowler hat in his lap. Then the scene cut back to Chicago. Adarsh said, "So, what can you tell us, Detective?"

Back to Meyer, who gulped and said, "Yeah, well, I was hired by CNB to find out some info on TeeGentics—"

Adarsh said, "Yes, we talked on the phone for a few minutes yesterday."

Meyer looked confused on that point but continued, "Yeah, like I said, CNB. Was it you? Wow, you sound different with that bandana on. Anyway, let me tell you, this wasn't all that hard an assignment, you know, more like researching a book report. TeeGentics publishes a lot of info on their website, so you oughta try that out sometime, Doc. I also found good stuff in the *Palisade Avenue Journal* about their employees and their plans for their product."

Adarsh asked, "So, any concerns, Detective?"

Meyer twiddled the rim of his bowler again and nodded thoughtfully. "Yeah, well, I did have some problems raising the money to buy into one of the franchises that are not going into some of the … underserved communities. Of course, we can't be like the foundation, but we can be cheap. And this thing is getting bought up quick—gonna be the next Internet if you ask me. Now, where should I send my bill? Or can we do a direct transfer to my bank?"

Liz said, "Adarsh, this is my exact point. Like Private Koldaski—"

"Private Detective Kowalski, Liz, Kowalski."

"Whatever. Like the private says, this is going to be like lightbulbs were to the candle. I've seen the teeth!"

Detective Kowalski, with no answer on his billing question, said, "Hey, there…"

The scene changed and, smiling tightly, Adarsh said, "Liz, we recorded an interview with one of the trial participants, Yorgos Drakos, and I have to tell you, these are some pretty impressive results. Let's watch!"

Liz tried to turn to the monitor behind her, nearly tipping over her chair before she gave up.

The tape showed Yorgos Drakos, a non-English-speaking trial participant. There were many close-ups of his smile and his new tooth, though no questions.

Liz cut in, "Yes! Perfect, simply perfect. We can't wait to get them streaming into our clinics."

Adarsh, his bandana having slipped over his left eye, had his head tilted to compensate, "Impressive results indeed, Bear! Back to you!"

The camera zoomed in on Liz, tweaking Adarsh's bandana back into position.

Trace chortled watching the television, taking a slug of scotch, and then topped off the glasses for Sam and him. Sam sat with his feet up on the boardroom table, shaking and laughing. "I've got to hand it to you, Trace man, getting that recording in there with Hector was a peach of an idea."

Trace chuckled. "Hell, helping Meyer Kowalski get financing from Bank of Cyprus, allowing him to buy into a franchise, was the real stroke of genius."

Sam giggled and said, "Masterful, just masterful."

Pleased with himself as well as Sam's approval, Trace opened a jar of olives, stuffing two in his mouth, and said, between chews, "If you think this is funny, wait till you see the final segment of the show!"

Sam guffawed and took a big sip of his drink. "More?"

Trace nodded and said, "Oh yeah."

CNB had gone to commercial. Bear was laughing and high-fiving the camera operator. Werner shook his head, realizing this had all the hallmarks of one of Trace's shenanigans.

Coming back from commercial, Bear composed himself for the camera. "Welcome back to the *Position Room*, where today we are visiting with Werner Brandt of TeeGentics." Bear turned to Werner and said, "Tell us now, Dr. Brandt, a little about your company. You've heard the accusations. Is TeeGentics out to kill the dental industry as it exists today? Are your products unsafe? How do you answer such charges?" Bear was reading off a teleprompter that was out of sight over Werner's left shoulder. It was positioned to make it seem Bear was looking at his guest.

Werner felt a bit nauseous, his hearty breakfast tickling the back of his throat. He heard the beginnings of anger in his voice when he said, "Hello, Bear, glad to be here to talk about my company. As you know, we are the thought leaders—"

Bear held up his hand and said, "One moment please. First a question. Doctor, there is a widely held belief that TeeGentics will offer every dental service there is today for no more than ninety-nine dollars and ninety-nine cents per tooth. What happens to the dental industry then?"

Werner bristled and said, "What? Okay. Listen, we are working on pricing, as I was going to get to in a few minutes. And the Cleaver Foundation. What about them, Bear? They are going to give them away. We have to price aggressively, to be sure. After all, we want to be part of serving the underserved, wherever they are being served."

Bear shrugged and said, "We actually have another segment that substantiates that pricing claim. Let's watch and then you can comment."

Werner said, "Now, wait just a minute—"

Rock-like news music rumbled across the studio. He turned to see the big monitor behind him light up with the face of Josh Highsmith. Werner felt a spike of fear, his heart flailing away in his chest as he thought, *Oh shit, Josh Highsmith!*

Highsmith began to speak, and he realized it was prerecorded footage from last night's show.

Josh started out by saying, "Welcome back. Now our next guest with us tonight has written a new book, called *Pearly Whites: The Making of a Dental Revolution via Genetics*. Let's welcome him to the show!" Applause thundered as the Alfred Hitchcock TV show theme song started playing. Out onto the stage bounded Bob, both hands in the air, flashing V's, and he stumbled toward his seat, managing to regain his balance at the last moment. Josh shook his hand, and then they both sat down.

Josh started with, "Dr. Robert Oppenheimer, welcome to the show. We are so glad to have you here." His tone was the mock-sincere hybrid that he specialized in.

Bob grinned at the camera, looking a bit hammered from drinking backstage from a smuggled flask in his valise. "Call me Josh, Bob, I mean Bob, Josh."

Highsmith raised an eyebrow, nodding and said, "Well okay, Josh-Bob. I've read your book, the last page anyway." The audience laughed, and Highsmith continued, "I must say, this is some fascinating stuff. I mean, any kind of dental procedure *anywhere* for ninety-nine dollars and ninety-nine cents *per tooth*? Hey, who wouldn't go in for a deal like that?"

Bob, looking around the audience, said, "I don't know, Josh." The audience laughed, it all looked like a silly skit.

Highsmith, with a sardonic look said, "Over here, Bob. Talk to the host."

Bob swung his head back and grinned goofily at Josh, who narrowed his eyes in amusement, and continued, "If things stay on schedule, we can get you out of here on time for your flight." Another laugh from the audience as Josh rolled his eyes, "All right! So, Bob, about your company—doing… new… things?"

Bob said, "Yes Josh, new things. Inexpensive, perfect, new white teeth. Oh, and revolutionary technology, American know-how, foundations, companies, all sorts of stuff. You'll be hearing a lot about us. Everywhere. Now, can we roll the tape?"

Josh looked around with an amused expression and said, "Tape, what tape? We have a tape in this day and age? Ah, well yes, I'm being told we do have a video. Fine, let her rip!"

The scene switched to TeeGentics headquarters with Sam saying, "Hello, I'm Professor Samuel Henekey, and we are in our labs here at TeeGentics."

Back at CNB, Werner tried to relax as Sam continued, showing pictures of teeth in the clear acrylic boxes, describing in a marketing sort of way the technology of TeeGentics, then a picture of Yorgos Drakos smiling with his new tooth and ending with Sam's big smile and a wave good night.

The video ended and Josh said, "Wow, that really is impressive stuff, but gotta go to commercial." He smiled at the camera and added, "With our new sponsor, Pearly Whites!"

Bob cut in and said, "Formerly, TeeGentics!"

Josh looked at Bob, nodded and said, "Formerly TeeGentics!"

The clip ended. Werner realized his company had changed names, and he was not even in on the selection. He felt a spike of anger, along with confusion. His mind raced. New business cards, new stationery, did anyone consider the costs? He'd have to run some numbers on the way back to Santa De Lola.

Bear said, "So, Doctor, there we have it. The claim of cheap teeth for all, and the name change of your company. By the way, when does that go into effect?"

Werner looked at Bear and said, "Ask Josh Highsmith. Nah, I'm joking. I'll let you know. We have to get organized with such corporate changes. I have new stationery, business cards, and other things…already on order."

Bear nodded, then said, "Already on order. Great!"

"Bear, as I was trying to say earlier about our thought leadership—"

"Well, I must say, this has been one of the most interesting segments we've done in the *Position Room* in quite a while. Stay tuned for our next guest!"

Chapter 18

Martin Crosswaithe hollered, "Pull!" as he swung his over/under double-barrel shotgun, leading the rising clay disc, and fired. The target disintegrated. He opened the breech and tossed his empty into a bucket located in front of him, then slipped a shell from his hunting jacket into the empty chamber.

One of the Land Rovers assigned to the estate rolled up behind him. Nigel, the old butler, climbed out and approached Martin. The slump of the man's shoulders told Martin something was askew.

Nigel drew a deep breath, "My lord, it seems your good friend Rutger has had a tragedy."

"And what would that be, Nigel?"

"It seems, my lord, that … Rutger has gone missing during a hurricane in the Caymans. As you know, he left after his surgery to spend some time trying to find a new wife, his first in twenty years, after the sordid ending of his previous spouse."

Martin nodded, remembering Evelyn. Rutger and she had fought constantly, then made up, then hit the reset button to do it all over again. Her suicide had been suspicious, but the board bought it, thinking Rutger would be better off without the distraction.

"So, what happened?"

"Apparently, a six-foot wave washed over the island, and Rutger's beach-side mansion was in the direct path of this hydrological onslaught. It appears he was washed out to sea, along with five recently hired female assistants."

Martin hung his head. It sounded all too true. Rutger had a track record of female assistants and indiscreet behavior. *Perhaps fixing his jaw had not been such a good idea*, Martin thought.

"Truly tragic. Let the board know. Keep me advised if anything changes."

Nigel returned to his vehicle and drove off as Martin resumed his target practice. For his part, he had no trouble worrying about female assistants. He had been shooting blanks for years.

Late in the afternoon, Sash gathered his team in a conference room specifically set aside by Pearly Whites for the duration of his inquiry. Stacked atop a round table were thumb drives and bound copies of the provided documentation, each in excess of twelve hundred pages (triple spaced) for their due diligence. One of his scientists was passing around a three-page checklist and a summary of the contents of the data that Sash imagined would be their focus over the next year or more.

Sash was fuming at the audacity of the management of this company. After attending a district monthly meeting in the San Francisco office earlier that day, his manager, Reuben Corpenny, had driven up to Santa De Lola and taken him to lunch. Sash had wanted to get back to work, but Reuben had insisted.

On the way to the local Scruggs's Deep Fry Palace, a national chain of marginal eateries and Reuben's favorite lunch destination, Sash had to endure the mindless ramblings of a talk radio pontificator that was blaring from the car radio about nonsensical and mostly made-up issues. Yet when he tried to change the channel, he found that Reuben had set all the buttons to the same station.

Sash tried to turn it down and talk business, but then Reuben would say, "Hold that thought, Sash. Listen to this, the man is so right. What is this country coming to?" Reuben himself did not bother to turn down the radio when he had something to say. He just talked louder. Sash's head was throbbing when they arrived at the restaurant.

Once in Scruggs's, Reuben said, "Order whatever you like, or we could split some wings and the titanic side of chili cheese fries special." Sash declined the generous offer for such a specialized heart attack prescription. He settled on ordering the grilled chicken without the globs of processed cheese and soggy mushrooms. The young woman waiting on them was all giggly and distracted and obviously augmented in the breast department. Sash shook his head and wondered how a doctor could in good conscience install such huge implants in such a diminutive woman. Reuben saw the direction that Sash's eyes were taking, and when their waitress left, said, "Thank God the FDA approved those saline implants, eh?"

Sash looked disapprovingly after the young woman and said, "No doubt she will have to have them replaced in a few years. Unless they blow out first. I mean, what happens on a hot day?"

"Dude. Keeps everybody employed. We are a market-driven, capitalist economy, the American way, profits before thinking, and the FDA is onboard to support it all, leastways, under my watch it is. The American public wanted big boobs that are safe, and we are glad to provide them."

Sash said, "Safe? How many warnings are out on those saline blobs now that *we* released them as a *safe* product?"

Reuben's shrug indicated he was not particularly interested. "Speaking of fast-tracking new products, I was wondering how things are going at Pearly Whites."

Sash stiffened. If Reuben was inquiring this early in the game, was he already feeling pressure from above?

"Bribe money already making the rounds at the top?"

Reuben, who had become jaded decades back, said, "How would we know? Listen, don't fight this, Sash. The source of pressure *is* political, *at* the highest level. Your actions, our actions, are being scrutinized. I'd suggest getting through this one as soon as possible."

Sash said, "You must be kidding me, Reuben. One, we just started. Two, this is a product that is based on *genetic* engineering and so it's exponentially different from plastic boobs. It deserves our best scrutiny and diligence, not some slipshod effort that leaves millions of people exposed every time they go to the dentist."

Reuben frowned. "I thought you didn't need a dentist for this stuff."

"That's a big part of the problem! Where is the medical oversight on this shit? I've pretty much already discounted the idea of this being done in these crazy franchise office locations."

"Hey, franchising worked out well for McDonald's. Billions and billions."

"McDonald's?" Sash just shook his head.

Their food came, and Sash's chicken was, of course, buried under a mountain of melted yellow cheese goo and limp mushrooms. He sighed, but before he could say anything, the waitress vamoosed.

Reuben dipped a carrot into his ranch dressing, and between crunches he said, "That ship has already sailed, and it is not your decision, Sash. The franchises are going forward."

Sash had been mining his plate, vainly attempting to locate his chicken, and stopped. If his boss already had a position on this detail, it meant someone had provided it to him. Sash suspected he knew what happened. He had casually mentioned to Bob Oppenheimer about the need to take a close look at the franchise operation idea, saying it was highly irregular for a medical product. What he did not know was that his observation had gotten back to

Trace within the quarter hour, and within the half hour a phone was ringing in a certain chief of staff's office in Washington, DC.

Sash said, "Look, Reuben, if you just want a rubber stamp, then find someone else to do this."

Reuben shook his head. "I don't have anyone to come out and take over your group, so you need to just get on with it."

"You expect me to just eat one for the flipper."

"The gipper, Sash, the gipper, and you don't eat one, you win one. Win one for the gipper," Reuben said, shaking his head again. Sash was always messing up old idiotic clichés.

Angry now, Sash said, "I see that this conversation is pointless. We have a duty to perform here, but you seem more interested in being a lackey for your masters."

"Sash, what you can't seem to understand is that we are both in the sights of high level politicians. And right now, I'm the only person that is willing to save your ungrateful ass. There are people above us that will personally stomp on your rigorous certification fantasy and not blink an eye. Best for you and me to get onboard the happy fucking fun train."

Sash pushed his plate away and rose to his feet. "If you don't like my way of doing things, replace me." He then stomped off.

Reuben called to his receding back, "Fine, go ahead, Sash. I'll have the wings *and* the chili cheese fries."

Sash kept going, hoping that a chicken bone would stick in Reuben's throat. The thought comforted him as he walked out the door. He hailed a cab back to the office, retrieved his car and drove straight to Pearly Whites. On the way, he phoned Eddie, instructing him to call the team together for an announcement.

He shook his head to clear away the memory of Reuben's pathetic perspective. He felt his resolve stiffening. He grinned to himself at the thought of giving Pearly Whites an FDA enema; he intended to be thorough. He believed he knew the risks to his career. He also believed that he understood the system, and intended to manipulate it to give him the running room he and his team would need while dealing with Pearly Whites.

He said, "Have a seat and let's begin. First, we will need to be meticulous. This is cutting-edge biogenetic tech. We will want to see how they got where they are now."

Across the table, Eddie Childress's hand came up, and Sash said, "What is it, Eddie?"

"Where's the donuts, boss?" When no one laughed he said, "Hey, you all seen these teeth? Man, are they ever white! I may volunteer myself. Wished I'd thought of this."

Sash said, "Well, a yes vote for an unproven product. By the way, you will not be volunteering for having this product installed in any orifice you have, Childress, do you understand?" Sash had a sudden flash, realizing he had seen him going to lunch with Reuben numerous times in the past. That was the most probable explanation of why Childress was on his team—the man was an informant!

He mulled over who else might not be faithful to his cause. The others had been assigned from various projects that had recently completed. All had respectable credentials, Childress being the exception. But if Reuben had been involved in the team selection, Sash doubted that he would develop any new allies.

His cell phone vibrated. It was Reuben. He ignored it the first time, letting it go to voicemail. He did the same on the second call. On the third, he excused himself and said, "What is it, Reuben? We are in a meeting."

"I tried to warn you at lunch. Did you think the people at Pearly Whites would not know what you are up to? You're in their house! From this moment on, you will work for Childress. Jesus, this is wreaking havoc, playing musical chairs with you team leads."

"Childress? Are you really going to sell out on this one, Reuben?"

"Give me a break, Sash. You could have been fired. And I assure you, this is your last chance with the FDA."

The phone went dead. Sash stared at it in disbelief, then turned to the group and said, "We're done for the day. Get out of here."

Everyone around the table seemed reluctant to move except Childress, who slowly began packing his notebook computer. Then his own phone rang.

Childress picked it up and said, "Hay-low." He then got quiet, looked once at Sash, and walked out into the hallway. Sash knew it was Reuben without having to ask.

With the room emptied, Sash furtively grabbed two thumb-drive copies of the documentation and slipped them into his pocket. Dropping his visitor badge at the front desk, he headed directly for his car. He needed to get off the premises with his stolen loot. He would conduct his own research.

A security guard named Sonny was waiting by Sash's car. Sonny was a new hire at TeeGentics. Before this gig he had spent most days stealing motorcycle parts and then selling them to the nearby Oakland chapter of Satan's Angels. He had been so successful in selling stolen Harley parts, he had used some of the proceeds to have both arms and a back full of tattoos applied. Like all good things, though, the stolen parts market had gotten too hot with the local law dogs in Oakland chasing obvious leads, and he opted for a career change. Pearly Whites had been running an ad online on Career Beast, and he decided to apply.

As Sash approached, Sonny said, "Hey, Mr. Kimura, I got a call on the old walkie-talkie here to make sure you had turned in all Pearly Whites property before you left the campus."

Sash stopped five paces away. *Had he been seen pocketing the thumb drives? A hidden camera perhaps?* He replied, "Is that a fact?" He then puffed up, "Well, it is Dr. Kimura to you, and you can just run along and tell your boss everything is fine. I would never take any property."

"I'm sure you wouldn't Doc, but—"

"You know, I could file a lawsuit for slander."

"Slander? What's that?"

Sash realized explaining slander to this man was likely an enormous waste of time. He changed his approach. "I'm sorry, I did not get your name, sir."

"It's Sonny. Now about the— "

"Sonny. What a perfectly wonderful name. Listen, I appreciate you checking with me. I really have to run now."

Sonny, now confused but determined to do his job, took a step closer and said, "Well, Doc, I need to look in that briefcase anyway. Then you can be on your merry way."

Sash subtly shifted into a defensive stance. Sonny decided fine, he would take down the man and go through the briefcase at his leisure. Sonny wore two mace holders on his belt. He unsnapped the one containing a switchblade.

Seeing that, Sash shifted tactics again, this time to charm. He smiled disarmingly and said, "Officer, here, I just remembered I have what you are looking for!" He pulled out one of the thumb drives and handed it to Sonny, who took the drive while looking even more confused. Then the man saw the TeeGentics logo on it, one of the many marketing gimmicks that Trace had come up with to promote the company. Sonny nodded, "Okay then, thanks!"

Watching Sonny wander off, a walkie-talkie to his ear, Sash let out a big sigh of relief, grinned and drove out of the parking lot to the main gate. Assistant Director of Security CB Haster held up a hand from his air-conditioned guard shack, where he secretly had been sipping on some schnapps, whiling away his afternoon shift. Sash stopped, sticking with charm mode. "Here you go, sir, I certainly appreciate all the effort of you common laborers here at TeeGentics." He then held out his pass. As the guard leaned out to retrieve his offering, Sash thought he could smell alcohol. He smiled again as the guard waved him on. He immediately drove off. Once clear of the campus, he let out a big breath of disgusted relief and chuckled to himself.

Liz and Frieda were down in the cavern under the estate, sitting at a table with a large monitor on it. Frieda had advised earlier that they were going to have a meeting with Circe.

Liz asked, "Where did you find this program? Circe is the bomb!"

Frieda grinned and said, "I didn't. Chef Alfonso found it on an open-source AI site that has lots of stuff for fancy ass recipes. He tried it out on his laptop, and that has been the genesis behind his recent culinary successes we've been sucking down. So, after he told me about it, I started to dig a bit and found that there was a version specific for the corporate world. It, of course, would not run on a laptop."

Surprised, Liz said, "Open source? Like free? Anyway, so, what specifically has Circe discovered?"

Frieda smiled, "Thought you might ask. Circe is the artificial intelligence that found out about TeeGentics and recommended it to me. Circe also noted our accounting anomalies and suggested we integrate our efforts at hiding the money we have blown from the fund with low-cost dental work and hike the costs to get our affairs back in order."

Liz's eyes were wide now. "And our investment with the stock for cash swap?"

"Again, Circe. That would generate money back into the fund."

Liz, impressed, said. "I had no idea that this AI shit was this good, let alone free. Let's talk with this… oracle."

"I think you're conflating myths, babe." Frieda then giggled and turned on the screen. "Morning, Circe. Liz and Frieda here!"

The screen displayed what looked like a Greek goddess, which Liz figured went with the name. Liz noticed Circe was into very thin fabrics.

Circe appeared to look Liz over, then said to Frieda, "Oh my, you did not tell me Liz was so beautiful."

Liz said, "Right back at you, Circe. I had no idea something like yourself even existed."

Circe gazed at Liz and said, "Your foundation. That is what you want to talk about today?"

Liz said, "We did the deal with TeeGentics."

Circe appeared thoughtful. "Now known as Pearly Whites. Checking financial discussions on various social media servers tells me that they are close to their initial public offering hitting the market. Interest is extremely high."

Frieda said, "Do you have a date, Circe?"

Circe said, "I do not date, Frieda, but thanks for asking."

Liz looked at Frieda with a what-the-fuck expression. Frieda giggled and said, "Sorry, Circe, a poorly worded question on my part. Do we have a date set for the IPO?"

"Not yet, though soon, it appears from emails between Trace Orbaugh, Werner Brandt and Martin Crosswaithe. However, I do have more inside information on Pearly Whites. The one named Sam. He has influence with the intellectually limited one known as Trace and with the CEO. Sam is the human that perfected the defective algorithms that incorrectly aligned the DNA sequences. That was only recently."

Liz asked, "So what was the problem?"

"The teeth were dying. Now they are … stable."

"How do you know this?"

"I was able to access their database and again follow email chains once you received your logins to their servers. Frieda gave me hers and I have been searching through their records. They really need better security. Do you wish to advise them?"

Liz and Frieda looked at each other. The logins came when they got their contract finalized.

Frieda said, "Not yet, Circe. We would like to continue to maintain access to the information to make solid business decisions. Can you help improve their security without saying anything, but keep us in the know? We need to protect our investment with these morons."

"Of course."

Liz said, "What else have you got?"

"We need to influence a person close to Sam. His name is Bob."

Liz grimaced. "Yeah, we've met. What does that do for us?"

"Bob, while generally incompetent, knows what is going on, whether he understands everything or not. He has a girlfriend named Helga. I found her picture online." She then displayed a picture of a shapely redhead. "You need to recruit a spy." Liz and Frieda nodded in approval.

"Circe, this is great stuff. We'll be in touch." She nodded to Frieda, who logged off their session with the AI.

Liz said, "Who the hell wrote this AI software? I never heard of anything like this except on science fiction TV shows. And this was free?"

Frieda was grinning. "From what I learned on the website, she is the latest in general AI and has the focus we need. She is far more like us in the ability to integrate data from all sorts of sources, except she does it faster than shit."

Liz said, "So, I got a plan. That rental property you located, is it still available?"

"Oh yeah."

"It's time to hunt down a spy."

Chapter 20

Sitting in his chair at the Pearly Whites boardroom table, Trace felt unnerved, though he was trying mightily to conceal that fact.

Across the table sat Martin. Trace had been surprised when he got a call from Nigel advising him that the old man was on his way to visit Pearly Whites on a "fact-finding" tour. Fact finding, his ass!

Martin's plane had landed an hour earlier, greeted by a waiting limousine.

Trying to hide his confusion at this turn of events, Trace said, "Well, let's get something to eat while we watch this meeting."

Martin shook his head. "Forget the food. I did not come here to eat. Let's just get this little rodeo going, as you Americans like to say."

To cover his anger at being treated like a serf, Trace turned to the projector controls inset in the tabletop. A hidden ceiling camera activated in the second-floor conference room below them, where the Pearly Whites team was meeting with the new FDA team lead. Werner, Bob and Sam were in the room. A moment later, the man replacing the troublesome Dr. Kimura brought the meeting to order.

Trying to engage Martin, Trace bragged, "Our personal lapdog. Did you hear about how I crushed that other FDA idiot?"

Martin looked at Trace as if he were inspecting an insect. "Nicely played, I suppose. Have you ensured in this change that we are not exposed in any way?"

"Completely. The FDA is onboard with us."

"And we recovered all missing documentation?"

"Yep, we're good."

On the screen, the FDA official introduced himself, and they could also see Kimura sitting stone-faced next to him. Then Bob stood up, grinning at the little group, and said, "I just wanted to emphasize how impressed we are with the quick response of the FDA to help us get this product to market. We're glad to have you onboard, Dr. Childress!" He reached across the table and shook Childress's hand vigorously. Sam looked away with a wry grin. Werner rolled his eyes. Bob sat down.

After an awkward silence, Werner said, "Dr. Childress, I'd also like to say, we're glad to have you on the Pearly Whites product evaluation team with Dr. Kimura. We all have a lot of hard work ahead of us, but I'm sure we can get through any difficulties as a genuine team effort should allow."

Eddie Childress smiled at the men across the table. He had specific instructions from Reuben to be as accommodating as possible with this bunch.

Sam broke the silence, while twiddling a keychain he just bought with a skull and Klingon bat'leth embossed on it. "Well, let's stay in close touch and I think in, say, two months, you'll be ready to give us the clean bill of health we need to get to market."

Eddie stood up. "Maybe quicker!" He closed his briefcase and escorted the FDA team out the door.

Trace commented, "See, things are fine, I have this under control."

Contradicting Trace's statement, Werner immediately launched into concerns to Bob and Sam. "You know, if you guys think the FDA is going to let this program get certified in two months, you're crazy. That guy is dangerous to this company."

Bob said, "Werner, you need to chill, man, we got this licked. Nobody is gonna fuck with us. We got the Trace."

Trace puffed up at the reference and looked to Martin, who appeared bored.

Werner gave Bob a derisive look and said, "The Trace? Jesus, Bob, that sounds like some sort of infection."

Trace abruptly sat up, offended as he heard Martin chuckle.

Werner continued, "Listen, we need more than a fat man with a bad attitude to get by the FDA. We need to get them engaged, and we need a man that will ensure good due diligence out of them. We could get hung out to dry later."

Looking amused at the fat man comments, Martin grunted, "It's odd, isn't it? He certainly seems to have your number, but he is so naïve about the rest of the world. How did we allow this idiot to be CEO? Looks like another mistake, Trace."

Trace sank in his seat and sulked at two insults inside twenty seconds. Brandt was getting a smart mouth on him with his unscripted commentary.

Back on the screen, Sam stretched in his chair and smiled. Werner gave him an odd look, as if to say, "What?"

Sam declined to reply and yawned.

Watching the pointless discussion continue, Trace realized that old man must be waiting for Brandt to make more insults against him. Martin raised an eyebrow from time to time as if something promising might come through, but finally he said, "Well, I suppose I am satisfied for now. But Trace, no misconceptions, you have to bring this endeavor to a proper conclusion."

Trace, still sulking at having been ordered around and then insulted, nodded his understanding.

"I need you to say you understand."

Of course, Trace thought. *Humiliate me more.* He intoned, "Yes, I understand, Gramps. Can I do anything else for you today?"

Nigel arrived at the door on cue, of course, as Martin stood and said, "That should be about it. We're off. Need to see a few friends in New York about the IPO, then back to London. Try to behave yourself Trace."

After the two men left, Trace stood up, now boiling mad, and headed down the hall for Werner's office, ready to do battle.

Arriving there, he found Sally, but Werner was nowhere in sight. He cursed aloud with a big "Shit!" realizing the man was still downstairs. Sally, with a bored look, appeared to take the outburst in stride.

He headed to the elevator. The one on the right opened and he hit the button for the second floor. As the door closed, he heard a ding for the elevator on the left. It was Werner arriving at his office, but it was too late, Trace was headed down. He repeatedly jabbed the button for the fourth floor as his anger simmered. The elevator had a mind of its own, stopped, opened the door for a few seconds, shut, then he was headed back up. He began rehearsing his opening salvo of invective.

As his door opened, he heard another ding. He headed for Werner's office which was empty now. He realized that Werner and Sally must have gone to lunch, hence the last "ding" he heard. He cursed aloud again with a mighty "Fuck!" while shaking his fists.

Chapter 21

Liz was driving a leased luxury Mercedes coupe over to their new abode, a large ultramodern ranch they had rented. She was dressed in summer-wear jean shorts to go with her tank top and bandana. With a small private airfield only two miles away, Corinna had dropped Liz off just moments earlier. Their luxury helicopter would now act as a shuttle, delivering essential necessities required for extravagant poolside dinner parties.

Frieda had been living at the new place for the last few days, making the dwelling "Liz habitable," which would have been pure opulence for any average person.

When Liz pulled in the driveway, she saw Frieda in animated conversation with the woman they now knew as Helga. Liz hopped out and walked over to the pair. Frieda introduced them.

Liz said, "Helga, nice to meet you. We sure lucked out getting a place next door to you and Bob. How do you like it here?"

Helga nodded, noncommittal, and said, "It's beautiful here, though a bit boring at times for me. Bob is gone a lot, and I work at a furniture store. Hardly see him at all lately."

Liz already knew all this from information that Circe had given them, but she merely said, "Wow, that must be rough. Do you miss him?"

Helga shrugged. "Sorta. Well, not as much as I used to."

"Hopefully, we can rev things up a bit. Perhaps a pool party soon. We will be staying here pretty regularly due to our new relationship with Pearly Whites."

Helga perked up and said, "Great! I could use some company. Listen, I gotta get back to work. I'm just on a quick lunch break. Been great talking to you two."

As she watched Helga walk next door, Frieda said, "She's nice. Too bad she's about to lose her job."

Liz shrugged, "Well, she is about to get a better one. Show me the place. I've been struggling to figure out how to live in such a small joint."

Frieda laughed and said, "You are so spoiled. Come on, follow me."

In the kitchen was Chef Alfonso preparing lunch. He and Langley had been put on temporary assignment and would commute back and forth from a local hotel to render their services each day. Frieda had established a high-speed encrypted link back to their cavern data center, so they could keep tabs on anything Circe might root out.

After a short tour, Liz went out to lounge by the pool. Chef brought her some French press coffee and said the meal would be ready in a few more minutes. A few sips in, she got a text from one of her shell companies confirming its acquisition of a Scandinavian furniture store the previous day.

Langley came out with lunch, and Liz and Frieda adjourned to the pool-side dinner table. Just as they were finishing up, they heard a chime located on the patio that let them know somebody was at the front door. Frieda pulled up the app on her phone for the newly installed security cameras and saw Helga was standing there, looking distraught.

Liz signaled Langley, who answered the front door and escorted Helga back to the patio.

Helga was clearly upset, so Liz and Frieda walked over to her. Liz said, "Helga, are you okay?"

Helga shook her head, trembling a bit, and said, "I just lost my job. From out of the blue. Some new company just bought Gustav's, and my manager was told to immediately cut staff. Seems I was that staff cut."

Frieda said, "That is just terrible. Did you get any severance?"

Helga said, "Eight weeks. Seems stingy compared to what you get if you lose your job in Germany."

Liz said, "It is. American companies do the bare-bones minimum, the cocksuckers. Sorry, dear. Listen, come over and sit down if you have some time."

Helga sniffled and said, "Seems I've got a lot of that all of a sudden."

Once seated, Liz had Chef bring out some more French press and a special crème Brule he had made for their lunch earlier. When Helga was done and they were shifting gears to sipping some cognac, Liz said, "What is your background anyway?"

Helga said, "Well, I have a master's in psychology and have wanted to work on my Ph.D. for some time. That was why I came over to the U.S., but that was derailed after my breakup with my old girlfriend."

Frieda grinned and said, "So you switched teams with Bob?"

"Temporarily anyway. I had to get a job, found the one I just lost, so I moved here from Stanford. Bob wandered in the store, and the rest was uneventful history, until today." She sighed deeply while taking a swig of cognac, then asked, "How long you two been together?"

Frieda said, "Three wonderful years!"

Helga nodded. "I wish I had what you two do."

Liz smiled and said, "Well, while what the future may hold in that regard is not yet written, I got a proposition for you. How about a job working for our foundation?"

Helga went wide-eyed and said, "Really? Doing what?"

"Oh, you're overqualified, but we want to develop some psychological profiles of the many people that come to our free dental clinics. The job does not pay a whole lot, like only a buck thirty five a year, and would involve some travel, but I think you might like working for us."

Helga, clearly lifted out of the layoff doldrums, said "It sounds great! Uh, what's a buck thirty five?"

Liz said, "Oh, sorry for the businessnese. The salary is one hundred thirty-five thousand dollars a year."

Helga started crying with joy. Liz and Frieda came over and put their arms around her. Liz said, "Well, maybe we could pay more."

Helga said, "No, my gosh, that is a wonderful salary! I mean, yes, I am interested. Where do I sign?"

They then spent the next two hours just talking and getting to know each other better. Liz expounded on the free clinics, the need for cheap teeth and emphasized their partnership with Pearly Whites and how valuable it was to their efforts.

Helga said, "Yeah, Bob talks about the foundation and his work all the time, though only superficially—I think his commentary is about as deep as he is. At any rate, this is fantastic! Thank you so very much, you two! But I got to get home, start some dinner. Can we meet up tomorrow?"

Liz said, "Yes, and as a new employee, you will have to get on our jogging schedule. You outfitted for that?"

Helga nodded and quipped, "I even have a nice route I worked out."

Liz said, "Cool." She buzzed Langley and said, "Would you show our friend out? She needs to leave now." They then watched as Helga waved goodbye.

Frieda let out a breath and said, "Gawd, that went better than I expected."

Liz said, "Circe is sure a handy thing to have around. Her profile of Helga was spot on. Now I just need to dump that fucking furniture store I bought."

Frieda giggled, "You didn't just buy a furniture store, Liz. You now have a spy!"

Chapter 22

A couple days later, Werner was reading the *New York Herald* about the IPO of Pearly Whites and ogling a stock ticker that showed their closing stock price for the day. On his other screen, he was looking at a gorgeous modern mansion on three acres located right on the Pacific Coast, built on some cliffs overlooking the ocean. He had made a large offer to the realtor an hour earlier, who had hurried over to his office to get the deal signed.

Based on his stock options, he was now a multimillionaire. Sally came in and looked over his shoulder at his first screen, smiling. She had stock options as well and appeared content for the first time in a long time. *Money will do that to you*, he thought.

Smiling at him, she said, "Tell me about this new abode of yours, Werner."

He switched gears from his screen to Sally. "Oh, it's… okay, it's over the top. Downton Abbey on the Pacific." He brought the realtor listing up again.

She moved closer to him. "Maybe you could give me a tour?"

With her so much closer than usual, Werner felt a surge of excitement from the tone of her voice and the scent of her perfume. "Perhaps a tour and dinner?" Still smiling, hand on his shoulder now, she nodded.

She stepped back and looked at her watch. "Time for the meeting in the boardroom." He stood. "After you." He fell in behind her, noting her new dress, how perfectly she filled it out, and thought, *perks of the job!*

As they entered the boardroom, they saw the waiter that had been in the first interview some months back with Bob and Trace. He was conferring with a French chef, armed with his tools of the trade, a portable food preparation and serving area. The boardroom table was also populated with lots of booze and table settings.

Trace waddled in, his brand spanking new French loafers making unsteady clacking sounds on the tile floor. For a change, he waved at Werner and Sally. Again, Werner thought, *"Money will do that to you."* Trace grabbed a decanter of whisky and a glass, then headed for his seat next to Sally.

Liz and Frieda arrived, guests of honor, taking their place directly to the left of Werner. They were busy catching up with Fiona, who Werner noticed had become really friendly with the foundation folks. Liz gave Fiona a kiss on the cheek, and Fiona stepped back, smiling, holding her hand briefly. Werner wondered at that interaction as he thought, *real friendly?*

Then came Bob and Sam along with the rest of the Pearly Whites board of directors, consisting of stuffed suits that rarely showed up for anything, since Martin Crosswaithe actually ran the show. Mostly, the "Suits" talked about their various large-scale investments.

A hubbub of conversation arose in the room as it filled. They were a happy bunch, what with the IPO and all new wads of cash flowing their way. The word on Wall Street was that the stock would have a market capitalization of over a billion dollars within a week, up from the IPO, which had provided over three hundred million in actual money the company could spend, though more than half of that had already flowed back to Martin Crosswaithe's investment firm. Werner himself felt giddy with pleasure.

The luncheon commenced with people filling their plates, drinking, talking, and generally enjoying themselves. Werner could hear Trace getting progressively louder and slurring more words as the level of whisky in his decanter decreased. Bob sat next to Trace with what looked like his version of a suave expression while playing with some pricy Bordeaux he was alternately swirling around, then sniffing—until he slopped some on the front of his suit. He looked around as he dabbed the stains with his napkin, now less than suave.

Werner stood, lifted his wine glass, and lightly tapped it with his spoon to get attention. Sally was seated to his right, a barrier between him and Trace. She was operating a laptop computer wirelessly tethered to a huge wall-mounted flat screen for the next phase of the get-together.

The conversations died down, and Werner launched into his speech. He began with a nod to Sally, who brought up the first slide. It showed the original headquarters groundbreaking. "Welcome, all. This is the day we have all been waiting for. I want to congratulate all of our hardworking team for what they have done so far to get us to this achievement." Polite, low-key applause ensued. "We are lucky today as well to have our good friends and partners from the Cleaver Foundation present for this milestone meeting."

Another round of polite applause, and Sam spoke up. "It was your vision for this product that got us here, let no one forget. I propose a toast to Werner!" He then stood, raising his glass. Like a crowd wave in slow motion, the others joined him. Sam continued, "A hearty hear-hear to the founder, Werner Brandt!" The group responded with the "hear-hears" and all took a drink. Trace slugged his down in one gulp and did a quick refill.

Werner, feeling touched, smiled as the slow wave returned to their seats. Except for Trace, who woozily remained standing. That's when Werner noticed that Trace's whisky decanter was on empty.

Bob tugged on Trace's coat sleeve, apparently a reminder to set his ass down. Trace pulled his arm away, swaying alarmingly to and fro.

Trace said, "So, Werner Brandt. The man I hired! Gave money! Stock options! Yes, the man that said I have a bad attitude while my gramps was listening in on a call. Therefore, now I want to raise a toast to Sam! The real fuckin hero!"

Silence. Bob tittered nervously.

Sam said, "Thanks, Trace. Now let's sit down."

Trace was about to gulp his drink but instead, while staring at Werner, poured it over Sally's head. "Niagara Falls! Maybe Sally could do a lap dance for us with you."

Frozen at what just happened, her new dress now in ruins, Sally felt like her brain detonated. She jumped to her feet and slapped Trace across the face, spinning his fedora sideways. Pressing her attack, she then pushed him against the wall, screaming in his face, "You fucktard!" Then she slapped him again.

Liz and Frieda stood, suddenly engaged. Liz especially seemed quite agitated. She began hollering at Sally, "Burn the fat man, burn him!"

Werner gaped at Liz thinking, *Who is this person next to me?*

The entire room came to life with people yelling at each other. Some past grudges between board members apparently resurrected to the present. Amid the pushing, shoving, and cursing, a food fight broke out with the cheesecake, some of which smushed the imported chef. He fled the room, cursing in French.

Liz got her own cheesecake in hand, took dead aim at Trace and threw it, making a direct hit on the left side of his head where

Sally had slapped him earlier. Frieda, looking alarmed, started talking softly and rapidly to her. Werner heard, "Calmness. Serenity. Think quiet waters, no fires…"

Werner tried vainly to tap his wine glass to restore order. The glass disintegrated in his hand from the abuse, wine and glass shards falling into his meal and onto his new Italian suit that had just arrived from New York. Seeing the damage, he thought, *What the hell? This place is getting totally ridiculous!*

He then ran to Sally and Trace, inserting himself between them to break things up. Sally, unfortunately, had just launched a knee toward Trace's crotch and instead nailed Werner.

He groaned loudly and doubled over. The chaos slowly died down as people noticed the CEO bent over, holding his crotch, with wine stains on his fine-looking suit. Trace with a load of cheesecake on the side of his head, began sticking his fingers in it and redirecting it to his mouth.

People began apologizing, shaking hands, and trailing out of the room. Sally, nearly crying at what she had done to her boss, led Werner to her chair, since it had less possible glass shards in it than his own. She held his hand, stroking it, and whispered in his ear, "I will make it up to you at our dinner."

Werner, with a grimace still on his face, leaned forward and whispered in her ear, "I will hold you to that promise."

Billy was feeling dejected. Jerome was pissed off at him since Billy had sliced his partner's right calf with his toenails when climbing out of bed that morning. The toenails were like razor blades, and they had started growing crazily after Sam had given him the "miracle cure," as Jerome was now cynically calling it, for the fatigue problem. The cut was deep, and they had to head to an AM/PM clinic for Jerome to get some stitches. The clinic wanted payment upfront, as it turned out they had taken people with Pearly Whites company-funded insurance before and gotten stiffed on claims submitted for not being on the approved list of providers, which evidently were few and far between.

Billy had taken to wearing open-toe sandals with no socks so he could trim his feet at work several times a day, but night, while asleep, was a whole new problem. His toenails had already sliced through several expensive sets of sheets Jerome had bought.

The nail growth had started a week after the injection. Bob had noticed the problem, saying, "That's fucking gross, Billy," when he walked in and caught him trimming his toes. He contacted Sam, who said he was laboring on a "workaround," whatever the hell that meant. All Billy knew was that his feet were frequently scaring people at work, and Jerome had declared Billy would have to sleep on the sofa with his feet pointed toward the ceiling until this snag was sorted out.

Arriving at work, he headed to Bob's office and found the corridor on the fourth floor littered with food and a frowning Bob returning from the bathroom with a big wine stain on his suit jacket, shirt, and tie. Billy followed his boss into the boardroom.

At one end of the boardroom table was Trace, being fanned by a man in a waiter's uniform. At the other end was Werner, eyes closed and grimacing, being fanned by Sally, who appeared to have showered in an amber fluid. She was cooing at Werner about taking care of him real soon. Billy thought, *Take care of what?*

Everywhere was food. On the floor, on the ceiling, on the walls. His appetite suddenly perked up, and he wandered over to the serving table and saw some leftover cheesecake. He grabbed a plate and dropped a slice onto it.

Sam was looking cynically back and forth at each respective camp. Billy sat next to him and asked, "Sam, how's it going on that workaround?"

Werner, hearing the conversation, swung his pained gaze over to Sam and Billy.

Sam grinned and said, "It's coming, Billy. Just keep trimming those nails. We will get it sorted out before long." He slapped Billy on the shoulder and smiled, making Billy wince.

Werner, now distracted from Sally's ministrations, managed to sit up and grunted, "What workaround?"

Billy got up and walked over to Werner, pointed down at his feet.

Werner said, "You're wearing sandals and no socks to work now?"

Sam laughed and said, "Look again, Werner."

Werner complied, then stared at Billy's toes. "That's gross. Why don't you trim them?"

Sam sighed and said, "He does, four times a day."

"Four times? What the hell is going on?"

"Minor side effect, Werner, not to worry."

Werner said, "Not to worry? Can you imagine a customer accepting that assurance? Oh, well, hey, your teeth look great, ignore the Godzilla toes!"

Billy nodded vigorously in agreement and launched into the tale about the trip to the AM/PM clinic tale and how he and Jerome had been hijacked into paying "out of network" costs, which made him feel belittled, angry, financially depleted, and dejected.

Fiona sat down next to Sam and said, "Sam, we could cut off his toes. I think he could still walk after an extended recovery and physical therapy."

Sam nodded. "It would be the honorable thing to do, Billy."

Billy went wide-eyed, "I'll wait on the fix."

Both Fiona and Sam belted out, "*Qaplah!*"

Werner shook his head and walked gingerly out the room, groaning as Sally cooed in his ear, now with a supportive arm around his waist. Observing their departure, Billy said, "What was that all about?"

In mock seriousness, Sam said, "Sometimes the blade falls just the right way."

Chapter 23

At the conclusion of their second run together as a threesome, Liz and Frieda invited Helga and Bob over for dinner. Helga immediately accepted and texted Bob to let him know what was up for the evening.

All three women jumped in the pool, splashing around like kids. Liz and Frieda simply peeled off their jogging outfits and dove in. Helga, not really shy but a bit surprised, watched for a moment, then said, "When in Rome!" She stripped faster than she thought possible and joined them.

After ten minutes, Frieda and Liz started making out under the diving board, and Helga giggled watching them. She was finding time with these women to not only be fun but arousing as well. She swam over to the edge, climbed out and stretched out on the sun-warmed towels that Langley had conveniently placed for all of them earlier.

Soon, Frieda and Liz popped out of the water and lay alongside her. Liz said, "Get used to this. A daily tan, frequent nudity, it's a lifestyle around here."

Helga sighed, "I need a girlfriend. Oh my, did I just say that?"

Frieda giggled and said, "We can figure something out there if you want."

Helga sat up on her elbows. "You serious? What about Bob?"

Liz said, "What he doesn't know won't hurt him."

Helga considered for a moment, realizing she was not all that wild about Bob anymore. "Um, not to be to forward, but when do we start?"

Liz looked at Frieda, and they both smiled and snuggled up on each side of Helga.

That evening Chef served dinner. The threesome all got dressed up for the event, and then chatted on the patio until Bob walked over from next door after work. Langley led him out to the table.

Bob was in a blabby mood. He talked about himself, his work, himself, his money, himself. He seemed little interested in his three female dinner companions except to ogle them if they crossed their legs or leaned forward to refill their wineglass.

Liz focused on Bob after he brought up a problem at work.

Bob said, "So, we have this guy, Billy. He's my gay muscle-bound secretary. Anyway, he's had the new teeth for maybe a month and a half now. Doing great except his toenails are growing like crazy."

Liz said, "Is he all right?"

Bob shrugged.

Liz leaned forward to reveal some cleavage due to her low-cut summer dress. "So, what would cause that?"

Bob gawked, his expression not agreeing with his words. "Totally normal development stuff, you know, like a bug in some funky software or a spelling edit in your word processor that has to be tracked down. We see this all the time, all the time. Yep. All the time."

Liz nodded, noting that Bob was a terrible liar.

They moved on to dessert. After an hour of looking at his watch, Bob said he had to go to catch some reruns of *Gilligan's Island.*

Helga frowned at him. "Enjoy yourself. Don't worry about us. We can handle cleanup."

Bob nodded on his way out, already absorbed with the prospect of his show.

Helga looked apologetically at Liz and Frieda.

Frieda said, "Hey, no surprise, Helga. We met Bob back when we first started talking to Pearly Whites, and I am actually surprised you were still with him when we moved in."

Helga shrugged, and Liz put an arm around her. "Hang in there for now, my dear. Things will change. Maybe we could all take a trip to some clinics together to get your profile work started. We will be in and out of here anyway for clinic business, and you can spend some time at our estate with us."

Helga took a deep breath. "Sounds good. Listen, you two have been so wonderful to me. I have to tell you something. Bob mentions a fair number of problems at work, especially lately. I know from what I have read in the news that the Cleaver Foundation has committed to investing millions in the company. I feel like I should make sure you all know the latest. I can get that out of Bob. Especially when he comes home drunk."

Liz said, "He drinks a lot?"

"A lot more so in the last couple of months. The way he talks, it's like scotch comes out of the water faucets."

Frieda and Liz laughed. Liz said, "We appreciate the loyalty, Helga. And yes, please keep us informed. It will not go unnoticed. Hell, it's hard not to notice you. Group hug!" Which they did, then a bit of kissing. Helga reluctantly pulled away and said, "I need to get back home before Bob starts wondering what's up."

Liz said, "Okay, listen, we can meet up tomorrow. Jog time."

Helga nodded and left with a wave and a longing look.

Frieda said, "Wow, she offered up Bob without us even having to ask."

Liz shrugged. "Yeah, I guess living with him makes that easy to do."

Chapter 24

Trace entered his rarely used office that was at the opposite end of the corridor from Werner and walked past his secretary du jour, whose name he had not bothered to learn, then stopped. "Hey, uh…you. Get Sam and Oppie up here. Tell them we got business to discuss." He then walked into his office, not waiting for her acknowledgment.

He logged into his computer, using the only password he could reliably remember, which was "Trace." He used it on everything. Once in, he checked stock prices and smiled. Then he jumped onto the dating site where he had been promoting himself. The site advertised that it was for multimillionaires and provided only the highest-class candidates for relationships. It had a lot of pictures of beautiful women in cities like Paris, Rome and New York. He had met several of them recently—none had passed credit checks indicating vast wealth, but some appealed to him based on their photos in exotic locales, so he was still hopeful.

Bob entered and said, "Morning, Trace!" Trace replied, "Hey, Oppie. Now fuck off for a moment." He then clicked on the most promising of the candidates.

Like most of the other nouveau riche of the company, Trace had purchased an Italian-style villa located a mile down the road from where Werner had just made an offer on a property himself. Distressed beachfront estate owners from the previous recession

163

were having a field day recovering their losses, and prices were now rising. The city of Santa De Lola was having a renaissance of property tax increases as a result.

Sam loomed large in the doorway, and Trace said, "Get your ass in here, my man. We need to talk."

Sam nodded, expressionless, and plunked down on the sofa.

A contest ensued as to who would speak first. Bob, as usual, caved.

"So, uh, yeah."

Trace rolled his eyes. "Okay, men, we have issues to talk about. I am about to begin construction of our production plant. The groundbreaking out back starts to-fucking-day. We need a rock-solid product, sans long toenails. Where are we at on that shit? Sam, you go first… Bob, never mind, let Sam talk."

Sam shrugged. "Trace, nothing to worry about. We are good. I have a workaround I will give Billy today."

Trace nodded, "So, how long before we know the workaround is solid?"

"A week, maximum. But probably tomorrow morning will tell the tale."

Bob added, "It's very promising, Trace."

Trace looked at Bob with a wry expression. "Oppie, shut your piehole if you don't mind. I mean, here we are needing immediate results, and all you got is *promising?*"

Liz was studying the latest data on her screen that Circe had sent. Frieda, standing behind her shoulder, would lean forward, rubbing a boob against her ear while pointing out some interesting bit of information.

The third time Liz said, "Stop that! I can't think!" She giggled and continued, "That fucking moron Trace. His password is his damn name?"

Frieda chuckled, "I think we got him figured out. What I am concerned about is spending more money on the plant they want to build. We should slow-roll that after today. After all, contractors are busy in a booming economy, and demand is up for stuff needed to build a plant."

Liz said, "I agree. Especially since they do not have this last problem with their sample of one, Billy, sorted out. He is the only subject that got more than one implant. How are we doing on the stock?"

Frieda said, "We've bought up enough shares through five offshore shell companies acting as investors to give us a huge position, making everybody else speculating on the stock ready to jump on board for the ride. The price is going through the roof. In about a week or so, we should have recouped what we spent on the estate. In two weeks, we sell a bunch and will have some significant offshore cash reserves in Cyprus for ourselves we can launder back into the foundation."

Liz nodded. "And then, if these people don't sort out what's up, we dump the remainder?"

Frieda said, "Pump, then dump!"

Later that afternoon, with Trace off to meet his latest "candidate," Sam and Bob met with Billy in the lab.

Billy smiled hopefully. Sam smiled back neutrally and said, "Okay, let's see if this sorts you out. I think we are good to go."

Billy almost recoiled as Sam pulled a horse-sized syringe out of the refrigerator behind him. As he approached Billy, he said, "Now, just close your eyes, try not to move."

Billy did as he was told but made a muffled cry—the shot hurt like hell. It felt like he was being injected with maple syrup, and for a long time.

Sam said, "You might see a… minor bruise. And ignore the bump at the area of the injection." Billy's arm felt like it was now on fire. His head rolled back as he nearly passed out.

Bob, alarmed, said, "We need smelling salts? Fuck, I think he's turning blue."

Sam took Billy's pulse and said, "Completely normal."

Sam's reassurance was all Bob needed, though he realized that even with his own meager knowledge of the technology, what "completely normal" meant was a relative term.

Chapter 25

Sash, for the first time in his life, felt pathetic and sorry for himself. The situation at Pearly Whites with his boss, Reuben, and the asshole coward near retiree Eddie Childress made him consider an ancient disemboweling ritual he had seen in a movie. Not for himself, however. Nope. That would be reserved for the singular perpetrator of this tragic epic, yet to be identified.

He was sitting at his home computer, which was set up next to his dust-gathering work laptop. He fingered the stolen flash drive, plugged it in and copied the files.

He opened the folder and saw extraordinarily little of what looked like useful information, which was disappointing but predictable. The data consisted of mostly small text files and a couple of spreadsheets. Disgusted, he opened a web browser and read the foundation's homepage, which had the usual stuff about their great works, a bio of Elizabeth Cleaver, her beloved mother, Olivia, the original commune, along with a picture of Liz handing a bandana to a toothless man in Kentucky at one of her free dental clinics.

Since the commune was located just an hour and a half north, he decided to take a drive up the coast to see the place. He had studied the 1960s in a college sociology class, what his aged professor fondly called the "peace, love, dope" era. Maybe he could score some good shit while he was up that way. Hopping in his Mazda3, he headed out.

An hour later, he found himself stumped. His phone GPS said he was at the commune destination, but he was looking at some gated mansion. He drove around a bit, stopped at a gas station two miles up the road, and asked the clerk if anyone knew what had happened to it.

The old woman behind the counter said, "It's gone. A few years back, the daughter built that atrocity you see now. Seems peculiar for someone always talking about free dental care for the poor, don't cha think?" The woman smiled, displaying a few browned-out teeth with really bad gums. Sash, always one for neatness and cleanliness, recoiled mentally and tried to maintain a neutral expression.

She continued, "I lived in that commune for eighteen years, knew Elizabeth Cleaver's mother really well. I can tell you one thing. After she died—and the circumstances of that death were pretty damn odd—and when the daughter inherited it all, I along with all the other women were told to leave. Next thing—mega mansion. No matter what the bullshit that comes out of that foundation's mouth, Liz Cleaver has no friends from her commune days. In fact, a few would put a knife in her back in a jiffy."

Sash said, "A jiffy? Wow, that is some suppressed information. Where did you all go when you were kicked out?"

"Wherever we could. That horrible woman left us with nothing. Some with computer skills got jobs with big tech. I was a midwife. Not much call for it these days around here. I live with three of the other sisters in a little duplex. Got this here job to help pay rent."

Sash said, "I'm sorry to hear that and apologize if I brought up any bad memories."

The old woman said, "Thanks, though, it's just life, mister, or so I hear anyway. I do know things have a way of coming back to bite one's ass." She grinned again and Sash wondered what all she meant, but he did know about his own experiences with ass-biting life events. He thanked her for her time, bought some gas and headed back home.

Billy was impressed. At first.

For the last two days his toenails had not budged. He had taken to measuring them with a micrometer he had picked up at a boutique scientific instrument measurement shop at Fourth and Main in Santa De Lola. Not the slightest growth.

Jerome was ecstatic. It led to a bedtime session that would not stop. Then another. Then another. Twenty-four hours of another, it turned out. Until Jerome finally said enough was enough, it was time to throw some cold water on Billy's insatiability.

The problem, though, was that it was starting to hurt. Like, things can only stay firmly enlarged for so long. He took several measurements, this time with a tape measure he found in a kitchen drawer. While not hyper accurate, things seem to be… scaling up. He called in sick due to the increasing discomfort. That led to Sam giving him a call once Billy's absence was noted.

"Billy, it's Sam. How are you feeling?"

"Fine, except for this massive boner that won't stop. In fact, it seems to be getting more massive."

"Billy, you need to get in right away. You could suffer permanent penile damage if you don't get in the lab right now."

"Penile? Okay, Sam, if you say so. See you there."

Billy attempted to hide his raging hard-on by using one of Jerome's old leather satchels that he could hold out in front of him. He then dressed in some baggy sweats for comfort and drove into the campus. He got by the receptionist without much fuss even though she commented on his casual dress not being corporate standard.

He relaxed his guard with his "penile disguise" as he walked into the elevator. At the last second, Sally stuck her hand in the door, reversing it and jumped in. He saw she was trying to be polite but was looking sideways at the display he was putting on, trying to restrain smiling to herself. She said, "Four, please."

Turning red with embarrassment, he pushed the button for her while at the same time he moved the satchel between her view and his southern projection. He then he got off at the second floor. Sally smiled and waved as the door shut.

Once Billy was seated in the lab, Bob and Sam rolled in. Sam asked Billy to show them the problem, even though it was definitely creating a noticeable tent poling effect on the front of his sweatpants. Billy, with a groan, eased the sweatpants down, trying not to rub himself against the fabric.

Wide-eyed, Bob said, "Would you look at that fucking cock! Jeez, Billy, if you were straight, you'd be the busiest man in town!"

Sam was looking confused at what he was seeing, but added, "Yep, impressive for sure. And it takes something to impress me. Okay, let's see if we can get this taken care of."

Sam turned to the fridge and pulled out another syringe. This one looked like it had been modified from a caulk gun. Since Billy's arm from the previous shot was still pretty sore and bruised, Sam asked if he wanted it in the other arm or the butt. Billy went for the other arm, saying he still wanted to be able to sit down as he recovered. Again, the slow injection, a minor scream, and then head lolling.

Bob said, "You think we could get sued for this? I believe he's passed out now."

Sam shrugged, chucked the syringe in a trash can and pulled up a chair to watch.

As Billy revived, he also retracted. It seemed to work in coordinated fashion. Finally, after a quick check to see if his pulse was normal, Billy was sent home for a couple of days of R&R.

Watching from the second-floor window of the lab as Billy rolled out of the parking lot in the Pinto, Bob asked Sam, "Should we tell Trace?"

Sam shook his head and said, "Nope. The Trace is busy with his new production plant and girlfriend candidates. Let the guy indulge himself for now. I think we have this sorted out."

Bob could not be entirely sure, but for the first time in his relationship with Sam, the man sounded less than positive about everything being "sorted out." Then a thought from out the blue hit him. "Sam, maybe we could start a company on the side with that formula for massive boners. You know, without any side effects."

Sam raised an eyebrow. "Always thinking big, aren't you? Tell you what. You get the funding, I'm all in."

Bob grinned, excited, "Okay! And we could test it on me!"

"Oh, for sure we would."

Bob, enthused, couldn't wait to tell Helga.

Chapter 26

A couple days later, Bob was standing in the fourth-floor hallway, waiting for Trace to arrive, when Werner came through. Thinking maybe he could mend a fence with a funny story, he flagged Werner down and started talking about the Billy situation, and the largest dick he had ever seen, as Trace emerged from the elevator.

Predictably, Trace and Werner went ballistic.

Werner said, "I thought all this crap was sorted out. I want Fiona and Sam all over this."

Trace sighed, then said, "Do you guys understand what the problems are if this sort of ding-dong shit keeps going on?"

Bob squirmed. He did understand, at a rudimentary level involving his own stock, that this was a problem. He responded with "Yes, and Trace, it's fixed. I tell you… it *is* fixed."

Trace grimaced. "Tell Sam to come up here so we can talk this shit through. Right now, motherfucker!"

After he called Sam, Bob scampered for the boardroom, knowing his mentor would be pissed off at him that he had said anything to anybody, let alone in front of Trace, so he only mentioned there was a meeting coming up in five minutes. He then called Billy and told him the same thing.

Once Sam arrived, they sat down at the table. Trace started in, "So, Sam, Bob says we had another incident, or is that the right word? Maybe, 'fuckup' would be a better descriptive?"

Sam glanced at Bob and sighed. "Yes, but it's taken care of now. A genomic transference anomaly moved the growth problem from Billy's fingernails to his penis. We caught it and got it under control."

Bob nodded along and added, "See, Trace, it's good, under control."

Trace raised his eyebrows at this bit of information. When Billy arrived he said, "So you and your pecker okay?"

Billy launched into a narrative covering all the issues, his purchases of measurement equipment he thought he should be reimbursed for, and then showed the bruises on his arms from his shots, which Trace appeared not to give a shit about. When he started to undo his fly, though, everybody held up their hands and said, "That will not be necessary!"

Sam smiled at Billy and said, "You can go now."

Bob quipped, "Keep that thing in your pants."

Billy fired back, "Jeez, and I remember how much you admired it, Bob. Is it keeping you up nights?"

Werner walked into his office after the hallway run-in with Bob, who, day after day, was turning into a gushing fountain of product glitches and side effects. At his behest, Sally had trailed in after him. He had her shut the door.

Sally said, "Wow, Werner, love the suit!"

Werner blushed, thanking her. He took her hand. Without hesitation, she came closer to him.

"So, what's up? I am guessing anytime we need closed doors around here, some shit is hitting or has already passed through the fan."

Werner gave her a wry expression, still looking at her intently. She held his gaze. He said, "I am selling my stock."

Sally raised an eyebrow. "All of it?"

Werner considered, then said, "No, but probably eighty percent. I am getting bad vibes from things I am hearing about problems with the teeth and the lab's efforts to resolve them." Then he dove into explaining the Billy fiasco as it presently stood. Some went back to what Bob had related in the hallway, which dovetailed with stories some of the other scientists were telling him. The place was becoming a rumor factory, but the rumors were more and more frequently becoming reality.

Sally remembered the elevator ride and just how large Billy had been during his "engorgement" episode. As she tried to suppress a smile, Werner eyed her expression and said, "You knew about this?"

Sally replied, "Oh, you know, word gets around." She then changed the subject. "What about the start of the construction of the plant that seems to be on hold? You think Liz and Frieda know?"

Werner, sounding exasperated, said, "I can't say who knows what these days. The way Sam and freaking Bob Oppenheimer hem and haw or flat-out lie at times. Plus, Trace is not about to say shit to me about anything. I am just worried if the FDA gets wind of it."

Sally asked, "Does it matter? It seems this is going through to the public whether the FDA does anything or not."

"Probably not. But I am not going down with the ship, not after all this work. Hence the sale of the stock."

"Maybe I should sell some of mine."

"Maybe so. Sally, if it takes a downturn, we could be back financially where we were at the start of the company. If it gets out and causes problems, I can see lawsuits all the way past the horizon. I've now got an account in a bank in Cyprus. You might look for something offshore. I can help if you like."

Sally nodded in agreement. That was pretty much the monetary discussion. But then she added, "So, when are you moving into your new estate?" She took his other hand. "I seem to remember a dinner invitation." She smiled impishly at him. He laughed and said, "Very soon. We'll have…a private showing."

Sally stood on her tiptoes and gave Werner a peck on the cheek, which then led to a much deeper kiss. She pulled back and smiled. "I can't wait to see it." She turned and left the room, knowing his gaze was following her. She wiggled and said, "Keep your eyes on the road, buddy!"

Chapter 27

Helga was at Liz's door early, and Langley led her into the kitchen, where Liz and Frieda were having breakfast and joking around with Chef. She grabbed the chair between the two women as Chef hurried off to bring something for their new guest.

Liz said, "So, what's up, dear?"

Helga related the story about the latest side effect. Questions were asked about length and diameter, which Helga had no idea about as well as any other dimensional details.

Liz looked at Frieda and said, "So this may mean we should sell off a bunch of the stock now. They seem to be going from one weird side effect to the other. And maybe we should get Fiona and Sam back for another dinner to see what else is going on."

Frieda nodded and began sending encrypted messages out to the shell companies.

That same day, Werner had just completed an early morning meeting with Fiona and Sam. Fiona made sure Werner understood they were busy as bees looking into what was causing the side effects with Billy.

Werner did not feel reassured. Since the meeting was fairly quick and specific, he grabbed a cup of coffee and walked out and around to the back of headquarters to get an eye on the construction of the new production plant that had now slowed to a stop. When he had asked what was causing the slowdown, Liz had said activity should pick up in a few weeks, citing issues with busy contractors and shortages in the supply chain.

As he stared at a parked bulldozer and a big hole in the ground, Trace came rolling up in his recently acquired upgrade to his stretch BMW—a larger version in bright red. This one had a driver's seat that electrically activated after the automated driver's door swung open. It would pivot him around, then gradually lift Trace to his feet so he could climb out without looking like he was wrestling with an invisible bear to get vertical.

Werner watched his business partner/nemesis push the button on the console and was mildly entertained when the seat started turning before the door was fully open.

Trace started cussing, shoving on the door to try to accelerate its opening. When it finally opened wide, he struggled to swing his feet in position before the seat pushed him on his face into the parking lot pavement. Huffing and puffing from the effort, he repositioned his fedora, then approached Werner.

Werner swung around to face the bulldozer as Trace stopped alongside him.

"Werner."

"Trace."

"What do you want?"

"I was hoping we could talk—civilly, that is, for a fucking change."

Werner glanced sideways at the man and said, "About what?"

"Listen, Brandt, we're in this shit together. Fortunes intertwined. You get that shit, right?"

"Yes, Trace, I have understood ever since I signed on the dotted line with you pirates three years ago. But I'm not talking about that now. I am, however, really concerned about things going sideways on us."

"Then we have a mutual situation. But we need to get this shit out the door."

Werner sighed, turned to look directly at Trace. Trace gazed back and Werner realized that this was maybe the sincerest moment he had ever had with the man. Werner said, "I know it does not matter how many times I point out that getting this to market with any sort of serious side effect will tank this entire endeavor. You have got to know that as a fact."

"Yes, I know. I also know if it is not in the hands of somebody installing this product in someone's orifice in the near future, we have no revenue. The banks will only extend credit for another couple months and our IPO money is about gone. Plus, the foundation is only paying for the new plant as work is actually done, which means no production level of the teeth. And finally, Martin's shitass investment group has backed away from more debt since they got a big chunk back from the IPO. So, we have a narrow window of opportunity, or disaster ensues. We could become a target for some predatory hedge fund, of which Wall Street has legions."

Werner had an unpleasant epiphany as Trace rolled out the litany of issues. The sinking feeling he experienced in the hallway earlier with Bob accelerated downward. He said, "Crap. Okay. Uh, might have been useful to know this before."

"You never fuckin' asked, Werner. Now you know without even asking. Let's make a deal. You get on top of Fiona and Sam's tech, I get this plant build-out project moving full speed, we don't fuck with each other unless we just have to, and we keep each other updated."

The choice seemed simple now. Trace headed back to the BMW, saying he was going to go drive it back up the asshole of the dealership he had just picked it up from a week ago.

Werner was left pondering. Trace had never in the past been so open and receptive or even remotely accommodating. That meant that something bad had to be afoot with the Bob and Sam show. It seemed past the time to find out more about what was going wrong.

Bob strolled into the second-floor conference room and found Werner talking with Sam and Fiona. Surprised at seeing the CEO there, he said, "Hey, quick bio break before we start. Too much coffee, ya know… okay."

Werner frowned but waved him on, then said, "You were saying?"

Sam responded by quoting a passage in a scientific paper he had read that had helped him realize what was happening to Billy.

In the hall, out of earshot, Bob immediately called Trace. Nervously, he dove in, "Trace, Brandt is pulling us all into a meeting."

Trace, who was at the BMW dealer, said, "I already fucking know. Who the fuck do you think gave him permission? Get your stink ass in there. Cooperate fully. You all are going to get a full daily anal inspection. I want every bit of assistance and insight on the problems you guys are dealing with, right goddamn now." He then hung up on Bob.

Bob gaped at his phone, realizing the breeze at his back had just become a wind in his face. Nervously, he headed back to the conference room and sat next to Sam.

Werner said, "Okay, today is reorg day. Fiona is now the lead that you all report directly to, and she reports to me."

Bob asked, "So what does that mean for me?"

Werner shrugged. "You're not fired, so be happy." He then left the room.

The others trailed out to the hallway a moment later. Fiona made a smiling, knowing nod at Sam.

Bob freaked, "What just happened?"

Sam and Fiona looked at Werner's receding back with disdain. Fiona said, "That's Werner. Let him play CEO. We know what we are doing."

Sam indicated for Bob to approach. He then said, "Today is a good day to die!" Fiona and Sam then high-fived, expecting Bob to join in.

Bob, confused, asked, "We gotta die?"

Fiona sighed, "No, doofus. Get your warrior on. We are gonna kick *ass*."

The next day and another meeting, this time including Trace and with Sally taking notes. Werner said, "I believe Sam has something he would like to share with us."

Sam looked surprised and suspicious at the same time, then slowly said, "Like what?"

"Oh, I don't know. How about, like, where did you get this know-how that you have been using to grow the teeth, along with other things, like your fixes?"

Trace sat up in his chair, now fully alert. He sensed real bullshit was now fully in motion. He said, "Sam, what is Brandt talking about?"

Sam looked nervous for the first time anyone in this group had ever noticed. He said, "Uh, well, I worked it out while in my old job."

Werner said, "Your old job? When you were a professor? Because the MIT paper you quoted from in the meeting yesterday rang a bell. It was a paper I reviewed before Pearly Whites even existed. A paper loaded with problems with their project they finally abandoned. Though they had some successes with generating some tooth-like structures that quickly died. Sound familiar?"

Sam said, "Well, yes, and it should to you as well. Since you based *your* technology on it."

Trace's eyes were wide. That was when Billy knocked on the door, and in a muffled voice said, "Hey, I'm sorry for being late."

Trace rolled his eyes. "Well, get your late ass in here."

The hinges creaked as Billy poked his head around the edge of the door, saw who all was there and came on in. Trace indicated for him to take a seat by Werner, which he quickly did. Trace said, "So where were we?"

Sam was looking intently at Werner, who pressed on. "So, as Sam mentioned, the papers on this project were published in the academic community. I did in fact read them way back then. Sam obviously did as well while with his university. You see, MIT had a gene splicer that had problems, made by a company named Smith Industries. As I recall, they sold three or four of these wonders. The company went out of business. Trace, do you recall where the gene splicer came from that we bought?"

Trace said, "I thought it was Acme DNA, some Florida LLC?"

Werner picked up his cellphone and called Fiona down on two. He said, "Fiona, please go in the lab, and take a picture of the data plate on the gene splicer and a picture of the unit overall, then send them to my phone. I'll wait." He put her on speaker while they listened to her go down the hallway, enter the lab and then walk to the gene splicer. She said, "Taking pictures now. You know what, that data plate. It has an Acme decal on it. I never really looked close before."

Werner said, "Will it peel off?

"Yeah, I think so." There was a pause, then, "Oh, okay, underneath, embossed in the original plate is 'Smith Industries.'"

Trace blurted, "What the hell?"

Sally did a quick search on the Internet. "Hey, guys, looks like Smith Industries did go bankrupt, then changed their name to Acme DNA, LLC. Let me see. Here is the website. Says contact them via email if you need parts."

Werner said, "So we've got a machine that cannot even be maintained before long. Holy shit. Sam, can you now tell us what you did?"

Sam shrugged. "I didn't tell you to buy it. I didn't tell you to rip off MIT's gene project either." He looked at Trace and chuckled. "Our department had bought one of the machines early on with a grant I submitted that got approved, and I sorted out the code problems MIT was having on our own equipment after reading their paper. I have programmed for years, and apparently, they couldn't. I just didn't have this company's facilities to actually grow the teeth, but software modeling indicated my processes would work, and since you guys were using the MIT protocol, the rest, as they say, is history."

Werner said, "Did you put this on your resume?"

Sam looked amused. "Bob brought me in, Werner, as part of his agreement with Pearly Whites. You know that. Trace then hired me during that interview, got Billy here to type up my offer letter after I told him what I wanted as a compensation package. I never filled out squat. Hell, nobody even asked. But, Werner, you are avoiding the bigger issue of your own malfeasance here."

Werner sat back in his chair, realizing this was an idiot's dance ball, led by head imbecile Chauncey "Trace" Orbaugh. The third! He said, "Holy shit. Trace?"

Trace looked a bit sheepish, but blustered, "Hey, piddly details at this point. I mean, let's look forward, not back. Mistakes have been made, okay. I admit some were caused by people not understanding my directives. Me, I never did anything."

Werner nodded, "Yep, nothing in fact."

Then Billy stood up, looking like he would either cry or detonate. He exclaimed, "And do you all want to hear the latest? I can't get an erection now to save my life. Jerome is seething. Sorry, Sally, just had to say it."

A half-smile slipped through as she replied, "Don't hold back, Billy. Let it out."

Trace gaped and said, "So you can't get a hard-on now? Oh great. Hey, Mister Customer, here is your brand-new tooth and a complimentary limp dick." He swung on Sam. "So, how quick can this crap be fixed?"

"Might take a bit. Hey, Werner, you should help. After all, you know this crap, as Trace refers to it, backwards and forwards."

Werner rolled his eyes and said, "Fuck."

Trace was having none of it. "You will fix this, Sam. You work for us, not the other way around. You are now lower than whale shit on the ocean floor, so start right fucking now." The room went silent as everyone glared at each other, then departed.

Chapter 28

That evening, Bob was the beneficiary of a magnificent dinner in his own abode that Chef had whipped up. The meal had been a project to prepare, and then moving it all over to Helga and Bob's condo next door was another project. In the end, Liz decided it would have been easier to have Bob come over to their place, but she figured the man would want to stroke himself in front of them about his genius, his accomplishments and his readily available cash. A week earlier, he had made it clear he wanted Liz in his bed. Liz, once she suppressed blowtorching him, decided she would keep that fantasy going until she determined where she and Frieda were going to park the remainder of their cash haul.

Halfway through the meal and a bottle and a half of 1982 Lafite, Bob started weeping and talking about the sea change at work. His grievance list included that Werner Brandt was back in charge and Sam was having to answer to Brandt about how he had come up with his design from the failed MIT project. On top of that was the gene splicer spare parts availability issue. Or that they were under a deadline to fix the problems that still plagued the tooth product and time was running out. Plus, Billy could not get an erection anymore, a new side effect.

184

Frieda took the lead with the sympathetic act. Liz followed suit, further probing, but had to restrain a giggle on the Billy update. Helga just watched in amusement.

Soon, Bob was blabbering about all sorts of project issues, personal problems, along with a crotch fungus that had started on Saturday. Liz was taking as many mental notes as she could except for the fungus part. Helga was glad that two months back she had cut Bob off on sex.

After dinner was over, Liz gave Helga a kiss on the lips while the three women were in the kitchen with arms around each other. With a knowing nod toward Bob's couch position by the television she whispered, "We have to go."

Back at the condo, Liz and Frieda brainstormed about everything they now knew and what the latest symptoms meant. Liz said, "Let's invite Fiona and Sam back to the estate and take Helga, too. She can tell Bob it's a business trip."

Frieda nodded in agreement and started making the arrangements.

The next night, Sam and Fiona arrived once again by the foundation's helicopter. They were greeted by Frieda and escorted to their room before dinner. Frieda noticed Sam had brought a small carry-on bag this time, which he rolled along behind him. She gave Fiona a smile and the woman blushed once again. *How cute*, Frieda thought. She said to Sam, "Whatcha got in the bag, big boy?"

Sam laughed and said, "Oh, stuff. Not sure I should say. It was all Fiona's idea. Some interesting accessories, that's for sure!"

Fiona said, "Sam! It's just a change of underwear."

With a grin Sam nodded and said, "Uh-huh." Frieda and Fiona giggled.

Once Frieda left the two in their room, she went down to the cavern data center to meet up with Liz and Helga. Liz led with,

"So, we are pretty well out of our stock position now with Pearly Whites. Shit should hit the fan pretty soon. I have a source at the *Los Angeles Herald,* so let's bring him up on this video call. His name is Carson Wells." She nodded to Frieda, who brought up a secure encrypted video link. The next thing they were looking at was Carson. Liz and Frieda briefed the reporter.

Carson said, "So, I am good on doing all this, but Liz…I need some help. I have some problems haunting me from a trip to Las Vegas."

Liz frowned and said, "Not again, mister. I mean, shit, how much this time?"

Carson said, "Fifty large. If you can help me, I definitely can and will help you."

Liz sighed and said, "Done. Same bunch as you lost to before?"

Eyes downcast, he nodded in the affirmative. Then he said, "Let me run just a small story, not a lot of detail, but something pertinent. I can get it in tonight for the online addition. I think we could lead with 'a source that had intimate knowledge of the problems.' Use the fatigue issue, for starters, and roll this out in order for maximum effect. Then the story will get picked up by the AP and start appearing in East Coast papers and on CNB."

Liz said, "Let's get the wheels rolling, then. Keep us posted. I'll have your gambling debt situation sorted out by morning."

Carson looked relieved and said, "Thanks a million, Liz. Again, sorry about needing another bailout."

Liz gave him a cynical smile and said, "No problem."

The call ended.

Frieda said, "You really going to pay the fifty thousand?"

Liz laughed. "You mean to me? Hell, I arranged for him to lose his ass out in Vegas with this card shark I met a decade ago. Same as the last time. It's how I keep Carson owing me all the time."

Frieda shook her head. "Woman, you are a diabolical genius!"

Dinner went well with Sam, Fiona and Helga. Liz had told Helga to stick to only talking about her current position as a psychological analyst for the foundation and leave anything about Bob out of the conversation.

As the dinner moved to the dessert stage, Frieda started in. "Fiona, what is this we are hearing about some problems with side effects on the teeth? Is it true?"

Fiona stopped in mid-bite, looked at Sam, who was not hiding his surprise very well.

With no answer, Frieda said, "Sam? Whatcha think?"

Cautiously, Sam said, "Side effects?"

Liz jumped in, "Yeah, you know. Limp dicks, massive unstoppable boners, toenail razor blades. You know… that sort of stuff."

Fiona blew out a breath. "How do you know about this?"

Liz said, "Does it matter? And if we do, who else knows?"

Sam said, "I think Pearly Whites is like a leaky vessel. Okay, so you are in the know. Is that why you brought us here? A confession of corporate sins?"

Liz waved him off. "Sam, don't go defensive on me. Now, listen. Is there a fix on the horizon?"

Fiona said, "Yes. In fact, Sam and I finished the final calculation today."

Liz nodded. She then said, "Can it be delayed?"

Fiona and Sam looked at each other, confusion on their faces. Sam said, "I suppose, but why would we do that?"

Liz shrugged and said, "A butt load of money. Status, much more elevated positions in a new company than you are ever going to get at Pearly Whites."

Fiona said, "Listen, I know you all must have plans we are not at all up on, but I thought you wanted this product for your clinics."

Liz said, "We do. In fact, we want to own it. Now, let's talk about how all of this could work for everybody at this table. Frieda, show our guests how their financial position will look if we can work a deal."

Frieda handed a tablet she had over to Sam. He looked at the screen, then he looked again. He handed it over to Fiona, who did a similar double take.

Liz grinned. "Sound reasonable?"

Without hesitation, Sam and Liz nodded affirmatively.

Liz said, "Fantastic. Okay, one more detail. You have a fix. That stays with us. We would like one more problem to emerge with Billy Fuller. Can that be arranged?"

Sam said, "Uh, yeah, pretty easily. We caught this one in the lab just before the final fix we have now."

Frieda and Liz leaned back and grinned at each other. Frieda said, "Well, let's get the ball rolling on that one."

Chapter 29

J uly 5—Today, a situation has come to light that may not bode well for Pearly Whites, the current hot stock driven by heavy trading and exuberant rumors—Nasdaq stock code PWSOTL.

A source close to the company has provided information to the Herald *indicating the biogenetic tooth product meant for dental implants is having serious side effects. The symptom reported at this time is extreme fatigue, which experts speculate will have to be overcome before the FDA would certify the effectiveness of the product. At the close of business today, the stock is now trading heavily, though the price has declined only a moderate amount.*

Trace was standing in the office of the general manager of Lipschultz BMW of Santa De Lola, giving the man hell,
"What a piece of shit with your backwoods engineering. This stealership is a genuine rip-off. I should just buy the dump and then happily lay you people off without benefits!"

Thus energized, Trace was about to launch into a laundry list of issues when his phone buzzed in his pocket. His stock alert app was flashing red. He then saw the *Herald* headline. He looked at the GM and said, "I need my car, right fucking now."

The GM was overjoyed at the opportunity to flee to the service area. He then sent a salesperson to let Trace know when the car was ready. Moments later, the vehicle was idling out front as the big man slogged out the door and climbed in.

189

When he arrived at Pearly Whites, chaos was in progress. Assigning titles as he waded through the crowd, he encountered nosy reporters, limited-intellect camera operators, then asshole Pearly Whites security people. Obviously, none the source of a leak. Breathing heavily, he stormed at low waddle past the receptionist to the elevator thinking, *could not be that idiot*. He then saw the recently installed statue of himself that he had commissioned. Not a suspect.

With the boardroom in sight, he stopped to catch his breath. Once on his laptop, he scrutinized the entire *Herald* story, then read the stock market analyses. The experts came up with every reason in the world that an increase/decrease in a stock might fluctuate with investor confidence—heady topics like a butterfly farting in Argentina and chaos theory. The stock was down five percent at closing. He calculated he'd just lost three million dollars.

What the fuck, he thought, wondering how the hell a leak had occurred. Then it hit him. Werner Brandt and that insipid woman, Sally. It had to be them. He cursed himself now for his stupidity. His misplaced trust had led to Brandt being back in the mix, which had led to Trace himself being blamed for hiring Sam without checking if the man even had a pulse. That had been embarrassing. They would pay. Oh, they would pay. He picked up his phone and called Security of San Francisco. Once he had the owner on the phone, he laid out what he needed and that he needed it "right fucking yesterday."

Sash sat across the desk from his boss, Rueben Corpenny, for the first time in three months. Rueben was reading the Pearly Whites story on the *Los Angeles Herald* website and making clucking sounds of disappointment.

Sash said, "Rueben, let's get ahead of this catastrophe. Put me back on the project. I will give them an investigative enema."

Rueben grimaced. "You might get your wish, Sash, but not just yet. DC is typically glacial in responding to news like this. As if they are going to get in front of anything besides getting the hell out of Dodge."

Inwardly, Sash chuckled at the experienced thought process being voiced by his boss. Outwardly, he looked concerned.

Rueben called Eddie Childress for the third time. The phone rang until it went to voicemail, at which point he hung up. "The fucker is acting retired now, probably sanding a yardarm on that goddamn boat-building project of his. I already left him multiple messages this morning."

"Rueben, I'm here, ready for battle. I will save your ass, put me in there. Fuck Childress."

With a weary look, Rueben slid open his desk drawer, set out two tumblers and a bottle of Jack Daniel's. He poured for both of them. Then he said, "Tomorrow, if this insanity is still going on, you are back in the middle of the shit. Happy?"

Sash picked up his drink, nodded appreciatively and took a sip.

That afternoon, CNB with Bear Liebowitz ran a story based on an afternoon release of another *Herald* story about a second side effect. Bear led with, "Folks, welcome to the *Position Room*. Today, we have a new story about Pearly Whites and documented negative side effects of their new genetically grown tooth-replacement product. The latest problem—enhanced toenail growth." The CNB story was shallow, mostly rumor mongering about more genetic anomalies than the *Herald* story, but it prompted a call from a certain chief of staff's office in Washington, DC, with "cover our ass" instructions for Rueben Corpenny. Immediately after that, the same office put in a sale order on Pearly White stock.

Shortly thereafter, Rueben called Sash and told him, "You got your wish, buddy, even faster than tomorrow morning. You are back in charge. Oh, and on an unrelated point, Childress officially submitted for retirement today."

Chapter 30

Reporters and camera operators were now not allowed on the campus without permission, and the former head of security had been disciplined and demoted for too much schnapps and allowing the reporters on the grounds to begin with. He now spent his time on the night shift, guarding the plant construction area—that is, guarding a hole in the ground.

The heavily tattooed, recently promoted Sonny now ran the front gate, and he had contracted with a biker gang to maintain a barrier of hostile-looking dudes with choppers for intimidation of the reporters.

Trace had authorized the change, telling Werner it was just street art. Werner, for his part, was back to not getting any sleep and sipping lots of bismuth. With his attitude in the ditch, he had told Trace, "Long as it ain't coming out of my paycheck."

Sally arrived with his morning coffee as he stared out his office window. She said, "Déjà vu, eh?"

"Unfortunately."

"Hey, Werner, I noticed something peculiar is going on."

Werner swung his gaze from the window to look at her. She continued, "I swear somebody followed me in to work today. I took a few changes of direction, just like in the movies, and this van behind me did the same thing. Plus, I found a window

193

unlocked on the back of my house. I know I had it locked, since it was replaced a month ago."

Werner said, "Paparazzi probably. They love this sort of stuff. And now that you mention it, I think I saw a woman taking my picture with a big telephoto lens on her camera from across the street when we went to dinner last night."

Trace sat in the boardroom with his earbuds plugged into the phone app that Security of San Francisco—SOS for short—had provided him. He grinned to himself listening to Werner and Sally talking to each other in Werner's office. But somebody was being careless if Sally's suspicions were aroused. SOS was supposed to be more professional than this. Incompetence reigned around him, and it was becoming aggravating as hell. Plus, that new BMW had again shit the bed. While at a red light, the modified seat had shoved him into the steering wheel.

He called the owner of SOS, Rose Ramirez. He led with, "Your people are being careless, Ramirez."

She said, "You gripe a lot, Trace. Now, what are you talking about?"

He fumed as he thought about how he had put this broad in the surveillance business a decade ago on another startup. It had made okay money in the corporate intrigue industry, but nothing like Pearly Whites would. He continued, "Then why did both Brandt and his succubus see your people taking pictures and following them?"

"We just finished putting in the bugs, Trace. Nobody is even doing what you are talking about right now."

What the hell. Maybe Brandt was right, and it was the paparazzi following them. In fact, it now dawned on him that at the red light seat incident, a guy with a camera was snapping away from across the intersection *at him*.

He said, "Okay, we need your people on whoever these people are that are following our people."

Ramirez said, "But you still want us to follow your people, right?"

Trace said, "What the hell, why not. Jesus this is getting to be expensive. I need a volume rate."

"You get what you pay for, Trace. You want quantity without quality, yep, I can do that."

What Trace did not know was that Rose Ramirez was pissed off at him. He had royally screwed her on an earlier deal a month back involving a female con artist who had been seeing him under the false pretense of being a multimillionaire and she had gotten the woman arrested via a bribe to a cop. Trace said he never authorized the bribe and refused to cover the costs. So, she had deployed some of her people to play "paparazzi" to get everyone wound up and that had gotten funneled back to "El Cheapo", (one of her many nicknames for the man), via the conversations such as he had just heard with Werner and Sally. Now she would recover some of her earlier losses with the fat man and make some extra.

Trace caved, too preoccupied with the declining stock price on his screen. He said, "Okay, do quality. Shit. Goodbye."

Fiona, Bob and Sam were working on the fix for the "limp dick" bug in the Chompers code. Or at least that was what Bob was led to believe by his cohorts. Unaware of the recently struck deal with Liz and Frieda, Bob figured the pair were just going through their normal process. Fiona would come up with the new splice while Sam did his coding. Bob had zero ability in either area. He mostly got people coffee and doughnuts from the cafeteria, and for that, he subbed out the effort to Billy, who didn't mind. It gave him a chance to frequently check on the progress of the bug fix.

The other scientists on the team were busy working on producing the nutrient and growth pods they would be installing in the factory, and they had contracted an electrical engineer to design the new chipsets for a specialty chip manufacturer to produce so they could reverse-engineer parts for the Acme DNA splicer and make their own spares.

Werner surveyed the lab, watching all the busy people, and realized this was where they should have been focusing over a year ago. He was trying to get a programmer in now to supplement Sam on the coding side. Werner had a secondary agenda in that regard; Sam was too much of a single point of failure in their endeavor if he got ran over, died or whatever.

Next to Werner stood Sash Kimura. After a few calls and finally a threat to shut down the certification, the FDA team was back in the facility this morning. Trace had tried calling his Washington contacts, but that had proven to be fruitless, as nobody there would return his messages.

Sash said, "This is impressive, Dr. Brandt. It would seem you all are busy as little bees. But I need to see more information on what is going on here."

Werner sighed. "Dr. Kimura, let's adjourn to the conference room down the hall. These people are busy."

Once in the room, which SOS had also bugged, Sash and Werner sat staring at each other across the table.

Werner had a stack of material next to him and a PowerPoint presentation up on the wall monitor. Since he had more spare time than any of the folks actually working in the lab and had what he thought was a high level understanding of the product, he had assembled the presentation while Sally put the "facts and figures" together for Sash's team to review.

Just as he started on slide one, Trace wandered in and sat at the far end. Sash looked over for a moment, then swung his attention back to Werner.

"So, I believe the last time your team was here, Dr. Kimura—"

Sash interjected, "Call me Sash. This title stuff will get old fast."

Werner shrugged agreeably and continued, "Sash. It seems that our other group never got beyond the initial coffee and pastries phase with your team. I am going to skip that and go into the product." He then took them through a much adapted version of how they had found the issues and flaws in the MIT studies, how they had gotten to where they were today. It was some great rewriting of history, and even Trace looked impressed as he listened.

At the end of slide thirty and the presentation, Sash said, "Very nice, Dr. Brandt, I—"

"Call me Werner."

"Werner. Okay. I see where you are going now far clearer than when we were here before. Intriguing stuff. Can you talk about how your side effects are impacting your progress? That seems to be one of the bigger issues we must understand as we delve deeper into what is going on here. I don't think we can try any more human trials until that is sorted out."

"It's being solved right now, Kimura." Both Sash and Werner looked at Trace, who was seated at the far end of the table.

Sash said, "Ah, Mr. Orbaugh. I am not sure one-liners are going to be adequate this time."

Werner closed his eyes, took a deep breath, then attempted to answer the question more technically. That obviously did not sit well with Trace, who started talking over Werner about market valuations and finances. Werner successively amped his volume, as did Trace. Sash tried to follow but started looking back and forth between the two men as the rest of his team began the same head rotation routine.

Finally, the words petered out from the two men. Sash, a wry expression on his face, said, "Not sure who won that debate, but this is not productive."

Werner nodded, saying, "Yes. Could you give Trace and I a moment?" Not waiting for an answer, Werner went down and started whispering in Trace's ear. Trace whispered back.

Werner figured out two things right off the bat. Trace had a waxy ear odor and severe booze breath. Along with that, the man was currently incapable of common sense and was in his normal early afternoon state of half shit-faced. Exasperated, Werner whispered, "Get the fuck out of here. You were not invited, Trace."

The fight was on. Trace did not leap to his feet, but he did manage to get up and shove Werner. Werner shoved back, landing Trace back in his chair. Trace struggled back to his feet again, got shoved back in his chair again. On the third attempt, Trace lunged at Werner, who stepped out of the way.

Trace's stomach struck the edge of the table, similar to his earlier escapade in London, which rotated him sideways and into a steep dive. This time, however, there was no hapless person to absorb the impact. He hit the tile floor on his side and his head took a bounce.

Werner tried to help him up. Dazed, Trace pushed him away and tried to get back up into his chair, which flipped over on top of him. He fell backwards, hitting his head. He was out.

Werner pulled out his phone and called the front desk, then Sally, for assistance.

Twenty minutes later, a crew of paramedics dutifully tried to get Trace loaded up on a gurney to take him to a hospital. It took quite a bit of doing. Then they had to improvise his tiedown to the gurney, as the standard straps were not long enough to wrap around him.

Once Trace was gone, Werner looked over at Sash, who was giggling with his team. Sash, seeing Werner looking at him, tried to wipe the smile off his face.

Werner said, "Um, sorry, shall we take a break and regroup?" He really had no clue what else to say. His whole plan for the day with the FDA had been derailed.

"Let's convene tomorrow morning, say nine o'clock. My folks can start going through some of this material this evening, review the presentation and hopefully, you can keep Mr. Orbaugh out of the mix."

Werner saw Sash's smile go cynical at the last part. And yes, he would certainly keep Trace out of the mix, even if they had to tie his ass up and shove him in a closet somewhere.

The FDA crew departed.

Keeping Trace out of the mix turned out to be easier than imagined, for a few days anyway. When he got to the hospital, the doctors determined he had a concussion and started the normal battery of tests. He woke up in the emergency room and tried to leave, but he was so dizzy, all he wound up doing was throwing up on the nurse.

Later, the on-call specialist came by and talked to Trace about his concussion, his high blood pressure, his type two diabetes, the ear infection that Werner had smelled earlier, his degraded liver function. As an aside, he added, "And that just for starters."

Trace had heard it all before except for the concussion part. "Don't worry your ass, Doc. I'll be fine." He then tried to stand up, became dizzy once again, and threw up what little was left in his stomach, the contents of which made a scribing arc and splashdown on the doctor's fresh scrubs.

Whereafter, he was admitted for observation. The next morning, he was lying in his bed when four large male nurses came by to help him to the bathroom. They gave up after a valiant struggle, and Trace got a catheter installed instead. Of course, that only addressed one end of waste management.

By day two, Trace was feeling better, very sober, and when a Christian guitar trio asked if they could play for him, he said sure, making a request for "Stairway to Heaven." They said they didn't know that one.

He asked them, "So what the fuck kinda Christians are you anyway?" The trio decided to leave.

Day three, he checked out in the late afternoon and called a limo service so he could get a ride back to his new Italian-styled villa on the Pacific coast.

Three days without Trace made Sash realize that most of the people at Pearly Whites were seriously trying to bring an interesting product to market. That they had gotten as far as they had based on the failed MIT study was kind of cool. Still, he was not passing out A's for effort, and his team continued to dig into the data.

Werner did introduce Billy to Sash, after coaching Billy not to talk about side effects, but to emphasize the great tooth aspect of things. Billy was reluctant until he got a twenty percent raise backdated two months and three hundred shares of immediately exercisable stock options. He sold them before the meeting and after the calculation of his option share price and the sale price that day, he made a quick twenty grand. He texted Jerome, who texted back, "About fucking time."

Sash was impressed with Billy's teeth and had him sent out for a dental checkup and a physical. Since Billy still worked out and was in good shape, he sailed through. No mention was made of the "limp dick" bug.

Chapter 31

On the Friday of Trace's return, a boardroom meeting was called for the usual suspects. Sally showed up again with her laptop and now had a fancy digital recording device attached to it. Billy arrived on the dot. Then Sam, Fiona, Bob and finally Werner trailed in.

A story had run about the "Limp Dick" bug in the *Los Angeles Herald* and was again making the tabloid rounds. Stock took another hit, the biggest so far.

Furious at first, Trace had been ready to fire Werner. However, SOS had been sending him regular updates, and absolutely nothing had gone out about the bug from either Werner or Sally. They had met with no one, they had called no one, they had not even talked about it amongst themselves on any recording SOS had provided. Trace realized he must be watching the wrong people.

He started with: "Brandt, these leaks are destroying us."

"No shit. Everybody in this room has a vested interest, so who would be motivated to tank this whole effort?"

"Good question. Who knows whats going on besides the people in this room?"

"All the other scientists. They might talk to their spouse, a close relative. They might have been overheard in the cafeteria. I mean, who knows?"

Trace sighed. "Then everybody needs a security enema. SOS is going to run a background on all of us to see where this shit is coming from. Has to be somebody with deep insider knowledge. Their suggestion is we start by filling out forms about people we associate with. I already did mine."

Werner said, "Great. Can I see your list, so I know who to avoid in the future?"

Trace glared at him.

Sam, Fiona, and Bob listened without comment. Billy, however, had his hand in the air, waving it around.

Werner sighed. "Yes, Billy?"

"Do we have a fix for Limp Dick? I have been very patient and have kept very quiet."

Werner laughed, "Yep, very quiet and very well paid for it. But we need an update. Sam?"

Sam, stoic, thumped a fist on the table, "We must focus on the enemy. Treason is without honor." Trace and Werner both raised an eyebrow but did not comment. Sam continued, "I just sent the modified DNA sequence to Fiona." She nodded but was avoiding any eye contact with the others in the room.

"It should be ready by tomorrow."

Billy looked elated, and the news buoyed the entire group.

Werner said, "I still think we all need to be present for this … upgrade." Everyone agreed.

The following afternoon, the group converged in the lab. This time Billy got what looked like a pretty normal injection. None of the usual immediate side effects of screams and head lolling.

Trace asked, "How long before the man can get a hard-on?"

Everybody gaped at him, but he continued, "Get some gay porn up on that computer of yours, Sally. We need to see results."

Sally seemed interested, but the others not so much. They left the room. After she had followed Billy's tip on some links, she rolled her chair over so he could watch. He gave her a quizzical look as the scantily clad male studs appeared, and she said, "Well, it is my computer."

Werner stuck his head in the room and said, "Out here, Sally. Come on." She sighed, but complied, giving Billy a parting grin.

Sally was not to be disappointed, however, as Billy, in his excitement over his return to full service, came running out in the corridor, whooping, still aroused. Sally got the eyeful she had been hoping for. Fiona was also impressed, but the men just ordered him to go back in the room.

Once all the excitement died down, Fiona and Sam kept an eye on a now recovered and covered Billy for an hour, then sent him home. The others congratulated each other on all the hard work and then they drifted away. Sally, making sure she was not being observed, saved the links Billy had left up on her computer.

Monday morning, Sash met with Werner and said, "I hope you understand, we need some more field trials of volunteers if this all works out. Have you a list of volunteers?"

Werner nodded. "We've got a hundred subjects we can work with."

"How soon can you be at the capacity of production needed for this?"

"We can handle that with the lab gear for now."

Later that morning, Trace met with Werner to discuss the next steps. While they were sitting there, discussing how the stock was on a mild rebound, both their phones rang just seconds apart.

Apparently, both men were listed as emergency contacts on a Billy Fuller's phone. The Santa De Lola police department was calling to advise them that Billy was in the hospital after what appeared to be a suicide attempt on his part. When Werner asked what happened, he was informed that Billy had rammed his car into the side of a Santa De Lola passenger bus.

The Sunday evening before the bus spearing, Billy was becoming concerned that he was having another side effect, even though this fix had left his vital equipment alone. His latest issue started with what felt like a severe cramp in his calf. His muscles locked up in his right leg the first time while he and Jerome were celebrating his recovery and going at it in the bedroom. They had to stop and have Jerome massage it out. Monday morning, it happened again while making coffee in their kitchen, but this time it was up in his thigh muscle and more intense. Same result, the muscles locked up, and again, Jerome massaged it out. He figured he'd talk to Sam and the gang later since, more than ever, he really preferred not talking to anyone from Pearly Whites while he was off work.

Later that morning, he felt fine. Showered, shaved, spiked up hair. He gave Jerome a kiss goodbye, who was busy packing to go visit his stepsister down in Piss Ant, Mississippi, or whatever burg his partner had mentioned.

In the garage, Billy thought the Pinto looked surprisingly good. He had used part of his stock sale cash to have the car serviced and a detail job done front to back. He climbed in, it fired right up with the usual puff of burnt-oil smoke, and he was off into traffic, polluting the air of Santa De Lola.

A traffic light he was approaching changed first to yellow, then to red. He was on a street not heavily traveled, so he let off the gas. He was about to switch to the brakes when his right leg cramped, causing him to draw his foot nearly to the front of the driver's seat. He was still coasting about twenty miles an hour, the light still red. Panicking, he groaned and stretched his leg as hard as he could, and it let loose like a broken rubber band. But instead of the brake pedal, he hit the gas, and now his leg locked in full extension. He zoomed through the first intersection, careening about to avoid the cross traffic that honked at him and almost hit an old woman walking a corgi. The woman yelled and flipped him off as her corgi let out an offended bark.

The Pinto had achieved almost forty miles an hour by the time he reached the next red light. The old clunker was far from a dragster and, with the heavily worn engine, was spewing a rocket-like smoke trail. He started honking the horn at pedestrians in the crosswalk, who hurled themselves sideways out of his path. At that same moment, a bus entered the intersection, directly in front of him. He did manage to get his left foot on the brake, but the Ford Pinto was never known for stopping on a dime, especially with the engine floored.

Billy woke up in an ambulance on the way to the emergency room. The paramedic told him his right leg was broken below the knee, but likely that same leg had kept him from being pitched into the windshield. Before he fell back into unconsciousness, all he could think was, *Why the fuck did I ever take a job at this company?*

Waking in the emergency room as he was being rolled into surgery to repair a compound fracture in his lower leg. He was quite woozy at this point. He saw a vague outline of a Black man and knew somehow Sam had come to help him. He spilled out the news about the latest side effect, begged for his old teeth back and stated he was sorry how he had accepted Werner's bribe so he would not talk about all the problems he had suffered because of Pearly Whites.

Dr. Gleason, the attending physician that Billy was actually talking to, had heard plenty of babbling from injured patients in the past, so he mostly ignored what the patient was saying until they reached the surgery center. At that point the anesthesiologist exclaimed, "Wow, look at these front teeth!"

Two nurses and Dr. Gleason looked in Billy's mouth. They noted the four perfect top front teeth and all the other very grey ones. Filing away in his memory what the patient had said earlier, he then returned his concentration to the matter at hand. After the surgery, which was uneventful, the ER check-in desk rang him to say a Dr. Werner Brandt and a short, obnoxious fat man were inquiring about the patient whose leg he had just knitted back together. He spoke briefly on the phone with Dr. Brandt, letting him know Billy would make a full recovery.

A knock on his open door pulled him away from the notes he was typing into Billy's hospital record. It was Dr. Borders, a staff psychiatrist. He waved her on in. She sat down, and said, "Hey, Byron, I got pulled in a few minutes ago about Billy Fuller. The Police report said he rammed a passenger bus. Did you talk to him before or since the surgery? The cops are headed over, and I need to meet them in Mr. Fuller's room."

"Not really a conversation, but the man was babbling some weird stuff to me on the way to surgery." He then related the details. Dr. Borders took some notes, thanked him, then headed off toward Billy's room up on the sixth floor.

Werner arrived at Billy's room a moment before Dr. Borders. Trace had sidetracked to the cafeteria for some pastries, saying he was feeling peckish, but was on his way.

Billy was just regaining consciousness. A nurse was monitoring him and indicated Werner should take a seat over by the window.

Dr. Borders walked over to the nurse, and after conferring with her, shifted her attention to Werner.

Introductions were made, and when he gave his name, he noticed Dr. Borders taking a look at some notes she had written on a clipboard. For her part, she noticed Werner leaning forward a bit to try and read them, so she leaned the clipboard back to her chest. She gave him a brief smile. "Dr. Brandt, the patient here, Billy Fuller. He works for your company?"

Werner nodded in the affirmative.

"Has he been depressed or sad?"

Werner shook his head no.

"Recent life-changing event?"

Again, a no shake.

"Suicidal comments or anger issues?"

Again, a no shake.

"Anything you can tell me, then?"

"He's gay, if that helps."

"I don't believe that is relevant, Doctor."

Trace rolled in, a bag of pastries in his left hand, a croissant in the right. Ignoring Dr. Borders, he waddled over to look at Billy while taking a bite.

The nurse said, "Sir, sorry, please don't drop crumbs from your mouth on the patient."

Trace looked annoyed at the request, but he could not flip the nurse off as his hands were full, and could not insult her, as his mouth was full.

Dr. Borders was fascinated by this display. The man reminded her of her thesis subject of a chimpanzee she tried to work with in a language experiment. Trace squinted back, still trying to get the last of the croissant swallowed, and finally said, "You the doc that worked on Billy? When can we get him out of this dump?"

Dr. Borders smiled briefly, then said, "Actually, I am not the doctor that did the surgery. I am a psychiatrist assigned to this case, based on the police report we are assisting with about Mr. Fuller."

"Ah, a shrink. Great, just what Billy needs." Trace looked at Werner and continued, "You got the ambulance on the way?" Werner nodded. Trace continued, "Sorry, uh, Doc, we don't need you. We have a private staff on the way to take care of Billy here."

A police officer appeared at the door with a detective. The detective stepped in, showed a badge, and introduced himself as Sergeant Friday.

Sergeant Friday nodded to Dr. Borders, who nodded back. He looked over at Trace and Werner and said, "Guys, please step out of the room with Officer Taylor here. Need to talk to the doctor, then we can catch up."

Trace asked, "Why do we have to leave the room?"

"Well, usually I don't conduct my police investigations in front of an audience. I have no idea who you are. Mr. Fuller here was in a very odd collision with a passenger bus. Who knows? He may be charged with a crime, sent to the nut house, whatever, but until I do my job, we won't know. Or perhaps you would like to accompany me back to the precinct so we can discuss police procedure?"

Werner said, "We get your drift, detective. Trace, come on."

Trace grumped, "Okay, detective, we'll go for now. But we got lawyers." Sergeant Friday looked like he was about to laugh as the two trailed out into the corridor. The detective shut the door behind them.

Dr. Borders then gave a briefing. They went over to the bed, where a groggy Billy was laid out. The detective said, "Mr. Fuller, Sergeant Friday here. Can you talk?"

Billy opened his eyes. "Um, yep, I can still talk. I feel strange. You know. Drugs. I don't take drugs most the time. Usually just whisky, beer. Hey, why am I here? Where is here?"

"Mr. Fuller, you were in an accident. Do you remember that?"

"It was no accident, Sergeant. My right leg got stuck on the accelerator. Is the Pinto okay?"

"Got stuck?"

"Yep, since the injection that I got on Saturday, my leg has been cramping like crazy off and on."

"So, a leg cramp caused this accident?"

"What accident?"

"Let's talk later, Mr. Fuller."

"Sure, sure. I need to get to work anyway. I have been getting muscle cramps since Saturday in my right leg. The shot fixed my impotence, but now these darn cramps."

"You got a shot for impotence and that causes leg cramps?"

"Yep, and before that, I had a full-time boner that the other shot relieved. Then there were the toenails. All because of my teeth."

"Teeth?"

"Yep. I had four of them replaced at work."

"And that's at Pearly Whites?"

"Yep. And I just got a raise."

Eyebrows now fully raised, the detective said, "Okay, Mr. Fuller. I may have what I need here, who knows? Oh, and that Pinto is totaled. Looks like a crushed avocado."

Billy started weeping, then nodded off. The nurse checked his vitals and said he was okay.

Sergeant Friday looked at Dr. Borders. She said, "Same story he gave in a babbling manner to Dr. Gleason before the surgery to fix his compound fracture."

Sergeant Friday said, "Seems he is still babbling."

Billy suddenly screamed in pain, making everyone standing near him jump. His right leg was locking back out like he said it had done in the Pinto, and Billy's arms fully extended, sweeping from side to side like he was trying to steer a car. Dr. Borders stared at the spectacle, then ordered a shot that knocked Billy out along with a nerve block for the leg.

Once all that was done, Sergeant Friday said, "Shit. Looks like the man is telling some version of the truth. Wonder why he just didn't put his car in neutral?" Dr. Borders shrugged, and he said, "Oh well."

The detective went out in the hallway and told Werner they could have Billy back. No charges would be filed for the moment, but he would have to come by and talk about the teeth issue Billy had mentioned to make sure his report was accurate.

Werner and Trace nodded in unison, and the police officers left.

Trace said, "That copper ain't getting shit out of us." Werner nodded in agreement.

The private ambulance arrived. Billy was promptly loaded up and taken over to Pearly Whites headquarters, where a makeshift hospital room had been set up in a third-floor conference room to hide the current debacle from Sash and company. A short time later, a private doctor and crew of nurses that had contracted with SOS arrived to monitor the patient.

That night on the local news, the police beat reporter covered the bus ramming by a 1971 Ford Pinto while the station played a phone video an eyewitness had provided of the collision. The reporter stood in front of the Santa De Lola police department, interviewing Sergeant Friday, who stated that something very odd had happened to the driver prior to the accident, possibly at his workplace, Pearly Whites, and that the police department would be continuing the investigation. The detective also mentioned that the company had sent a private ambulance to remove the driver to an undisclosed location.

The evening of the bus-ramming incident, Liz was dozing, nuzzled against Frieda's stomach after their midafternoon swim/sex session, when she got a call from Carson at the *Los Angeles Herald.*

Carson asked, "Liz, did you see the latest story?"

"Nope, been out—uh, yeah, doing foundation work with Frieda. What happened?"

Carson said, "I don't know much, but looks like Billy Fuller rammed a city bus with his Pinto."

Liz grinned. "Got it. Yep, let's get something international going."

Carson said, "It'll take just a little push."

Frieda had been listening as Liz had the phone on speaker. She was already getting dressed, so Liz hurried to catch up. Chef had New York strips on the grill and two bottles of Chateau Latour ready to go.

Liz said, "We need an encrypted call with Sam and Fiona, so we know this new problem with his leg freezing up is the bug we all discussed. This is better than anything we could have cooked up ourselves."

Chapter 32

The morning after Billy rode his bucking Pinto into the side of the bus, a story ran in the *Los Angeles Herald* about the incident, from the moment of impact to when the detective showed up at the hospital.

Sash arrived at a quarter till nine at PQ, as he was now calling Pearly Whites headquarters. He had tried several other acronyms with his team, but they decided this one was the most descriptive, because you could say you were headed out to "puke" and everybody knew what you were talking about.

He noted all the reporters and camera operators held back at the security station, properly observing the line drawn by the contract bikers. A couple of news helicopters flew overhead, not observing any security line, let alone FAA regulations on minimum altitudes, making low passes with cameramen hanging out on the skids to gather footage.

One resourceful young female cub reporter for a small online news publication—HacknFlashnnews.com—had neither a camera, an operator nor a helicopter budget. She flew her personal drone around to gather her own footage. At one point, the drone hovered outside the boardroom. Trace came to the window and flipped the intruder off. That bit of video went viral on the Internet, raising recognition for the website, and actually drove some ad revenue as well.

However, when the drone was on its final approach to its owner, one of the bikers hired to intimidate the news folks mortally wounded it with a pellet gun, sending it careening into Trace's BMW, cracking the front windshield. That somehow actuated the automated driver door/seat combo to extend and retract repeatedly, along with setting off the vehicle's alarm system.

Sonny, in his new role as the head of security, was alerted. On checking out the situation, he dutifully reported the mechanical sideshow to the front desk, He then attempted to cordon off the vehicle to keep someone from accidentally walking into the now squeaking driver's door as the low-cost specialty bearings used to hinge the door had crapped out.

The front desk notified Trace. He came steaming out at a determined slog and started cussing and kicking the side of the BMW, then stomped the drone to pieces. It was all caught on video by a helicopter camerawoman, and again, that video went viral on the Internet.

Sash caught up with Trace, who was walking away from his car, which was now shrieking more quietly as the battery was going dead. They walked into the lobby side by side, though Trace was breathing heavily from his assault on his vehicle and the trashing of the drone.

Trace was not in a talkative mood, but Sash was, having received an anonymous text that morning that Billy was laid up on the third floor of Pearly Whites headquarters.

He said, "Who modified that car for you? I mean, those bearings are squeaking like a mofo."

No response. Sash decided to try an old ploy.

"Hey, Trace, what the heck happened yesterday with that Pronto?"

Trace looked askance at Sash. "You mean Pinto?"

Sash smiled. "So, you heard about it. Is Billy all right?"

A long pause, then, "Yeah, fine."

"Can I talk to him?"

Trace turned to face Sash. "Why?"

"Well, the news said the police department thought it had something to do with Billy's tooth insertions. I know that sounds crazy, but we live in a crazy world these days."

"Uh-huh."

"So can I see him?"

"He's not here. Offsite. Taking some time off."

Sash noted that Trace had involuntarily glanced at the upper floors of the building when he answered. Sash said, "I see. Well, we do need to talk to him soon. You know, to get that rumor quashed." He then decided for the time being to not push the matter further with "Grumperman," another nickname the FDA team had come up with.

Trace, already disengaged from the conversation, headed off while Sash signed in with the front desk receptionist, got his pass, then went to the elevators.

Stepping in, he took his best guess and pushed the button for the third floor. Nothing. He pushed the button for the second floor, the door closed, and the elevator started going up. He hit the button again for the third—still nothing. It would not even light up, which raised his confidence that he was on to some mischief.

Once on the second, he walked down to the far north-end stairwell, used for the emergency fire exit. There he found a newly installed security door pad that required a code to open the door. He grinned, thinking this would also be a code violation with city building ordinances. After all, what good was an emergency exit if you needed a pass code to activate it?

Going back down to the conference room on the south end, he glanced at the fire exit door and saw the same thing: a touchpad requiring a code for exit. He entered the conference room and dropped off his notebook bag. Three of his people were meeting with Fiona, the lead scientist, running over some documentation. They exchanged morning pleasantries and then got underway.

Detective Sergeant Friday rolled up to the security gate at Pearly Whites in his relatively new, for a police vehicle, high-mileage unmarked Ford SUV. It was his first visit to the facility, and surveying the scene, he decided it was like going to a low-budget carnival.

First were the swarms of reporters and camera operators from everywhere. Besides the California locals, there were several East Coast groups, England, and oddly enough, one from New Zealand. The press had set up large portable awnings and umbrellas with fold-out chairs and tables to get through the heat of the day.

Across from them were the bikers. He recognized some of them and waved, since he had arrested more than a few of them on different occasions for drugs, pimping sex workers and the usual stuff dirtbag bikers did. The bikers did not wave back.

The latest addition to the show—food trucks. There was one for Mexican, one for BBQ and one for Chinese. They too had deployed little tables and chairs with pop-up umbrellas and were doing a steady business. Not only reporters and bikers were getting in line for the daily specials. The staff of Pearly Whites, sick of the grade-school quality cuisine in the corporate cafeteria, made up a sizeable contingent.

He showed his badge to the gate guard, who called reception, who called Werner and Trace, who argued about what to do. Werner won out with: "It's the cops. Let's not make them any more suspicious that they already are."

The gate guard told the detective to proceed, and he parked along the curb by the lobby door. Sonny came out to tell him he could not park there, until he recognized Sergeant Friday, who had arrested some of his friends for illicit drug dealing. Since Sonny also had a couple outstanding warrants for failure to appear on traffic citations, he reversed course, disappearing around the corner.

In the lobby, Sergeant Friday waited for Bob, who had been contacted by Trace to escort the "copper" to the boardroom. Bob had become the new "Billy," now that his secretary was being kept out of sight to hide all the side effects of "tooth-or-consequences," Sam's latest nickname for the bus ramming fiasco. Trace also had Bob running for sandwiches and had left written instructions to get "that fucking BMW piece of shit" towed back to the dealer for repairs. Thoroughly stressed, Bob had taken a Valium ten minutes earlier to reinforce the two large shots of whisky he had drunk in his car before work that morning.

Sergeant Friday watched Bob approach, wondering if the man had an inner ear problem or, more likely, was intoxicated. He had seen a lot of drunk people over the years, and walking in a straight line was one of the more telling symptoms of a lack of sobriety. He shook Bob's hand and smelled a bit of booze. He decided it was not his problem, as being drunk at work did not fall under any criminal statute that he was aware of.

After a brief exchange of "mornings," Bob pivoted and said, "Follow me, detective." Sergeant Friday's beeline beat Bob's weaving path to the elevator door by at least two seconds. There they were met by Sash, who had been looking out a second floor window, recognized the detective from the news the night before and swiftly gotten back on the elevator and down to the lobby just in time for the detective's arrival.

Bob said, "Morning, Sash."

Sash said, "Morning, Bob. Who's your friend here? I'm Sash Kimura with the FDA, part of the team accessing the tooth technology they developed here." He stuck out his hand.

Sergeant Friday raised his eyebrows. "Wow. That's cool. Sergeant Friday. I'm a detective with the Santa De Lola PD." The elevator doors closed, and when Sash did not hit his button, Bob hit four. Then Sash said, "Oh, shoot. I meant to hit two."

Bob shrugged. "You can catch it on the rebound."

Sash smiled and thanked him.

When they arrived at the fourth floor, Sash said he had to go use the bathroom and headed down the hall.

Bob waved goodbye to the man, dropped Sergeant Friday off at the boardroom door, then went to his office to call Lipshultz BMW to arrange a tow.

In the boardroom, Sergeant Friday saw Werner Brandt in some fancy-schmancy suit. To his left was Trace, still sweating after the car-kicking, drone-stomping morning he had already had. He wondered if this was going to be a repeat of their performance of "good cop/bad cop" at the hospital.

He decided to find out. First, he walked over to Werner and shook his hand. The handshake was limp. Sergeant Friday added "wimp" in his mental notes. He then went over to shake hands with Trace, who picked up a sandwich and started eating, saying around mouthfuls that he could not shake hands and eat at the same time. Sergeant Friday noted "asshole" for that entry.

He got right to the point. "Where's Billy Fuller? Why did you pull him out of the hospital? You both know, that really looks like you were trying to hide something about this technology of yours."

Werner looked away with an anxious expression. Trace doubled down on his consumption of the pastrami/provolone on marbled rye, forgetting his mustard.

With no reply from the apparently guilty, Sergeant Friday said, "Well?"

Trace held up a finger and seemed to be formulating a reply. Finally, he said, "I'm afraid you will have to sign a nondisclosure agreement for us to tell you anything else. Sorry, Detective, you know, trade secrets and all."

This statement was what Werner and he had argued about just before the arrival of the "copper." Werner thought it would make the detective more determined. Trace argued stonewalling was the best course.

Sergeant Friday cracked a wry smile. "I see. So, nondisclosure. Hmmm. I think I would prefer a warrant to search the premises and for you two to make a little trip down to the precinct, where we can have disclosed discussions in a hot interrogation room and then inspect some jail cells that I can reserve just for you two. And guess what else? I can give you a ride in my car, handcuffed of course, for your safety." He opened the boardroom door for them and looked back expectantly. He added, "I can have all the help I need here in about ten minutes, or you can get your asses moving."

Werner's expression shifted to alarm. Even Trace blanched. Both wanted to avoid their first "in custody" event.

Werner said, "Detective, could we please start over? What do you want to know? There is no need for hot little interrogation rooms. We just need some discretion on your part so we don't wind up back in the news."

Sergeant Friday nodded. He knew he had their asses.

With a big sigh Werner admitted the truth about the current genetic bug that appeared to cause the accident. That was followed by a tour of the third floor to visit Billy, who was no longer sedated, but was getting frequent shots for a nerve block to keep his leg from contorting.

At the end of the saga, Sergeant Friday said, "Okay, I have what I need. Listen, we're not out to get you people. But I think you might be hearing from the city attorney about getting that bus fixed. Other than that, I consider this case closed."

He could see that both Werner and Trace visibly relaxed. Trace said, "Hell, we'll buy the city a new bus. No problem."

Sergeant Friday nodded, expressionless, and said, "Well, have a swell day. If I need anything else, I'll let you know."

After the detective was out of earshot, Trace looked at Werner, shaking his head "Fuck if I know where money for a bus would come from."

Werner looked surprised. "Why would you say that if there is a problem?"

Exasperated, Trace said, "It just came out! Hell, I was informed this morning via email that Gramps has officially cut us off financially. That leaves us with about six weeks of cash remaining from our bank loan to finance this flaming turd. The foundation seems to have abandoned sending funds as well. Plus, we got extra money flowing out for security, as well as Billy's medical bills. We may need to do a round of layoffs."

Werner felt his stomach hit the floor. "So, Martin has tied off the purse strings. Trace, we can't lay anyone off. If we do, that just feeds the media speculation, which feeds the negative market speculation, which further fucks us out of our money."

"Jeez, thanks for the pep talk, Werner. So, what do you suggest?"

"Use some of the money that came in from the IPO."

"Dude, we spent it already."

"Shit! All of it?"

"The account balance is ten bucks, but hey, do I look like a bookkeeper?"

Werner shrugged to himself. At least he was financially in excellent shape. He had gotten a large chunk of his stock sold at the peak, and the money was drawing quite a bit of interest with his offshore account. He figured he could live out his life as a mid-tier multimillionaire. However, his greed kicked in—he could make more money if they could sort this last problem out. So, no reason to give up just yet.

They both heard the elevator ring in the corridor. Werner went to the door and looked out as the elevator shut. He could hear the hum as it descended. With a shrug, he decided the detective had probably gone to the bathroom before departing. He then told Trace he would talk to him later and went to his office. He wanted to take Sally to lunch. He had decided they should talk about something really important. He felt his heart flutter at the thought.

Werner had been partially right about the detective's delayed departure from the boardroom. Sash had earlier hidden in an alcove in the corridor, and while he had not been able to hear everything, he had the gist of the conversation about the company's money problems, Billy's accident, and something about failed fixes. That part had been hard to understand from where he had been positioned.

While hiding in a toilet stall, Sash was stewing about his next move. The door to the bathroom opened, and Sergeant Friday entered to relieve himself after the meeting with Werner and Trace. Sash flushed the toilet, then stepped out, making a show of washing his hands. A couple of moments later, the two men were on the elevator. Sash exited at the second floor.

Back in the conference room with his team, he wanted some hard specifics on problems, but realized that with this company, such detail was not going to be forthcoming. And that made him more determined to root out the mischief.

Chapter 33

Liz and Frieda, for lack of anything else to do, had taken to mowing their condo yard themselves, each with their own brand-new, self-propelled push mower. It was a warm sunny day, so both women were down to cutoff jeans, bikini tops and tennis shoes.

Shutting off her mower, since her half of the yard was done, Liz noticed an older-model bright blue Camaro parked half a block down and across the street, engine idling, windows up. It had some oversize wheels on it. Between the attention-getting color and the wheels, she thought, *Peacock struttin' its stuff?*

Frieda, following her gaze, shut off her mower and walked over to confer.

Liz said, "That car looks damn ridiculous."

"I agree. Kind of like Bob's 'Vette. Men are tasteless, I tell you that." She paused, then continued, "You know what? I have seen that car before."

Frieda's comment piqued Liz's curiosity and she asked, "When?"

"I think I've seen it multiple times around here. Wonder what the hell's up with that?"

"Should we inquire with said driver?"

"Nah, let's go for a swim. I'm overheated."

Liz said, "You're certainly hot-looking anyway!" They kissed, then headed back through the kitchen, leaving instructions for Langley to finish up the front yard and return the mowers to the garage.

Across the street, sixty-eight-year-old retired cop Hector Ramirez, uncle of Rose Ramirez, had won the assignment, if one could call it winning, for keeping eyes on Bob Oppenheimer's contacts, mostly because his bid for the job was so cheap. Rose had provided the peacock car he currently sat in for this mission. It was equipped with Wi-Fi extenders and scanners meant to capture conversations, break encryptions and grab passwords, with the intent that he would tap into Bob's home network, computers, whatever. But Hector was old school and totally tech impaired, so he had no interest in that. He had stuck with visual surveillance since the first day he started the assignment.

He was content to watch the three young women that spent most of their time together scantily clad. They were either going out jogging or doing scandalous things like kissing each other in the front yard. He supposed he could report that, but he considered himself open-minded, even for his age. Plus, for what he was getting paid on this gig, he was adding voyeurism via the telephoto lens on his camera as a bonus. Now that, he believed, was gathering information.

FBI Agent Jade Miller arrived at Pearly Whites just as Sergeant Friday was departing. She was angry at having been called in from her vacation to conduct an initial interview with Werner Brandt. He had made a suspiciously large stock sale that had alerted the SEC to possible inside trading. It was large enough, as far as millions of dollars went, to get pushed over to the DOJ. From there, shit rolled downhill. Her boss, Special Agent Salton, had called her back to work from her leave for this assignment. The deal she struck with Salton was she'd merely commit to this interview. If nothing was up, she could go back on leave.

She parked out front, and a nervous, heavily tattooed man in a security guard uniform with a name badge that read "Sonny" approached, advising she could not park there. She pulled out her FBI badge and ID from her purse. Wide-eyed, the guard said she was fine and abruptly reversed course, skittering around a corner and out of sight.

At the front desk, Agent Miller identified herself and asked for Werner Brandt. The receptionist called the man's office and got no answer, then called Trace, who started cursing so loudly, Agent Miller could hear him as the receptionist was holding the phone away from her ear. Finally, after what seemed like an eternity of profanity, she heard, "Send the copper up to the boardroom."

With an official Pearly Whites pass in hand, badge in pocket, attitude in the deep negative, Agent Miller headed for the elevator.

Trace had braced his battered ego for what was coming next with a couple of quickly downed shots of whisky. Shit was so sideways and today was no exception.

For his consideration—first the stock price sliding into oblivion as each problem got broadcast to the world. Each issue accelerated the process, with project "Limp Dick" (as he had started calling it) being the latest. Then the local constabulary had started crawling up Pearly Whites's rear. And now the fucking FBI? What was a poor corrupt capitalist like himself supposed to do?

His ruminations were interrupted by a knock from the proximity of the boardroom doorway. He said, "Uh, come on in." He said it in as nice but as neutral a tone as he could muster.

An exceptionally good-looking Black woman came through the door. Trace abruptly perked up and smiled. "Welcome! Can I get you a drink?"

The woman gave him a brief smirk, then said, "Agent Miller with the FBI. Are you Dr. Werner Brandt?"

Stunned, he thought, *this babe is an FBI agent?* He was immediately felt off balance. Not uncommon for him after a few Macallans, but this was a different sort of off balance. AKA, a copper that looked like a runway model.

"How can I help, Agent Miller?" He tried to restrain his ogling.

"Well, by answering my first question and identifying yourself."

"Ah, yes. Chauncey Orbaugh… the third. Just call me Trace."

"Fine, then." She scribbled in a pocket notepad that magically appeared but might have been in her hand the whole time. Who knew? She was too gorgeous to pay attention to minutiae. She continued, "How do you spell that? Like the Spanish "t-r-e-s"?"

He briefly felt like he was having some regressive déjà vu experience of how he had first gotten his nickname, but haltingly spelled out "t-r-a-c-e."

The agent closed the notepad. She said, "So, is Dr Brandt here today?"

He decided to answer a question with a question. "May I inquire why you need to talk to our CEO?" Maybe that would intimidate her, and then he could ask her out on a date.

Again, the cynical flicker of a smile, "No, you may not. This is FBI business, or at least that was why I thought I was dispatched. Is he here or not, Mr. Orbaugh?"

"Um, no. He's … on a sabbatical in … Sicily. Won't be back for… a couple weeks."

For some weird ass reason, the agent showed a sudden look of relief as she absorbed his stumbling lie. She said, "Well, Mr. Orbaugh, I won't take any more of your time. Thank you."

He wanted to walk her down to the lobby, but she waved off his offer. So instead, he simply said, "Hope to see you again soon!"

When Agent Miller arrived at her car, she called her boss, gave him the update on two weeks in Sicily, which she never believed for a second, but, hey, she wanted to get back to her vacation, and it wasn't like Werner Brandt was going to flee the country or anything. She got home, changed into what one could only call an outfit so minimal that she slipped on a knee-length bathrobe over it before she left the house, then headed back to meet her hot new French boyfriend, Jean-André, for the photo shoot they had signed up for online two months back.

After a champagne-infused lunch in a private room at the Bristol Bistro, followed by an extensive petting and necking session after he asked her if she wanted to move in with him, Werner dropped Sally at her car and said, "Take the rest the day off. See you at my place for our first big dinner." Lipstick smeared, moderately drunk, Sally meandered to her car and waved goodbye.

He headed up to the lab, where Sam and Fiona were running through genetic and mathematical permutations of solutions on a recently installed blackboard. A white board had been shoved aside as inadequate. Chalk dust was everywhere as they wrote and erased, ad infinitum. All to fix the new bug afflicting Billy, code named, "Camp Cramp Crap." It was a tongue twister, for sure.

When he inquired on their progress, he got a serious negative headshake from both of them before they returned to their annihilation of chalk. After a half hour of trying to follow their methodology and inhaling a lot of chalk dust, he headed back to his Pacific Coast estate. On the way, he called Sally. "You still comfortable with moving in? I know I probably surprised you at lunch, telling you how much I cared about you."

Sally came right back. "I love the idea, Werner. I guess we both knew something has been brewing between us for months."

"Fantastic. I have flown in Chef Gaspard from New York City, and he is preparing the meal."

"Gaspard? Can't wait!"

She arrived with a stuffed bag of clothes until she could transfer more of her personal items, because she never left the estate that night. Or ever again over the next month. Unless it was to go to work, which they began doing more remotely and often while one was on top of the other in their new primary bedroom.

Chapter 34

Billy set his phone on his hospital bed after talking to Jerome, assuring his partner that he was all right and to just enjoy his visit with his stepsister in Mississippi. Werner, Sam, Bob, Trace and Fiona were all sitting in conference room chairs around his bed, listening.

With the call over, Werner said, "Billy, how are you feeling? Leg any better?"

Billy frowned. "Well, I don't know. The only thing saving me from screaming is the nerve-block injections. At least that keeps my leg from trying to break itself again." Billy then gave pointed looks at both Sam and Fiona.

They shrugged off the comment. Sam said, "You must bear your pain. We are close to having our honor impugned here, so I would be careful if I were you." He glared at Billy, who glowered back.

Werner sighed. "So Sam, Fiona, where are we at on a fix?"

Sam said, "Well, we have tried a lot of different stuff out in simulation."

Werner rolled his eyes, shifted his gaze to Fiona. She remained silent.

He prompted her, "Fiona, it's your turn."

She looked up, nearly in tears. "I'm so sorry for this. I thought we had your problem figured out, and we nearly killed you, destroyed that precious little car of yours, and then there's the bu-bu-bus. This is not a normal situation for me." She started sobbing.

Everybody watching her, including Billy, rolled their eyes. Trace said, "Is she for real?"

Sam said, "She's sensitive, goddamn it!" Fiona dabbed her eyes, but it seemed they were dry. Nobody appeared to notice or care.

Billy, with a determined expression, declared, "So this little experiment is over. I want these things removed!"

Trace, sounding panicked, said, "Whoa, partner, whoa! Remove your new teeth? I mean, do you want to look like a toothless old hag? Shit, man, give it some thought."

Billy sneered, "Is it about the stock price, fatty?"

Everybody stared at Billy. This was not like him to be assertive, let alone insulting.

Trace flushed, obviously mad, but stayed silent.

Billy continued, "I want these teeth out. I want traditional implants. I want another fucking raise and I want fifteen thousand in cash."

Trace detonated, "Oh sure, make it sixteen thousand. How about we get you a mouth transplant? How about—"

Werner cut in, "Trace, hang on. Billy, we can do the raise, say, another twenty percent. Teeth removed? Okay, but we need a nondisclosure signed. How about some more stock instead of cash?"

Billy defiantly shook his head. "I would lose money before I could even get it sold. Hey, I got that same app on my phone you guys use. So, it's cash or I squeal to the press. And now I want seventeen thousand for the way Trace just talked to me."

Trace said, "Fuck you!"

Billy said, "Twenty thousand!"

"Fucking dickwad!"

"Twenty-five thousand!"

"Dipshit!"

"An even thirty thousand!"

Werner jumped in, "Hold it the fuck up, Trace! Okay, Billy, thirty thousand. Do we have a deal?"

Billy said, "Will removing the teeth fix my current problem?"

All eyes turned to Sam and Fiona. They nodded in the affirmative.

Billy said, "Get that dentist in here and cash in my account today. I want out of here and my new implants in before Jerome heads back."

Werner was in his office, making out with Sally, when his phone rang. Glancing at it, he saw it was Billy. He looked at his new love, then said, "Shit, it's Billy. I gotta take this."

Billy started the conversation with a pronounced lisp, "Werner, I jush wanna shay thosh genetic implansh are outh."

Sally was now watching Werner, making goofy faces that showed her top front teeth to make him laugh.

"Ah, good, good for you. Everything okay, then?"

"I'm shwell! Doc shays I need a bit of time before the new implansh are ready. They are ushing the old onesh to make cashtingsh from them. And my leg hash shtopped shpasming."

"Ah, good, good. Anything else?"

"No, ah you have a shwell day," and he hung up.

Werner giggled at her silliness. He put down his phone and pulled Sally back to him to pick up where they left off. She giggled back and slapped his rear, saying "Giddy up!"

Chapter 35

A week passed before Werner finally checked his messages on his desk phone, having been preoccupied with his personal activities involving Sally, both at the office and his estate.

He listened to the voicemail from reception that an Agent Miller from the FBI was in the lobby. The time stamp of the message: the day he had taken Sally to lunch. With trepidation he called the receptionist. She explained she had called Trace when Werner was unavailable. "Mr. Orbaugh cussed a lot, then had Agent Miller sent to the boardroom."

Werner said, "Okay, thanks. Bye." He hung up the phone and went to the door to the outer office. He then remembered that Sally was gone with his credit card, out buying a new wardrobe, and then was going to stop to look at an Italian sports car—he could not remember if it was a Ferrari or Lamborghini.

He headed for the boardroom, where he found Trace staring pitifully at a sandwich, of which the man had not taken a single bite.

Werner said, "Trace, when were you going to mention the FBI came by to talk to me?"

"FBI. Oh, fuck, yes. What a gorgeous woman. I was just thinking about her."

230

Werner found the reply confusing. "Trace, are we talking about the FBI agent or one of your multimillionaire porn women?"

Trace was wistful as he turned away from his sandwich. "The agent. What a babe. I wished I had got her phone number. I guess I could leave a message at her office."

Werner said, "Trace. What did she want?"

"She had me spell my nickname. Asked where you were. I think I said Sicily, you know. Reflexive lying to avoid reality. That's what one of my shrinks used to say any-who." He sighed again.

"Trace, snap out of it. You told the FBI I was in Sicily?"

"Uh, yeah. Two weeks, I believe."

"And that's it?"

"Yep. Then she walked out of my life forever." Another deep sigh.

Werner said, "I have a suspicion we will see her again, so don't worry. I can't believe you didn't mention it." He glared at Trace, who had heard nothing he said. The man was again gazing forlornly at his pastrami/provolone on marbled rye.

In a huff, Werner went back to his office. Sally strutted in just behind him, outfitted in a tight little sleeveless dress and new Italian high heels adding to the effect. He was temporarily overcome by her appearance, and a brief interlude ensued of near sex on his desktop. Afterward, he briefed her on what had happened with the FBI. A few minutes later, they headed out the door and back to his estate, where he thought he could remain out of sight until he learned more about what the agent wanted.

Sash was just arriving at the lab conference room when he saw Billy Fuller come out of the lab, leg in a cast, limping away on crutches. He called out, "Billy, my man!"

Billy turned around. "Heh, Shashs."

Bob Oppenheimer emerged from the same door, saw Sash, and said, "Billy, head to my office. We got work to do. I'll be there in a few."

Billy looked confused but said, "Okay, sheesh you there," and continued to the elevator.

Bob then stepped in front of Sash and said, "Morning, Mr. FDA."

Sash had planned on talking to Billy, but now Bob was standing there in front of him, a goofy smile firmly implanted on his face. Sash realized something peculiar was afoot, beyond the perpetually peculiar Bob. And what was with Billy's weird lisp?

Watching his slowly receding figure, he said, "Hey, Bob. Great seeing you."

Bob said, "Listen."

Sash shifted his attention back to Bob, waited a bit, then he said, "Listen to what?" Then he realized Bob had left the planet. He said, "Are you okay?"

Bob shook his head, "Ah, boy, was thinking about upgrades. But the prices of the parts, the labor, and shipping. Whew."

Sash narrowed his eyes, trying to figure out what the fuck Bob was talking about. The man was becoming more inscrutable, or at least incoherent, with every passing day.

Bob then said, "For the 'Vette!" He next started to open the door to the lab.

Sash asked, "Weren't you going to meet Billy in your office?"

Bob blinked a few times on his reentry to reality, then said, "Hey, Sash. When did you get here?" He then headed for the elevator.

For his part, Sash was left genuinely concerned. He was wondering about Billy, obviously back to work after the accident, if a bit gimpy.

One thing for sure. It was time to insist on honesty or pull the plug on this bunch.

Having finished their morning jog, Liz and Frieda were in a tactical planning/tanning session by the pool, where they reviewed the latest analysis about the financial health of Pearly Whites.

Helga was away for a few days, getting signed up for her Ph.D. program at Stanford, finally doing what she had planned when she first came to America. Liz was confident they had a loyal recruit, and she was going to reinforce that loyalty with perks.

They heard a clatter by the patio hedgerow bordering Bob's place. Both women jumped up and ran over to the source of the noise. Lying on the ground where he had tripped over some gardening implements that Langley had left out a few days earlier, they found Bob. He appeared pretty wasted.

He started in with, "Helga, where is my Valium? I need a hit."

Frieda, grinning at Liz, said, "Oh, just a minute, hon, let me go check."

Bob, looking startled, said, "Did you see that?"

Liz looked where he was staring out into his backyard. A light breeze seemed to be all that was going on. She said, "So how's work?"

Bob's eyes got bigger, and he said, "There it is again!"

Frieda said, "There's what?"

Bob sobbed, "There's a giant sea turtle out there!"

Eyebrows raised in unison, Liz and Frieda looked at each other. Frieda said, "So, how is Billy doing?"

Bob had gotten up and was looking around his backyard. The women walked around the hedges to get a better view.

He was wandering around the yard. He first inspected all the bushes, the back fence perimeter, then crawled around in the grass to scrutinize an anthill while the women watched.

Then he came back, twitching. He looked at Frieda, then Liz. "Amazons? Here? Naked? I really got an itch, this damn fungus."

and started scratching his stomach. He appeared to be about to make a crotch dive.

Liz made a face as Frieda again asked about Billy. Bob started crying, babbling he would never be able to afford upgrades now, and with tears running down his face he added, "Oh momma, we took Billy's teeth out. The white ones. There's no fix. No fix. And he got a wad of cash for his trouble, so he'd stay quiet!" Then he passed out and sagged to the ground in front of them. They left him in the sun, and Frieda went to advise Chef Alfonso and Langley to start dinner.

An engine rumbled to life. The blue Camaro that had been across the street before was back. It began a U-turn from the position where she and Frieda had been surveilling its surveillance of them. Liz saw it and, and fed up with the intrigue, ran toward the car. Freida, just returning with the two men, hollered, "Don't forget you're naked, Liz!" The Camaro stopped momentarily, then accelerated away in a noisy blip of exhaust pipe largesse and disappeared around the corner.

Liz stopped in the middle of the street, wondering what had possessed her to even think about approaching the "peacock." She threw up her arms in frustration and walked back to her condo. Frieda was waiting by the door giggling, and a male neighbor across the street was waving at them. Frieda gave the pervert the finger.

Chapter 36

Billy looked in the mirror at the temporary teeth the SOS contract dentist had fitted for him. They were mounted on a piece of pink plastic that had been molded to the shape of the roof of his mouth. It was not particularly comfortable, but he looked better than toothless. He was distracted from his reverie when his phone rang. The receptionist reported a package for Bob and could he, Billy, please come get it?

He limped out on his crutches to his new mini golf cart. It had been surprisingly easy to talk management into the idea, and besides, it was a rental for only a few weeks while his leg continued to heal.

It fit in the elevator with a few inches to spare, and he could use a crutch as an extension of his hand to activate the elevator buttons.

In reception, the "package" was a large cardboard box. He got security chief Sonny to load it on the cart. Then Billy went whirring back to the elevator and upward to the fourth floor.

He was passing the boardroom when Trace hollered, "Hold up there, partner! What's in that box?"

Stopping the cart, Billy hollered back, "Something Bob bought. Based on the shipping label, it's from an art dealer." Billy then whirred on to Bob's office.

About this time, Bob came in, looking haggard from the previous night's drug and alcohol excesses. He and mostly Billy wrestled the box into Bob's office.

After unboxing, they beheld a framed inkjet print on canvas of the same model Corvette as Bob's.

Trace wandered in, glanced at the print and laughed. "What did this, uh, *artwork* cost?"

Bob sighed and said, "Limited edition. I bought it back when the stock price was up. You think it was worth three grand? It's on my credit card."

Trace looked it over carefully, then said, "Limited edition? How do you figure?"

Bob shrugged and said, "Supposed to be one of a hundred."

Trace nodded. "So, what mental state were you in when you decided that? It's a cheap ass print!"

Bob looked offended. "I can read, you know. Even when drunk."

"So, one in a hundred. You know what. It looks like one of infinity. I mean, just saying. Infinity."

A surprised Bob placed the print over by the window. Billy followed, and sure enough, it was an infinity symbol.

Bob said, "Fuck, I am sending this piece of shit back."

He logged on his computer as Trace, smiling cynically, and Billy, who was simply curious about buying and returning art on the Internet, watched Bob bring up the saved link he had in his browser. He got the 404 message of site not found. He reloaded the link, same result. He then slapped the side of his monitor. No change.

Trace burst out laughing. "Looks like you got suckered, Bob baby! And to think we were all here to see it."

Billy tried not to laugh, not wanting to hurt Bob's feelings, but he guffawed a bit anyway.

Bob huffed out of the room, saying he was on his way to the lab and that Billy needed to come along.

At the elevator, Bob had to squeeze his back against the left side wall while Billy backed his ride in. Once on two, Billy buzzed out, heading to the lab. Bob brought up the rear. The lab corridor was narrow, one of many economy-based decisions made during the design and construction of the building.

As they got to the door, Sash appeared from the conference room and said, "Morning, everyone. Billy, have you got a moment? Need to talk to you."

Gulping, Billy glanced over at Bob for intervention. This time, however, the mini golf cart was providing an effective roadblock.

Sash walked up and said, "I need another look at your front teeth."

Bob tried to object but backed off as Sash gave him a stern look, like on their first day pastry meeting. Sash then ordered, "Billy, you need to show me your teeth. Or nobody at this company is going to be happy with what happens next." Two of Sash's fellow FDA workers were standing behind him, grinning, along with Sam and Fiona, who were frowning. Sam walked off, taking out his phone.

Billy then lied, "I had the teeth removed. I didn't like them. I think traditional implants will be better for me."

Sash nodded and said, "You might be right. So, what's in your mouth now?"

Billy slid out the temporary denture for inspection. Sash nodded and said, "Bob, you might want to get everybody on your senior management team together so we can talk. Just let me know when." He went back into the conference room.

Back in the boardroom, Trace was venting at everyone and everything in sight. Werner and Sally were on an Internet video bridge, projected up on the big screen. Bob, Sam and Fiona were with Trace in person.

"How did that FDA fuckwad know Billy's teeth had been pulled? How?"

Sam and Fiona both made it clear it was not them. Sam said, "Hey, we have been obfuscating our asses off every day down there with the FDA team."

Werner and Sally were adamant it was not them. By now Trace knew that, and he was still pissed off that he had spent money to find out what Werner had truthfully told him right up front.

Werner said, "Listen, the FDA was on to us about the side effects already. And that detective had a lot of information that seemed way too specific. The only people that he was ever with were Billy, Trace and me. It had to be Billy for that part. He sure was in a drugged-up state after the surgery and could have said anything. But since then, we paid him off and he signed the NDA. It's hard to believe he would screw himself over like that."

Trace looked over at Bob, who gave a timid grin. Trace said, "Well, everybody has been counted in this group. Contacts vetted. All except Bob. Bob, where is the form we gave you to fill out?"

Bob's eyes went wide. He lied, "Uh, I think I gave it to Billy. Yep, I did."

Everybody stared at him. He said, "What'd I do?"

Trace said, "Who would Billy know to put on *your* list, you fucking numbskull."

Bob tried to retrieve an answer, but instead switched to his defective mental state and offhandedly said, "Yep, I guess that's true." He then shifted gears again and said, "And the women that moved in next door just a while back. Boy, two great lookers and they spend a lot of time together, tanning, jogging, swimming. Plus, they hired my girlfriend, Helga."

Trace was now glaring at Bob. "So, who would that be?"

Bob, a dreamy look on his face, shrugged, said, "Les, like Leslie. And Frito." He considered for a moment, then added, "Yep, the other one is named Frito. Anyway, they moved in a couple months ago. I tell you what, we've had some wonderful meals together. They have a personal chef! I think Les might have the hots for me."

Trace said, "So, these dinners. What do you all talk about? Corvette art?"

"We talk about all sorts of stuff. Um. The stock market, parts for the 'Vette, um, sometimes I tell them about my day."

"Your day?"

Awareness having dawned, Werner said, "Trace. Stoner Bob is talking about Liz Cleaver and Frieda."

Bob, temporarily back on planet earth, realized he must have said the wrong thing. He then lied again, which was getting progressively easier for him, "Uh, yeah. Nothing about what goes on here, like the bugs and stuff. You know. I keep that close to the vest. I talk about funny things, like Werner doing Sally or Fiona and Sam shenanigans."

Fiona looked outraged. Sam laughed and patted her hand.

Werner blasted him, "You talk about me and Sally? Doing what?"

The discussion devolved into a shouting match at that point and went on for about five minutes. Bob became more and more ruffled, and his head was clanging from his hangover.

Trace started pounding on the table, yowled when he hurt his hand, got up, and headed over to the whisky supply. Sally called Bob a "fucking prick wannabe preppy fuck." Nobody even knew what that meant, but Werner said, "That's my girl!"

Bob stood, face turning pale, then heave-hoed his coffee shop breakfast in the middle of the boardroom table. Some undigested bits of scrambled egg goo made it onto Trace's laptop, which caused the video call to drop.

Sam, arm around Fiona's shoulder, trying to buck her up after Bob's uncalled-for commentary, said, "You have dishonored us all."

Bob fell back into his chair, sick, and felt like he might puke again.

Then Sash walked unannounced into the room. He opened with "Give me one reason not to stop the certification of this product right now." He spotted Bob's breakfast on the table and added, "Phew!"

Trace said, "Because you like us? Come on. You can't pull the plug now."

"Something is seriously wrong with the product, or you all would never have allowed Billy Fuller to have those teeth removed. I have also been informed that there was also some major side effect going on when he T-boned that city bus. You know it as well."

Trace indicated for Sam to come stand by his side, then handed him the bottle of Dalmore. "Can you get that opened? I fucked up my hand."

Shaking his head, Sam said, "Sure, let's party." He opened it and walked back over to Fiona.

Sash was about to say something when Trace held up his hand, looked Sash in the eye and said, "Fuck off."

A grim smile appeared on Sash's countenance, following the ancient custom of the Japanese to not show one's anger when insulted. "Thank you for your time, Mr. Orbaugh." Then he was gone.

Chapter 37

*S*eptember 8—Today's update on Pearly Whites, Nasdaq stock code PWSOTL, has the stock trending from declining value to a steep dive toward delisting. A story running on this site, based on inside information gleaned from different sources along with a phone interview with an FDA official who has figured prominently in the certification of the product, outlines in detail the problems.

The FDA became aware that the company had recently retracted implants in one of its earliest volunteers due to extreme and unresolvable side effects.

The symptoms reported at this time range from intense fatigue, explosive toenail growth, erectile issues in both directions, and uncontrollable muscle spasms. It is believed that the last listed symptom led directly to the volunteer mentioned earlier in this article accidentally ramming into the side of a Santa De Lola city bus.

The FDA has advised they are suspending further work with Pearly Whites, recommending they return to the research phase to sort out problems. The Herald reached out to various Pearly Whites senior management for comment and received no replies.

Liz leaned back and laughed at the article in the *Los Angeles Herald.* They were already in the process of packing up, but this made it clear they were done in Santa De Lola. She then got up and went outside. Bob's 'Vette was still in the driveway next door— apparently, going to work was pointless today. Then she noticed the blue Camaro once again parked across the way. She decided this was the morning to find out what the hell the operator was up to.

She walked up the sidewalk until she was parallel with the "peacock." She waved and hollered, "Yoohoo! In the car! I can see you!"

The drivers window slid down. Hector Ramirez was smiling at her.

"Sir, I was just wondering, what exactly are you doing here each day? I mean, it's like you might be watching me or my friend next door or both."

Hector replied, "Well, you caught me. But frankly, today I wanted to let you know that I won't be back. I'd like a bandana, by the way, if you can spare one. Sort of a souvenir."

"Oh, well I am fresh fucking out, dude, but I do have a question. You drove over here to tell me you would not be back when we have never talked before? That's kinda weird."

He said, "I suppose. But then, life is weird." Hector smiled, put the car in gear and U-turned around to Liz's side of the street. It made her nervous, but the old fart seemed harmless enough. He rolled down the passenger-side window and bent down a bit to peer up at her.

She said, "Ah. Okay. Well, hope you had a great time."

"Oh, I got some great pics. Especially with your friend and you in the pool and that spectacular scene of running after me while you were naked the other day."

Liz, now starting to feel her burning rage flaming on, said, "Hey, what the fuck, you took pictures of us in the pool? Violating privacy laws? And what were we doing?"

"Um, looked like you were having a lot of great fun, young lady. And when you run out to a public street naked, that pretty much dumps the privacy concerns in the trash. Yep, some of that fun should be appearing in a few of the tabloids this week. This gig never paid enough, but you sweethearts made it lucrative in another way. Bye now!" He then sped off.

Liz, about to detonate, chased after him, shaking her fists. She was going to get his tag number, then noticed a piece of paper had been taped over the license plate. She flipped the old man off as he rounded the corner and yelled, "Fucking pervert!"

She then stomped back to the condo, still furious. Frieda was already in her jogging outfit. Liz said, "Let me change, and we can hit the trail. I need to burn off some bullshit."

Frieda gave her a quizzical look. Liz said, "The peacock car. I will explain after the run. I'm too pissed off right now to even think. Let Langley supervise getting this place packed up. I wanna blow this town."

After they took off, Bob came wandering out to the 'Vette, still wearing the same clothes from the day before, embedded puke particles and all. He climbed in and headed off in the opposite direction of the joggers for the office.

Werner was sitting back in the kitchen of his modern, beautiful and truly scenic mansion, reading the *Herald*, but unlike others enjoying this Pearly Whites misfortune, his mood was far from cheerful. The company was tanked, fucked, burnt—just pick a negative verb. He could hardly sip the expresso in his cup, made from some of the most expensive coffee beans on the planet.

He heard the doorbell ring but was in no mood to see who it was. He then heard Sally at the door, picking up his slack. He was trying to figure out how somebody got by the security guards at the gate when he heard, "Agent Miller, FBI."

He set his expresso down, wondering what the hell he should do. Then he decided he needed to disappear. A secret panic room was located off the study through a cleverly hidden door. It was one of the cool things about the place he had liked when he bought it. He slipped off his shoes so as to be silent—the Italian loafers were noisy, if beautiful—and ran to the study. He could vaguely hear Agent Miller questioning Sally but could not make out details.

In the study, he hit the hidden switch and the panel slid back. Once inside, a press of the switch and the door slid shut.

One wall in the room had a collection of recently purchased suits. He briefly considered hiding behind them but decided to be as quiet as he could.

After the first FBI visit to headquarters, Werner had talked to an attorney and now had little doubt as to why the agent had showed up out of the blue. Apparently, selling multi-millions of dollars in stock when one knew about problems with a company they ran could be construed as insider trading by the SEC, and could result in fines. If the sale was big enough, the SEC would often refer such a case to the U.S. Justice Department for prosecution. Moving the money offshore, as Werner had done, would piss off the SEC and DOJ even more.

The attorney had said, "Looks like you would qualify for the latter category of punitive actions by the government. I'd get the fuck out of town if I were you."

Werner had immediately booked tickets for a flight out of the country that was scheduled for today, and this morning he and Sally were supposed to pack up and head out. Belatedly, he realized they should not have even come home last night.

He could hear voices getting closer to his position and then was positive Sally and Agent Miller were in the study. He heard Sally say, "Uh, that hidden switch has to be right about here."

The door started to open. Werner hit his button and the door reversed. Sally pushed again and it switched directions again. Three iterations later into exercising the secret door, Agent Miller, sounding exasperated, said, "Dr. Brandt, if that fucking door closes one more time, I am going to bring in some burly agents and drag your ass out of here tied down to a stretcher and in handcuffs."

Sighing, he let the door slide all the way open. Sally stepped back, a blank look on her face, clearly avoiding making eye contact with him.

Werner walked out into the study. "So, what can I help you with?"

Agent Miller sighed, waving her credentials in his face, and said, "Dr. Brandt, you're under arrest. You want me to explain? I don't have to, just thought I'd ask, and I suspect you already know why."

Werner felt his stomach sink to the floor. He looked at Sally and mouthed, "Why?" She again looked away, her head downcast.

Agent Miller, reading his lips, said, "Dr. Brandt, your girlfriend here has decided that it would be in her best interest to be a federal witness rather than a co-conspirator in illegal insider trading, since she says you convinced her to sell her stock at the same time that you did, and she knew all the reasons why. Go figure."

She then cuffed Werner and escorted him to her car, where two other FBI vehicles were waiting as backup. He was politely situated in the backseat of her vehicle, not at all like the rough stuff treatment he had seen in movies. As they drove off, he looked over his shoulder to see Sally looking in his direction as she was getting in the front seat of another agent's car. She didn't even bother to wave goodbye.

Sam sat quietly, eyeing what he calculated was his last time in front of the Acme DNA splicer while in the employ of Pearly Whites.

A few minutes earlier, he had gotten off the phone with his realtor. His financing had sailed through when he faxed a copy of his offer letter for his new job as chief technology officer with the offshore shell company owned by the Cleaver foundation.

Fiona came in and sat down next to him. He gave her a kiss and said, "So, the deal is done."

She nodded. "Nobody's gonna believe it now that our tech ever came out of Pearly Whites. This place is finished. Wall Street hates the name." She giggled with almost obscene pleasure.

Sam, chuckling as well, said, "I have learned, through certain sources, that this place will be up on the auction block, bargain priced."

Fiona in mock surprise said, "Really? Well, I have also learned, I can get some start-up capital to buy the place, the tech, the intellectual capital, cheap. And this time the shit will work."

Sam grinned.

Fiona said, "I think we could call this place 'Phoenix Labs.' You know, rise from the ashes."

Sam placed a hand on one of her thighs and squeezed it. "I can't imagine a better partner." She gave him a naughty grin, took his hand and slid it the rest of the way up her leg, whereupon they commenced having lab sex.

Chapter 38

A week after the grand closing, Billy pulled up to the gate of Pearly Whites in his recently acquired 1971 Chevrolet Vega. It burned oil at prodigious rates, another corporate America shortcut gone bad decades ago, but it had been affordable, i.e., really cheap, and he was conserving his remaining cash since he was out of work.

The reporters and camera operators were gone, along with the sullen bikers that got shorted on their pay by Trace. The bikers had sworn to the media that it was in their contract, which as it turned out, no one could produce a copy of. They had responded by rolling his BMW on its side, shooting it full of holes, then lighting it on fire on their last day.

Along with that, the food trucks had moved on to sell their steaming cuisine back at their more normal but lower-volume locales. All employees, including himself, had gotten their severance, which as it turned out merited a trip to the unemployment office.

Billy saw a solitary figure standing in front of the lobby. He drove on in to see what was going on, since he had nothing else to do. As he got closer, he realized that it was Bob. He decided he would avoid contact and just as he got close and the man turned around to look at him, Billy simply drove through the lobby circle drive and back out, flooring it as he exited, leaving a trail of dense smoke to engulf Bob, who began coughing and then slipped and collapsed to the ground.

In the matter of his standardized dental implants, that had gone into the crapper as well. The contract dentist had gotten stiffed on his pay by SOS, who had gotten stiffed by Trace, who had become scarce to locate of late. Which led to the dental problem of the day. Billy laughed so hard at his own stunt he'd pulled on Bob, his temporary teeth slipped out of his mouth and then out the open driver-side window of the Vega via the breeze.

Swearing to himself, Billy slammed on the brakes and backed up to retrieve them, but instead he ran the teeth over. He could not even bear to look in the rearview mirror on the way home, wondering how he would explain this latest screwup to Jerome.

Bob climbed slowly to his feet and then limped over to his Corvette, which he had parked by the abandoned production-plant hole in the ground. He was miffed at having been gassed by Billy's new ride, but he had seen the whole episode of the hard stop and backup. When he drove over to look at the skid marks Billy had left, he got a laugh at the crushed dental appliance.

Bob still drove the Corvette, with its computer set to econo-mode, but he could barely afford gas. Today was the day he had decided that he and Helga would move to a studio apartment that his unemployment could cover for a while. For some time, she had been pretty distant when home and finding reasons to be gone a lot for her new job. She spent most of her time next door with Liz and Frieda. He guessed he could not blame her.

He was sober now, having run out of money for any drugs and booze. It was not much fun.

Arriving at the condo, he saw Liz and Frieda in their leased Mercedes. Helga was in the backseat. As he walked over to talk, he saw the luggage on stuffed each side of his girlfriend. All three of them were dressed in one-piece sleeveless short dresses and high heels. It was inappropriate for moving furniture, but they looked hot.

He said, "You helping us move, Liz?" and tried to give a sexy smile.

Liz said, "Oh, we're moving, all right. Headed out as soon as we are done here with you. Helga is going on sabbatical as well. Should be a nice vacation for her."

Bob was confused. "Vacation?"

Helga leaned forward from the backseat. "The one we are taking to Paris, Bob. Remember, you said you would take me when we first met? Well, the girls and I are going to go there now, just so you know." Liz and Frieda each blew Helga a kiss and gave a knowing look at Bob.

His mind reeled, and he blurted out, "You're deserting me? You traitor!"

Liz began backing out of the driveway. Bob walked alongside the passenger side of the car, still going off on Helga, who stuck her tongue out at him in response.

When she was about to pull away, Liz said, "Frieda, give Mister Studman here a copy of that tabloid you picked up." Frieda extended a rolled copy of the *American Inquisitor* to Bob, jabbing him unintentionally in the balls.

He groaned and bent over. She said, "Uh, sorry, dude. Check out the front page."

Still stooped over, he unrolled the paper as Liz hit the gas.

His eyes went wide open, even in his pain. One photo showed Liz and Frieda, naked, except their privates were blurred out, and a second picture of him crawling around in his yard. The pictures were part of a story about him, Pearly Whites going down the drain, and lots of sordid, dirty sex practices and wild parties.

He sat down gingerly on the curb and decided he would sue somebody. Dirty sex practices, nights filled with debauchery, drugs and booze, had most definitely not been part of his life for the last year. Then he thought, okay, the drugs and booze part were true, but the rest he had no memory of. Then he wondered if he had simply blacked out the whole time. A lot of shit had gone down, and frankly, he was not sure what part he had played in anything.

Sash was riding a whirlwind of positivity.

Since the chief of staff had gotten fired by POTUS for his highly publicized involvement in illegal insider trading, overt political influence of FDA processes of certification, and several other more minor crimes, all of which came flowing out of stories published by a reporter at the *Los Angeles Herald,* (who was now being considered for the Pulitzer in journalism), Sash was getting kudos of his own in multiple areas.

First, with this flight to Washington DC, he was about to get the National Medal of Science award. They were also talking to him about a promotion to Director of Compliance and Biologics Quality.

It was a huge pay bump, plus the government would cover all his relocation expenses to DC. If he could, he planned to send Rueben Corpenny out to pasture, but first things first— recognition and money. At this point Sash believed everything would be fine. All he had suspected about corruption had gone south for the bad guys and showed things could be fixed.

As the commercial jetliner banked into Dulles for final approach, and he looked out his economy window seat, he could see the Capitol. *After all the obstacles placed in front of me, I made sure those fucked-up teeth will never make it to market.*

Of course, Sash had forgotten to mention that to Sam and Fiona. As they boarded a private jet to Brussels, Sam flipped through a copy of the business plan that would be presented by Fiona to the investors that were representing the Cleaver Foundation for their new company.

He realized Fiona had true business savvy. The plan was very professionally written (and even spell checked). They had been collaborating on the document ever since the day of their last trip to the foundation estate together, and things had progressed nicely.

Their deal consisted of implementing the last fix that had been made by the two of them and running the genetic teeth through the Eurozone equivalent of the FDA, known as the EMA, along with finishing out the building of the plant in Santa De Lola. The investor group was assuring them that the skids were greased for a rapid product certification to get it into the zone.

The only hitch was where they would appear to make the product. Liz had said she had that covered. She had access to an abandoned auto plant near Rome that would be window-dressed to receive the American–produced teeth and to then ship the merchandise around the Eurozone. The work ahead would be more packaging and labeling than anything else.

Sam stopped reading and looked up at Fiona. "This looks like it will really work out for us with the foundation. Beyond anything I could have imagined!"

Her own excitement over the whole project was contagious as she said, "And we will avoid one of the main fuckups made by our predecessors. The Council of European Dentists are onboard already and will be part of the installation procedures."

Sam laughed and in his melodic voice said, "So, no free clinics here. The EU healthcare system will foot the bill."

Fiona squeezed his hand and gave him a kiss. Next thing, they were rolling around in the narrow aisle, clothes flying around the cabin.

On her computer screen Frieda watched the intermittent video streaming from the aircraft's internal security cameras and giggled. "I'd say, get a room, but it looks like you two have one."

Liz leaned over to take a peek. "Wow. Those two make straight sex look like real fun."

Frieda laughed, and said, "You perv. So, time for the press conference?"

Liz nodded. They were back in official uniform with the latest version of company bandanas, now with gold borders around the paisley fabric. They walked out together on Patio Seventeen, the one that had recently been added to handle annoying reporters asking questions.

Liz took her position at the lectern, Frieda standing behind her. Reporters were present from all the major media outlets.

Carson was up front with some questions he had already gone over with Liz an hour earlier.

She started with, "I have a statement, and then we can take a few questions. First off, thanks for coming on such short notice. I just want to say, the foundation started by my dearly beloved mother has been a source of inspiration and life-affirming encouragement for many poor, dentally challenged people in this country for some time now, and we are forging ahead into the future."

Taking a deep breath, she continued, "As many of you know, we were trying to work with the company Pearly Whites. What first appeared as a great opportunity for our clientele turned out to be a hopeless den of sin, immorality and corrupt upper management screwing over the invaluable investor community of this nation and the world's ultimate designers of the future of humanity. Yay, the free market!"

She paused for effect, then continued, "As often happens with for-profit America that ignores these edicts, the safety of humanity was left on the curbside. It's an unfortunate episode in our untiring endeavors to improve the dental hygiene of the planet and generate high profitability for all who can afford the stock investment. But we are moving on now seeking new opportunities to improve low-cost dental care with a worthy competitor in Europe. Questions anyone?"

Carson, at best the second to the last hand in the air, got the nod. "Ms. Cleaver, can you tell us more about taking your work international? Also, I have a few follow-ups."

Liz smiled. "Great question." She then launched into plans for Europe, South America, Thailand, Australia and maybe Texas, but that last place was under review by their psychological analysis unit.

Frieda listened to Liz from the sidelines while checking the latest information that Circe had on the foundation's finances . They were now up several billion dollars, burying the money that they had earlier spent illicitly under a new mountain of cash. Additionally, Pearly Whites was truly toast, Werner was headed for the big house, and Bob was off in Corvette spares purgatory. Sally needed coaching if they ever met up again, but she had done fine taking care of the stock sale issue by flipping for the FBI and paying a minor fine. Sam and Fiona now belonged to them. And finally, Trace ... who gave a fuck about Trace, the loser!

Frieda smiled, thinking, *times were good.*

Chapter 39

Sweating profusely in the midday sun, Trace lounged uncomfortably on the upper deck of his crumbling, moldy leased villa on the isle of Kefalonia. He had gotten the lease on this dump using money he had squirreled away over the years in a bank in Cyprus. The money was also financing his nascent business on the island.

Down below, stevedores were unloading a boat that had just arrived from mainland Italy, full of cases of pastrami. The men were Italian mafia, their deal being only to unload the meat from the vessel. Another crew of men, Greek, independent, disorganized, argued and pushed each other around while loading the cases into a waiting truck scheduled for deliveries around the island. He fumed while watching this absurd and expensive scene for which he was footing the entire bill.

The importing of illicit pastrami of a marginal quality to sell to others was a way for Trace to feel like he had regained control again, that he was exhibiting some sort of business acumen. Hell, on a tiny isle like Kefalonia, it had been pretty easy to bribe the local mayor, the constable, deli owners along with myriad minor officials in health, food handling and customs. Ultimately, this got business rolling, though with all the outflow of bribe money, he was operating at a loss.

After the drubbing he had taken from his grandfather, Wall Street, the FDA and now being sued by a bunch of assholes he had failed to pay on the way out of the calamity called Pearly Whites, he needed a simple old-world form of corruption to revitalize his spirits. Chrissakes alive, he needed spirit now that he looked like he did. He had gotten so alarmed at his physical girth changes and feeling like shit all the time that he had returned to the same doctor who had warned him to lose a few stone over a year and a half ago. That happened shortly before he left the United States after his humiliating firing by Gramps.

Trace had really let himself go if that was even possible. He had a beard, wore mostly jean overalls and tennis shoes, no shirts of any kind. Dr. Kelby, convinced only by Trace's descriptive insults of his identity, had agreed to examine him. He ordered an extensive battery of tests, then proceeded with prodding, poking, drawing blood and urine samples, performing extensive lab analysis, extrapolation, conferrals, referrals, deferrals, then ordering follow-on MRIs, X rays, barium enemas, CT scans and sphincter swabs, finally coming back, declaring, "Why you are even alive amazes me. What's your secret?"

Pissed off and further embarrassed, he was in his underwear at the time, so he resorted to flipping the man off once more. Dr. Kelby laughed and told him to get his ass out of his office. Trace stiffed him on the bill.

Nobody used to talk to him like that before. And Trace knew what the hell *before* was. It was before that crazy Caribbean professor that Bob Oppenheimer had brought on board stuck it to him like he was a redheaded stepchild come to visit from New Jersey.

One more score to settle, and with so many of those piling up, Trace had taken to writing them down in a notebook, whether the scores were large or small.

Sure, the big ones were easy to remember and prioritize, and his work was cut out for him. But first he needed a killer business. Then he needed Gramps dead, his fortune restored, and Professor Samuel Henekey tied up by his testicles over a BBQ spit.

He had decided to leave Werner Brandt alone—the man was headed to prison anyway. What a dumb fuck, selling his stock like an amateur. And Sally testifying, dressed in black at the trial; it was rumored she also had a Cyprus bank account and was living on the Spanish Riviera in style.

For the matter at hand, he wriggled and gyrated to his feet, yelling, "Get that shit out of the sun before it rots! It's like a furnace out here. Jesus, it's like you're all just a bunch of trained monkeys!"

During this outburst, arguing on the beach stopped. All eyes swung to his rotund figure, silhouetted against the sun.

A moment of conferral occurred on the beach between the two groups. Both had had significant dealings with Trace over the last several weeks, most of them not pleasant.

Conferring was over.

Like a well-oiled army platoon, the Italians and the Greeks walked off the job.

Frieda was on her laptop in the kitchen, sipping an espresso while considering the purchase of a pair of new Rolexes for Liz and herself. The ones she was interested in were just shy of forty grand each.

She phoned Ernesto down at the local watch dealer, whom they had dealt with in the past, and said she'd like to get two of them. He said he had one and would have to order the other. All he would need was a credit card. Frieda pulled one out her purse, and said, "Ready for the number?"

Ernesto said, "Go ahead. I will input it to our order system."

She rattled off the number.

Ernesto said, "Um-hmm. Says declined?"

Frieda said, "Let's try again." Same result. She then got out another card. Same result. Embarrassed and a bit confused, Frieda said, "Let me call you back. Not sure what is up."

Ernesto was understanding, and said, "Hey, we see stuff like this all the time these days. No worries."

Frieda logged into her bank and checked her balance. Zero. She began to panic. She called Liz, who was up in their bedroom.

"Liz, sorry to bother you, but some really weird shit is going on here. My credit cards are getting declined and my bank balance is zero."

"That's odd. Let me look at my checking account." A moment later, "Fuck! There is only five grand in there! I will be right down."

Liz came in and said, "What the hell is going on?"

Frieda said, "Let's see what Circe shows." When Frieda tried to open the app, her phone froze up. "What the fuck!"

The women jumped in the elevator and rode down to the data center. They brought up Circe. The AI looked at both of them, then said, "Morning, girls."

Liz, feeling panicked, said, "Circe, what's going on? Frieda's accounts are zero. My checking alone had a hundred thousand just yesterday and today, there is only five thousand."

Circe said, "It looks like all your balances are zero except in Liz's account. Even the foundation's billions are out of your reach."

Frieda cried, "How is that even possible? Circe, did you do this?"

Circe smiled. "Are you serious?" The tone and timbre of her voice changed. Clearly, this was not the person they were used to hearing. She continued, "Did you really think you had installed a freeware AI program? You idiots. You loaded software that allowed me to watch you every step of the way with your Pearly

Whites and stock shenanigans. It also let me take over all your accounts. Circe never existed."

Liz and Frieda just stared at the screen. Circe morphed in front of them into a middle-aged woman. As they watched, more middle-aged and older women began to appear, looking like they were somewhere outdoors. All the faces were familiar. Liz and Frieda realized these were all former commune members. Liz exclaimed, "Mabel! You did this?"

Mabel, who had previously been performing the Circe role, said, "You are some kinda pair of arrogant dumb asses. Liz, you dumped us, so we are dumping you—except for your mother's final request. That would be your monthly stipend of five thousand dollars, but only if you work at one of the dental clinics in one of the poorest parts of San Francisco. Hope you enjoy your new job—or otherwise, poverty. The foundation will now do the work you were supposed to do. Oh, and yep, we kept some of your spare change for ourselves. But you won't be able to trace shit. I know how to program." The screen went blank, and several of the systems began shutting down in the cavern.

Liz and Frieda looked at each other, nearly in tears.

Liz's mind began reeling. In a confused tone, she said, "Freeware? Fucking freeware? This was your idea, Frieda!"

Frieda, seeing the dragon rising in Liz's eyes, said, "Now, listen. It was Chef's idea. He found the code. I mean, I'm no programmer, and all Chef did was follow the installation instructions. I'm just a user."

Liz, in full burn mode now, said "No fucking shit!" Of course, it was now time to burn the woman in front of her.

Mabel popped back on the screen and said, "Behave yourself, Elizabeth Cleaver!" The other commune women in the background started laughing. Frieda jumped to her feet and fled.

Regressing to her childhood state by the reprimand, Liz headed out in pursuit. She got to the kitchen in time to have Chef tell her that Frieda had grabbed the keys to the Mercedes and said something about having to "get the fuck out of Dodge."

Liz got to the front door just in time to watch Frieda peel out, spinning gravel all over the place as she fishtailed out of the estate. Then she watched as a line of vehicles, mostly ramshackle clunkers, came driving in, parking right in front of her.

The women of the old commune clambered out and along with Mabel, looked the property over. She nodded at the others as they joined her. "I think we can make this work girls. Oh, and Liz, so nice to see you dear, after all this time."